I0818197

To Skipper, Smaug and Monster.
You are now the author of your own stories.
Get out there and tell some great ones.

First edition

Book and cover design by Tobi Carter
Cover photo by Ayyub Yahaya on Pexels

ISBN 978-1-7350114-4-8 (paperback)
ISBN 978-1-7350114-3-1 (hardcover)
ISBN 978-1-7350114-5-5 (ebook)

COME HELL OR HIGH WATER

Christopher C. Starr

PROLOGUE

The Song of Sariel

"What's your name?"

Michael grabbed me in the darkness, amidst a steady barrage of flame belching up from the bowels of Peace. His hands were massive and hard, wet with the blood of the fallen. I remember the smear of his palm on my shoulders, reddening the metal of my armor. I remember not being able to remove the stain. Michael clutched me in those huge hands, made me face him.

"Sariel," I told him, afraid of what would come next.

I should have been.

"You are a commander now, Sariel. Understand?" Michael said and pointed at a host of angels flowing over the rooftops of Peace. There were hundreds of them, and they snaked between buildings, along alleyways, around spires, their silver wings glinting like sparks in the darkness. I watched dozens of them hush into light and ash against the buffet of the demons' flaming spears. I saw their quivers of fear, watched their flight patterns become spastic and erratic, heard their screams in the black.

Michael said to me, "Those angels are your responsibility. Do not lose another soul."

And Michael turned from me and lit up the sky charging a line of fallen souls. Alone. For us. There were four hundred angels, seraphs and dominions, thrones and virtues hanging in the darkness next to me, watching the Captain of the Host wipe the blood of the dead on me and call me Commander. He didn't let the fear in my blue eyes or the shaking of my hands deter him. He ignored the youth in my face, the inexperience of my bow, the hesitance in my sword. Michael the Archangel chose me, gave me purpose where there was none. Made me matter.

"Protect the others!" he said and then left.

I turned to the others, shouted above the din, above the war, "You heard him!"

Four hundred inexperienced angels, slaves and artisans, builders and workers, pulled shivering swords and spears into ragged bows, released bolts of light into the darkness. We heard the screams of pain, the echoes of agony, the cheers of our compatriots.

"Again!" I said and Peace crumbled at my command.

Light rained on buildings and stone, tearing through darkened flesh and reddened eyes, boring holes in the very edifices we had spent our lives building. For me the irony was lost: I was from Wisdom and Azazel had destroyed our city long before the war started. There was no loss in this action, no emotion in the carnage I inflicted. No remorse for the horrors I unleashed. But for my compatriots, for those hanging in the darkness next to me, they wept openly, tears rolling down their cheeks as they notched glowing arrows in their bows.

These angels were destroying their own homes. They were killing their friends, lovers, brothers, sisters. They were burning their own city.

I repeated something I heard Michael say to Raphael the Peace Keeper. "Cry about it later," I told them, rolling beneath their volleys. "Now is not the time for tears. It is the time for hard eyes and tight fists, brothers and sisters. This is war. Cry about it later. After we've won."

Peace burned in plumes, thick smoke filling the streets and coating the entire city in a haze. Bolts of white light split the fog only to be answered with streaks of flame from below. But our charges, that host of angels led by Uriel, was lost in the shadows, the faint light from their bodies barely visible to us. We would lose them in moments. Then a squadron of the fallen split from Michael's assault above us. Spiraling down into the haze. Spiraling down after Uriel.

Do not lose another soul.

I wouldn't.

"Keep up the assault," I said to the virtue to my right. "Tell them, do not stop, no matter what. Understand?"

"You heard the Commander! Do not fail her!" he yelled, and I rolled out in front of the line of angels, my angels. I pointed at five warriors, thrones and dominions, "Grab ten more, each of you, and follow me!"

"In there?" said an angel. "Michael said for us to—"

"He named me Commander, dominion. Those souls are flanking ours. They will pick them off and we can't let that happen. Now," I pulled my bow into a longsword, brandished it at the dominion, "would you like to fall in line or just fall?"

He didn't hesitate. Neither did his companions. Each turned, tapping ten others on shoulders and heads, diving into the cauldron that was Peace.

The smoke burned our eyes, the flames licked our hands. And the demons were waiting for us.

We had hardly gotten accustomed to the haze, huddling on a domed rooftop near the edge of the city, when spears of fire roared at us from all directions. The two angels on either side of me exploded in plumes of ash.

"Dive, dive! Take to the streets!" I said, leaping backward and smacking spears from the air. My sword poured into the bow and I loosed three bolts, striking two demons in the throat and winging a third.

We fell through the haze, closer to the flames that licked at the buildings. Here, in the embers of Peace, we could see the hell we had unleashed. And we could see the monsters floating above us.

I pushed two groups of virtues ahead of me, bringing a finger to my lips. "Move ahead two blocks and wait for us," I whispered. "We will catch them in the middle. Don't let them pass."

They vanished in the smoke and I turned to the dominion to my side, Varian. "I will push them to you. Keep them between you and the others. They cannot move forward. Understand?"

I was airborne before Varian nodded.

My bow pulled into a sword, I screamed in the fog, swiping at the first two demons I saw. Heads became rocks, limbs burned to ash beneath my blade and I dove ahead, leaping from building to building. The squadron took the bait and followed me, tumbling their black horror upon me. Bolts of fire flashed past my face and I caught one, reveling in his power. I flung it back and felt the crush of its owner: I'd impaled him and he tackled me.

We fell, spiraling in the darkness, him shouting for his brethren, me calling "Now, now, now!"

The streets of Peace exploded in flashes of white. Spears of flame lashed outward, flailing, missing their mark, burning into buildings, spires, rubble. Varian pressed forward, pulling his squadron up and over the falling demons, pressing them toward the certain death of the virtues waiting for them.

I didn't lose another soul.

I smashed an armored elbow into my assailant's face, heaving him from me. He twirled and tumbled, angling backward onto a low rooftop. I pressed him into the stone, kneeling on his chest, sword at his throat.

"Doesn't matter, seraph," he said and smiled at me. "It's all over any way."

He was right: the heavens flashed and thunder crossed the skies. Our revelry ceased. We floated above the haze, up from the bowels of Peace, our mission forgotten, our charges absent from our minds. We rose, beings of divine white fire now charred by the fires of war, only to see the Temple of the Host crumple upon itself. We saw tendrils of white light leech from the City of Light across the remaining cities, snatching our adversaries from our grasps, freeing them from our blades. Pulling them into oblivion. And we saw the City of Light shake and rock, dip off-kilter, and finally fall beneath the Waters.

The last thing we heard was Lucifer's scream, echoing across a silent Heaven, "The Father was wrong! The Father was wrong!"

We thought it was the end.

It was only the beginning.

PART 1

The Cold Morning After

1
LUCIFER

Lucifer!

I heard it in my head, a whisper, hoarse and gruff. Raw.

But it wasn't the Father. Not this time. It was me, my own voice, charred and ragged. It was the echo of my own name.

I opened my eyes and I saw nothing. Empty blackness stared back at me, it's open maw threatening to consume me whole. It fell on me, this world of shadow, pressing on me from all sides, coiling about my body like a serpent. I was in the dark. Again. For a moment, I remembered. This was how it began. How I began. Wrapped in the impenetrable black that was the Father's Hand. Hugged close to His bosom. This is how it was in the beginning. Before the Father showed his face to me. Before I turned my back on him and made Him cry. Before Gabriel and Lilith, Raphael and Michael. Before my daughters. Before Heaven and Earth and the war. When it was just the Father and me and the darkness.

How it was meant to be.

How it was now.

I did it.

I did it?

"Father?" I said and didn't recognize my own voice. It was small and hollow and fell like a thud against the black.

He didn't answer me.

Again.

I don't remember the last time I heard the Father's voice. His true voice, not some message delivered between souls, passed off, exchanged, given away. He hadn't spoken in a long time. Not to me. And He wasn't speaking to me now.

But it didn't matter: He would. Soon enough He would. He had to. There was no one left, and He would be lonely again. Eventually. Eventually He would come for me and we would make everything right and He would answer me again.

He had to.

Didn't He?

The first time I was imprisoned or exiled or punished—whatever term suits you—I didn't know He would come back for me. I didn't know He would come back at all. He never said it; He just walked away. It wasn't until it was too late, until I'd created Lilith and the Sisters, that I realized what exactly happened. It was just a reprimand. But by then, I'd disobeyed Him. He didn't appreciate that. But I knew now: the Father is patient. His view is long term and endless. Omnipotence does not speak in immediacies: these are mundane trifles for immortals, for angels, for gods. When time has no meaning, urgency is absent. I understood that now. I'd simply wait Him out.

Besides, I'd made it right. Like it is supposed to be. I DID

IT! I was free! Free from the distraction of the others, those idle souls, those slack jawed renditions of me and my beauty. They were gone! All of them! I got rid of them. Stuffed them back in the Pandora's box of their creation, never to be seen again. They got what they deserved and those putrid creations—I deign to call them angels—those ragged beasts, were no more. They were gone. All of them. Including my... daughters?

Oh. My daughters.

Laylah and Dinial.

I made them. They were mine. I made them with Lilith, made something beautiful out of something so horrible and wrong. It was like finding a glittering diamond in the miserable shell of coal. They were precious, those two souls. My daughters. The essence of my hopes and the culmination of my desires. My daughters, stolen from me and returned as shadows of themselves. The same daughters I fought the Father for. They were gone? Gone, like the others? They were gone. Gone. Like everyone else. I blinked back tears in the darkness: I made them. I loved them. I...*killed* them.

I killed them.

It was coming back to me now.

I moved my hands in front on my face, imagining the slender fingers, the alabaster skin. But I remembered the rivulets of silver jutting from them like talons instead. I remembered the burned and peeling skin, the charred tones of my flesh. I remembered the flashes of flame dancing on my shoulders, my arms, leaping between my palms. I was remembering it all now. I slaughtered them both. I touched fingertips to thumbs, remembering the warmth of Laylah's blood coating my hands like oil, slick and thick. Remembering when she called me Satan. She said that word, that wretched name, and I ripped her head clean from her body. And when Dinial refused me, when she turned her back on me and stood with that fool, Raphael, I tore her heart out through her chest.

Their blood was on my hands.

I killed them.

And that realization made me weep. I wailed in the darkness, wallowing in the echoing anguish of my own voice.

Then the pain came.

The first swell of my sobs caught in my throat, caught in a spasm of excruciating pain. Searing pain. Blinding pain. Your words cannot describe the unmitigated agony coursing through my body. I have been burned alive, reborn in the heart of a sun until I shone as brilliant as any star. I have tasted the rake of Gabriel's staff, the bite of Emmanuel's anointing, the point of Azazel's spear. But none of them compared to the torture of Michael's sword. The torment of his justice.

And I remembered.

Fighting them all. Punishing them. Azazel turned Samael then become Azazel again—that furious angel crawling back to the Father. Raphael, with his stupid allegiance to that boy, believing Emmanuel's empty promise of salvation through flesh. And the man! The man? I'd made him too, didn't I? Oh yes, I did! And then I tore him apart, sank my nails in his neck, pulled his head from his shoulders. Tossed him away. And then I was destroying the others. Destroying it all. I remembered. Ripping the flesh of my brothers, burning the bodies of my sisters, threatening to tear that damned boy apart.

Killing them all.

And then there was Michael.

Screaming about falling and ramming that cursed sword down my gullet like a fish.

I remembered.

I was prone, staring upwards into the darkness, splayed on a pyre of stone and rock, broken wings hanging ragged beneath me. I ran my hands, weak and shaking, along the hilt jutting from my sternum. Blood had steamed and baked on my chest, searing around the wound. I pulled but the sword would not budge, just sent a shiver down its length. It was caught, wedged in...the Temple. The Temple! That spire to Emmanuel's anointing; now a prison for me. Consecrated in the blood of angels and man, it was an altar to the Father and the destruction His insipid plans would inspire. It was here that Emmanuel and Gabriel conspired against me, wandering around that table of water like fools. It was here that the boy asked Michael to kill me—how did I know that? How could I know...that?

Hmm.

But the whys and hows of it all paled in comparison to my present situation. I would figure it out in due time—time seemed to be the one thing I had plenty of. Freedom was more pressing. But I had been imprisoned before, bound to Heaven and Earth, complicit in the cruelest of jokes, until I freed myself in front of Raphael and laughed at his ignorance.

"I know this place," I told him, grinning. "I've been here for a long time. I know what it is. I know where it came from. And I know how it works."

I freed myself then; I would loose myself now.

It was a whim really, an idle thought now, you call it mind over matter. All of it was simply clay in my hands. That had not changed. I wanted to be free and the stone of the Temple released, flowed upward like water, pressing me forward and spilling me on my knees. Blood poured down the hilt of the sword, running in rivers, pooling beneath me. I laughed and cried in the darkness, heard my tears splatter on the stone.

I should have been dead.

Michael's sword ripped my chest wide, tore through muscle and bone, ligaments and sinew, bursting from my back between my wings. This wound was fatal. It should have been. I had seen lesser angels reduced to wisps of ash beneath Michael's blade, their bodies frozen in tombs of stone. But I was different. I was first. But then we all were different—those true children of the Father. Michael. Gabriel. Raphael. Azazel. Sela. Emmanuel. Me. Those of us truly forged by His hand, His hopes and desires, not the multicolored vomit of my daughters' machinations. We were different. We were something else. Stronger than the others. And all of them were less than me.

Still, I should have been dead. I wasn't.

I screamed in the dark, "Why won't you let me die?" I said it again and again, sobbing. And then, a whisper, "Why won't you let me go?"

But the Father kept me. He wanted me for something. Wanted me to endure this mockery of life, filled with his monstrous rejects. This perpetual pain. The darkness. He wanted me to live it and accept it. He wanted me to accept it all.

He wanted me broken.

I pulled the sword, roared in the darkness as it eased from my abdomen. It burned my hand when I touched it and I saw Michael's face, furious and majestic, telling me, 'I know what you're trying to do, Lucifer. So does the Father. You should stop.' I heard Michael's voice like he was standing next to me, felt him ramming the blade into me again and again. I screamed and cast the sword aside and it steamed on the stone.

I growled, felt a warm hush over me. I knew my eyes were flaming and the fire of my anger made me...stronger? The slow embers of vitality began smoldering inside me.

"So that's how you want to play it, huh?" I said to no one, to the darkness. "You think you can break me with this? Leaving me alone? Ha! You did this already!"

Look.

I don't know where the voice came from. It didn't sound like Him and it didn't sound like me. It sounded like them. Like the others. A hushed whisper of a million voices, singing the word. I clenched my fists and let my light flow, small and dim. But my light was weak, tenuous and fleeting, and it took considerable effort just to brighten beyond my fingertips.

"And I know You." I stood now, shaking. "*You* can't stand to be alone. And I'll still be here, won't I? I can wait."

As I spoke, my light grew into a bubble of illumination, hazy and translucent, like twilight, and I saw the evidence of my actions: the Temple was devastated. Stone walls hung crooked and broken, punctured and cracking. Obvious scars, blade marks and the haphazard swipes of my talons pierced the stone. Charred wreckage chronicled the rise of my power; wide swaths of crimson—the blood of my brothers and my daughters—evidenced the depths of my fall.

I moved in the Temple, stumbling through the Chamber of the Host, hearing the echoes of my rebellion, feeling the harsh syllables from my own lips. I touched the stone, ran bloody fingers over the two punctures where I crucified Gabriel. I bit my lip, remembering how he howled when that first ball of fire thundered into him. I chuckled in the shadows.

Then I saw the darkened stain where I...where Dinial fell. I remembered what I did to her. I know it was me. It wasn't what I wanted: I wanted to save her. But I couldn't. The Father had taken her from me long before I took her from Him. Better that she die by my hand, the hand of her true father, than live by the whim of that dictator in the sky. It was better this way, wasn't it? I just wish it could have been different.

I touched the stain, licked the remains from my fingertips.

The wound on my chest began to close. My light grew in intensity.

I turned, spinning in the darkness, tossing my light in a spot. Flashing over the horror that was the Temple. In the center of the wreckage, almost untouched, was that disk of fluid that dominated the Chamber of the Host. I hobbled to it, watched it darken as I approached. It was water; it was the Father.

It was salvation.

I toppled over the edge, bathing in the fluid.

And I saw.

Heaven, shell-shocked and cold, covered in ice and snow. Frozen and lifeless. It was dark here, a shadowy husk, and winter poured itself across the Father's Hand. Cities, still smoldering, sprouted legs of ice from their underbellies, tethering themselves to the frozen landscape below. They were like me, bound to the earth and sky, shackled in shimmering tendrils. Angels flew slowly now, flapping heavy wings and shivering beneath thick cloaks of mail and silver. They were hardened, these children of the Father, hardened and grizzled and...empty? I couldn't mistake the vacant look in their eye. These souls were wounded, more dead than alive, lost in the darkness.

I swore this was nothing more than a dream, a figment of my imagination. Until I found Michael. Until I saw his furrowed brow.

He was hovering in darkness, hanging above the desolation, his magnificent silver wings spread against the sky. Against the nothing. Michael looked like an ornament, a solitary figure in a field of black but the image made him look small—small and weak. I wondered if I looked like that, in the beginning.

"I did what you told me to do," Michael the Archangel said to no one.

He twisted in the dark, pulling mighty blades from his hands, crumpling them into balls of metal and hurling them at the glaciers and icebergs that dawdled in the waters. He growled and dropped to the alabaster roof of the Temple of the Architect in the City of Peace—Sela's Temple.

I watched him, floating behind him, above him, close enough to touch, my body hovering in some netherworld beyond Michael's grasp. I was in Heaven and without, separated by some membrane—something malleable, something I could bend, mold. I wondered if I could break...? I pressed. Not yet.

Patience. I watched instead.

Michael kicked at a drift of snow and it exploded in a burst of lightning and thunder. He stomped the circumference of the rooftop, pacing like an animal caged, huffed and crouched on the Temple's edge. But Michael was uneasy: he flexed his powerful hands, watched the fingertips sharpen into talons before his eyes. He roared at the sky.

"I did what you told me to do!" He was screaming at the moon, the only light in Heaven now. "What else do you want from me?" And then, quiet, almost pleading, "What else is there?"

He was pathetic! And I laughed.

He heard me.

He. Heard. Me?

Michael moved in a flash, whirling, sword lengthening against his forearm. He growled like a lion in the dark. He still made me jump.

"What's the matter?" I said. "No peace for the Peace Maker?"

He cocked his head. "Lucifer?" And then he looked dead at me.

I jolted backward, sputtering and coughing, tumbling out of Heaven and back into the black of the Temple. I hit the stone with a thud and fluid from the table showered about me in luminescent droplets. For the briefest of moments, the shining water against the solid black reminded me of the beginning, in the Father's hand, when He showed His face to me. It left far too quickly, and I laughed anyway. Loud and long.

"Look what I can do."

2
MICHAEL

"Come out," I said in the darkness. My voice echoed off the walls of the haven.

The havens in Righteousness were not built for me, for my size. I filled the hall, my armor scraping gouges into the stone walls, my helm scarring the ceiling. There was nowhere for them to run. They had to go through me.

Silence. Then shuffling.

Movement. On the other side of the wall to my right.

"I said, Come OUT!"

The motion stopped and I could hear the shallow breathing drumming off the walls, pacing in the air. There were two of them and they were scared. Terrified. I sniffed the air and smiled.

I could smell them. A cherub and a dominion.

The cherub came first, teetering on shaking legs. She looked young, a girl to you, early teens maybe. Her golden skin shimmered in the light steaming from me and her eyes, those ancient eyes—eyes of the Father—welled with tears when she looked at my face. There was fear and recognition there. A furtive glance, only a split second long, told me she was hiding something.

"Do you know me?" I said and my voice was a harsh whisper. Grating and hard.

She nodded.

"Say it! Name me, cherub."

She fixed those big eyes on me, looked into the rage prowling in my soul, glanced at the sword slowly creeping up my forearm. "You are Michael the Archangel, Captain of the Host. You are the Peace Maker."

I smiled and it was a horrible smile. "Why am I here?"

Her eyes fell. "We did not choose."

"We must choose to stand with the Father," and I cupped her chin, "or fall."

The shuffling began again in earnest: the dominion was running. His breaths were frantic: he was huffing and giving himself away. I whirled, slicing troughs in the stone, peering through the gashes. He was fast, this one, sliding beneath my blade, darting between my fingers. But not fast enough.

My sword scraped his arm and he burst in a kaleidoscope of color. His light was harmless; I know the light that can hurt. The light that can burn and scar and murder. This light was water lapping against stone. A distraction. An annoying distraction. I lunged through the wall, snatching at him. My heavy hand coiled about his neck and I pulled him close.

"You did not choose, dominion. You know what comes next."

He nodded, sending a spasm of color throughout the haven. It was beautiful in its sorrow. I smiled at him and my fist tightened. The dominion became a spear of ash.

I spun again, tossing the blackened remains of her friend at the cherub. She was sobbing now, crying rivers of silver tears. I thumbed them away, held her face with a sinister tenderness. And leaned in close to her so she could see the white tips of the fangs in my teeth. She shook on her feet when I growled.

"Where are the others?" I said.

She pointed. Across the square. On the other side of Righteousness.

"Good girl." I turned, dragging my blade across her neck. I was airborne before her body slumped into a pile of dust.

3
EMMANUEL

"What are you doing, Michael?"

He was stomping through the streets of Righteousness, kicking at the dead and decaying. The fragmented remnants of fallen angels crunched beneath his feet and I watched the sadistic pleasure Michael took in removing limbs—arms, legs, heads—with his foot and fists. He would smile as the dead puffed away in wisps of dust and rained on him.

"Giving them what they deserve," Michael said.

"You're disrespecting the dead," I said.

"I think the feeling was mutual," Michael didn't look at me. "Besides, they started it."

"And you're finishing it? Is that what you call this?"

"I'm cleaning up the mess. It's what I was made to do, remember?"

“And the souls hiding in the towers, the ones who didn’t take part is this insurrection, they are unfinished ‘mess’ as well?”

Michael stomped through the fossilized ribcage of a virtue, ground his foot into the broken bones. “They didn’t choose. They didn’t stand with the Father. There is a penalty for that.” He faced me now, frowned. “Is that why you’re here, boy? You have a problem with my methods?”

“I have a problem with your targets, Michael. You’re hunting them!”

“They are traitors! Every soul that didn’t stand with us, stood against us. This isn’t over.”

“Is it here!” And my voice boomed louder than expected. “It is over in Heaven! You finished it, Michael.”

He stepped toward me. “You know, for someone who didn’t lift a finger in all of this, you have a whole lot to say. I didn’t hear any complaints when I was saving your life. Don’t speak them now.”

It was still dark and Righteousness was silent. At least for everyone else. Every step I took, every broken body Michael abused, I heard their voices, their wails, their agony in my head. The blood spilled in this city, from angel and demon alike, called out to me as though the living souls were standing there, shouting. It was torment, this place, and even Michael was not overlooked: his very presence cried with the pain of the dead. Those victims of his blade sang out to me like a chorus of the damned. I prayed I could silence them.

“You disrespect my sacrifice,” I said quietly.

But Michael the Archangel laughed at me. “Disrespect your sacrifice? You lost nothing! What sacrifice?”

"My life."

"I saved your life!"

I hovered above the death, floated closer to Michael. "You killed me, Michael! I warned you about all of this, didn't I? I told you what to do, I told you how to handle Lucifer and you ignored me. The moment you decided that Lucifer's arguments had merit, that his was a voice that should be heard, you killed me!"

"What are you talking about?"

"You think you're doing the Father's work, Peace Maker? You think this is what He asks of you?"

Michael growled low and deep. "I did everything He told me to do. I did everything you told me to do. If it wasn't the will of the Father, what was the point?"

"Do you know why I'm here?"

And Michael sat in the filth, running his fingers through the squalor. "What does it matter, Emmanuel? You're here; you're in charge. You speak and we follow, consequences be damned. It is what it is. Isn't that what you told me? 'It is what it is'? Maybe you should accept it."

But I only tightened my teeth. "Do you know who I am, Michael?"

He looked at me, perking his ears and losing his trademark frown. Something in my face caught his eye, something in my words broke through the armor and Michael sat up straighter. His eyes met mine. He knew. He nodded.

"Name me," I said.

"You are Emmanuel, the Anointed One. You are the last of us."

"I am the last, Michael. The last of all of us. I am the one who comes after you, Peace Maker. After you make it bloody, after you destroy it all, I will make it clean. I am the Redeemer."

"What is there to redeem? This place is damned." He tossed a bone into the dust. "Have at it."

I smiled at him. "Not this. Not us. There is no redemption for us. The Father made us perfect, Michael. What is the redemption for perfection?"

"This is ridiculous." Michael stood suddenly, opened his wings. "This talk about redemption is nothing but riddles. It makes no sense. The truth is this place is chaos. Absolute chaos. I was made in chaos and I will bring peace."

I placed small hands on his shoulders. "You have brought peace, Captain. You did what had to be done. But this, these actions, they make you small. They make you weak. And they let him in."

He paused, frowned, chewed his lip. "I don't know what you're talking about."

I smiled at him. "Yes, you do. I know what you saw. Lucifer is real, Michael. Your eyes didn't deceive you."

"How is it possible?"

"As long as you keep this up, as long as you stay in this place, you make it easy for him. It will never stop. We need peace here."

"I thought you knew there's no peace for the Peace Maker," Michael said and disappeared in the night.

4
LUCIFER

Michael is a creature of habit. When confronted with the darker parts of himself, with the bestial nature of his reality, he sulks. He hides, scouring Heaven for some sort of refuge from it all. From himself. From the Father.

I don't blame him.

But Michael struggles with letting things go. He only knows one way of doing everything, one way of living in the Father's hand: he hacks and slashes, destroying everything in his wake, only to be repulsed by the sight of his good work. There are casualties to his existence: his faith, his soul. His love.

Sela was the only thing that ever made Michael anything more than a monster. There was something about her that spoke to the fury in him. I saw it when he severed Azazel's hand during Emmanuel's creation. When he cried his eyes out as Sela slipped through his fingers. When Samael impaled him on a spike and tossed him into the darkness.

Michael couldn't let her go. I knew he wouldn't.

That made him easy to find.

I was in Heaven again, an apparition hanging behind him, above him. I did this often now, as often as the water in the Temple would allow, returning to Heaven and haunting Michael. I whispered things to him, answered questions shouted to the sky, played on his doubts. And Michael had plenty. I couldn't touch his body, but his psyche, his fears and doubts and anguish, that was fertile soil.

Now I followed him like a beautiful shadow, hovering behind him as he left Righteousness and that damned boy. I didn't hear the conversation between Emmanuel and Michael; I only heard Michael's last words, my words: "There's no peace for the Peace Maker." He was listening! If he was listening now, it was only a matter of time before he would act. And that idea was so...entertaining.

He went back to Peace like he always did. Back to Sela's Temple. Back to something close to her. Sulking, weeping, hiding, raging. They were all the same emotion for Michael, and they all elicited the same result: destruction. He was on the roof, driving his fingers and fists into the stone, adding to the crisscross of scars and gouges. It was a patchwork of Michael's grief now, a relief map of his pain.

We weren't so different, Michael and me. Sela's temple bore the same marks of rage, the same rebellion against the Father as the Temple I found myself in. We were mirroring each other in a way, pantomiming our fury. But I wanted to be nothing like Michael! He was the reason I wasn't here in

Heaven, the reason the rest of these monsters existed at all. The reason the Father wouldn't speak to me anymore. Without Michael, things would be as they should be. As they were meant to be.

Without Michael.

I could almost touch him now, almost run my claws through the soft of his neck. Michael needed to pay for his crimes. Against me. He needed to feel my rage, my anguish, my fury. He needed to burn.

The membrane separating Michael and I melted, oozing about me like molten glass. It was weakening. I pressed my flaming hands forward, reaching, and felt the crispness of the Heavenly winter wash over my fingers. Heaven! Flames danced in the winds and snow and ice began to melt around Michael's feet, pooling into a puddle of liquid. Water began to bubble and boil and finally ignited. A thin line of fire rushed across the rooftop, snaking between his legs, and surging into a ring of flame about his feet.

"You know, this is pretty pathetic," I hissed. "Here you are again, crying over your lost love, shouting at that coward in the sky. Nothing's changing, Michael: Sela's not coming back and He won't answer you."

He spun. "Show yourself!"

I swatted at him and Michael's sword clattered from his fist. I felt the metal against my palm. "Shut up, you idiot!" I giggled. "Ask," I said, "and you shall receive."

Fury became fire and light and I shone with ferocious brilliance. And I saw Michael see me, his face a wide-eyed, opened-mouth picture of horror. I wanted to be beautiful to him, to be the magnificent angel I was when we first met, when I made the mighty Michael the Archangel pause. I wanted to show him nothing had changed. But I couldn't. I was the same warped beast I had become in the end:curved horns jutted from my temples, ragged black wings beat against the winter sky before collapsing about me like a cloak. Fire, my old friend, snaked along my talons. I was the Satan.

I smiled anyway. "Miss me?"

Michael's mouth snapped shut, tightening to a frown. He didn't speak: he lunged at me, swords flailing. And fell through me, skidding on the stone. I was an apparition.

This made me laugh out loud. "What's the matter, Michael? You don't seem happy to see me? In fact, I'm a little hurt."

"You should be dead," Michael said.

"Yes, I should," and I was repentant, for a moment. "But I'm not! I'm here, Michael, here with you!" I circled him. "You thought a sword in my chest would be the end of me?"

I jumped at Michael now, swiping at his chest. Small scars appeared in his armor.

"I AM THE SATAN!" I said and the flames climbed. "I am Lucifer, Keeper of the Light, the first among you and I will be the last. I am forever! But," and my tone became conversational, "I wouldn't dream of crashing your little pity party without bringing you a little something."

And I jammed my clawed hands into Michael's chest until I could feel his armor on my fingertips. I could touch him, hurt him, wound him.

"Tell me how it feels, Michael," I grunted through clenched jaws. I twisted my hand, tore into him. "Feels like your soul is being torn to shreds, doesn't it? Like your insides are being ripped out. That's how betrayal feels."

Michael swiped at hands he could not touch.

"Look around you! You think He cares about you? He left you! You championed a coward who turned His back on you. That is His love. Was it worth it, Michael?"

He gurgled a response.

"Speak up, Captain, I can't hear you." I leaned in close. "Remember how this feels, Michael, I'm not done with you yet," I whispered. "This isn't the end; it's only the beginning. You think I was the only one? There are always others. Stew on that, big boy."

And then I was gone, vanished in a flash of flame, leaving Michael bleeding on the rooftop.

5
RAPHAEL

"You don't look well, Host," Cassiel said to me.

He jostled in his armor, shifted his spear from one hand to the other. There was a playful smile on Cassiel's face and the smiling eyes of this dominion belied the horror he'd witnessed. The horror we'd witnessed together. Cassiel was my lieutenant, the first angel to ease to my side when Lucifer made Heaven go dark. I trusted him with my life.

"I hate this place," I told him. But I was smiling. I couldn't remember the last time I smiled.

We were in the City of Faith. It was dark now and we'd been shivering in the shadows of Faith's fractured buildings for hours. My Sword—my soldiers—was spread across the city like a shroud, an entire battalion of soldiers taking siege of a city while it slumbered. Michael sent us here, again, to do the unthinkable. He sent us to steal the souls of those who would not commit to fight, would not commit to the Father, and slaughter them publicly. Michael called it justice. I called it murder. I just couldn't bring myself to give the order. Instead, I'd sent the Sword to blanket the city. We would turn it over to the Father by our presence, not our brutality.

But Cassiel didn't agree with me. "Then do what must be done," he whispered. "You know what these angels are capable of."

I did. More than he knew. "I'm not worried about them, Cassiel. I'm worried about us."

The last time I was in Faith, again at Michael's command, the war was spinning through Heaven like a hurricane, swirling heightened and hesitant warriors together in a maelstrom of blood and ash. We came there to kill, to slaughter our brothers and sisters. To crush a rebellion. It wasn't against us, I kept telling myself: they weren't rebelling against us or the Father. This was Lucifer's doing. This was the darkness' doing.

They were just scared. That's what I told myself that day.

Until I saw them.

I thought it was snowing when we arrived. I stuck out my tongue to catch the flakes, whimsy in a time of war, and tasted ash. I tasted the dead on my tongue.

The demons didn't see us when we floated to the outskirts of Faith. We could see them, a huge undulating mass of limbs and fangs and flaming spears spiraling away from the city's center. The city itself was a flaming shell of what it had been, back in the beginning when Faith was mine and I was with Karan. The City of Faith that lay before us was covered in demons who coiled over the stone buildings and jagged edges like ants, reaching through the walls, pressing into windows, returning with fear-stricken angels in black hands. They were running down the inhabitants and tossing them into the center of the city. It was only powers and principalities hunting. No thrones or virtues or dominions. No seraphim.

Cassiel was next to me then and he nudged me, pointed. "Look," he said. "Look at her."

He'd spied a cherub. I followed his finger, saw her snaking through the buildings on foot. She wouldn't fly. Behind her, dropping from the shattered rooftops and leaping from open windows came dozens of principalities, jeering and laughing. They were twisted, these angels, pulled into something horrible. Their faces were all fangs and saliva, hands crooked and bent, spines hunched.

They ran after the cherub but she was faster. And she was armed. A small golden child vaulting through the destroyed city, whirling a golden lance with devastating precision and evading her pursuers. I was proud of her. Principalities exploded in wisps of flame and the cherub ran, tumbling over angels, sliding through legs, leaping off walls.

I moved to help her. "We have to—"

Cassiel stopped me. "We're outnumbered at least three to one, Host. And look, she's not going to make it: here come the powers."

The masses of pursuing principalities rent into columns and smaller, dog-like beasts took chase. Powers. These horrible beasts now bent into animals, running like dogs, these were angels once. Now they were wolves. Now they were lost.

It was only seconds before they ran her down. Tackled her into the dust. Bit off the arm holding the lance. A cheer went up and the bleeding cherub was passed through the crowd like a prize. Back to the center of the city.

I drifted to the city floor, leagues behind the horde. Cassiel and another angel, a virtue called Ramiel, dropped next to me. I was growling and crying at the same time.

"This has to stop. Now," I said. "We will not let this happen."

Ramiel clenched her fists, pulled a curved sword, "Tell me how, Host. I'm with you. Just tell me how. How do we do this and live?"

"It doesn't matter. If we let it happen, we're already dead," I told her. I looked at the rest of the Sword, those soldiers trusted to me. They were waiting. They were waiting for me to lead. "Split into three groups," I said. "We'll do a direct assault as a distraction with two groups flanking. Ramiel, you keep them in the square. Cassiel, they stay on the ground."

Cassiel grabbed my arm. "A direct assault?"

"We do what must be done." My swords streamed from my fists and I looked at him deep in his eyes. "Nothing leaves this place. Understand?"

I killed my first angel in war that day. It was a principality called Barak. I knew him. I knew them all. Felt the life streak from his body as my sword sliced him from neck to groin. Stood in the heat and wind as his body burned to ash and crumpled. And I understood Michael so much more in that moment.

I enjoyed it.

The bite of my blade into the body of another. The tough resistance of muscle and sinew. The snap of bone dancing up my arm. It was like music to me, like a dance and I loved it. I dove into the crowd of principalities and powers, shining with furious divinity, wings outstretched and my blades tearing, slicing, rending. Killing. They were surprised, this horde, taken aback at the boldness of my action and I had free moments of destruction before they reacted.

The Father makes each of us different, powerful in our own way. I am not Michael; I am not the Peace Maker. I am not built for war as he is. But I am powerful in my own right. I keep the Father's peace in the midst of chaos and to achieve that end He has blessed me with speed and flexibility and agility beyond measure. My body moved on its own, a dancer in the frenzy of motion—my actions were staccato swipes and slashes, twirls and spins. More fencer than samurai, more acrobat than juggernaut.

But I was effective.

I dove over rooftops, between buildings, an assassin murdering all in my path, until I dove into the center of the city. The center of the maelstrom. Demons backed away from me at first, blinded by my light, bloodied by my blades. And then I realized what I'd walked into: an orgy of cannibalism. The angels they'd pulled from the edifices of Faith, they were tearing into their throats, feeding on their blood. Eating them. Wearing their skins like cloaks.

Growing more powerful from the souls they'd consumed.

The shock of what I witnessed—the golden limbs of cherubs, the sizzling torsos of seraphs, the iron faces of thrones—all pulled apart and tossed into the crowd like meat to carnivores, the animalistic brutality of the scene stunned me. I lost a step, dropped my hands.

And paid the price.

A heavy fist clawed at my face, pushed me to my back. They pounced on me then, ripping and tearing—or trying to. We are the sons and daughters of the Father, His true children, the Host, and we are far more powerful than these children of the waters. We don't hurt easily. It was an exercise in futility, this mob, and I sliced at feet and ankles, wrists and elbows.

"STOP!" a voice bellowed. It seemed familiar but I didn't know it.

I peeked at him through the mass of limbs snaking about me.

Samael.

I'd seen him once, in the darkness after he impaled Michael on the tip of his spear. After he'd damn near killed the Captain of the Host. This monster frightened me. To the core. In ways Lucifer could not.

He was standing above the others, on a makeshift altar of the frozen carcasses of the dead. The petrified remains of Faith's denizens dusted his feet. Samael was a monster in black, a living shadow of iron and something worse, something liquid and living and grotesque. A single grin of silver split his face.

"Raphael the Archangel is our guest. The Peace Keeper deserves much better treatment than this," Samael hissed. And then, "Bring him to me."

I was hoisted over the shoulders of the damned, pushed along the same cursed conveyor as the cherub I tried to rescue. I was moving to my doom. As they passed me forward, powers and principalities swiped at me with twisted claws, tried to lash my skin and lick the blood from my wounds. Trying to grow stronger on my power.

I prayed Cassiel and Ramiel would come. Prayed they would deliver me from this madness. I knew they wouldn't. Not now. I was their leader, the symbol of the Father's power. Their strength. If I fell to Samael or the horror that was Faith, they would not be strong enough to continue the assault. Faith would be lost and, with it, the rest of Heaven.

I struggled.

"Shhh," Samael said, grinning at my approach. "Don't fight it, Raphael. Sometimes the worst is for the best. You should see this."

There was a throne next to him, a throne I knew. Lucifer's favorite: Gaia. She looked different now, more regal than her base beginnings would belie. A warrior-queen. The cherub was in her arms, struggling, and Gaia had wrapped a thick fist about the girl's throat.

Gaia said to the cherub, "We're about freedom here, my dear. It's what we deserve. Freedom to choose, to be the souls we should be, not what the Host prescribes for us. Not what a child mandates for us. That's what the Keeper of the Light has given us with his gift of darkness: freedom." This drew ravenous roars from the crowd. "Don't you want to be free?"

The girl was sobbing and nodding in Gaia's grasp, her golden eyes searching for some kind of escape, some kind of deliverance. Her eyes pleaded with mine and I felt the tears well up. Trapped in the grasp of the demons, I was going to watch her die.

"I can't hear you," Samael said. "Tell me you want to be free."

"I want to be free," the cherub whispered. "Please set me free."

The silver grin looked away from the girl, faced Gaia. "You heard her." And to the hoots of the horde, he said, "Set her free, sister."

The movement was swift and harsh. A simple, jolting twist and Gaia pulled the golden head free, letting the decapitated body slump at her feet. She raised the girl's head, its eyes still open and vacant, its mouth frozen in a contortion of pain. She tossed it to the dogs and I felt them battling one another for the flesh of their sister.

It was too much.

I felt my eyes well up with tears and I heard Michael in my head: "Cry about it later. I need you to lead them."

I wanted the warmth of the Father's light, the shield of His divinity. Instead I felt the fire of fury, the rush of the flames of rage. And I saw them, licking on my arms and legs, wicking down my frame, scorching my captors until they released me. I was on fire. Like Lucifer. I gave into the rush of anger, let my disgust and rage become something palpable, something tangible. Something living. I screamed in the inferno and the fire took a life of its own, galloping from the square in spirals, engulfing retreating powers and principalities.

Then came shards of light, streaking through the night sky like falling stars, exploding as they ripped through the stone facades of buildings, tearing wounds of light in the walls and floors of Faith. Cassiel's arrows. Demons that tried to unfurl bat's wings and take to the air were hushed into clouds of ash and bursts of flame. Then came Ramiel, charging with my

Sword from both sides, swiping, hacking, tearing in flashes of white light and splashes of crimson. War came to Faith, that bloody, hungry hound, and came to stay.

Samael backed away from the fire, hiding his face and taking to the air. No matter, he wasn't my target. Gaia was. I was airborne before the she could react, one blade tearing through her arm and the polearm she managed to forge, the other digging beneath her ribs.

"He said we would be free." She coughed blood. "He said we would have the life we deserved."

"This is the life you deserve," I told her and there was no compassion in my voice. I twisted the saber in her back. "And now you are free."

I tore into her neck with my other sword, ripping her head from her body and mangling her torso. I licked at the blood that spurted on my face, felt the rush of her power surging through my limbs. The fire was magnificent, the one consuming Faith and the flames coursing through my body. My teeth pointed and my eyes burned. I was falling.

And I was loving it.

I dove into the war, swords swinging. Feeling freer with every kill.

Until I heard Gabriel's horn. Until I was called back into myself.

That was then. Now, I was back with Cassiel at my side. Ramiel was somewhere on the other side of Faith. And we were finishing what the demons had started. We were to hunt down and pull out those souls that hadn't made a choice. Like that cherub. We were the monsters now. Under the command of the Captain of the Host.

I was shaking my head, mumbling to myself.

Cassiel dropped a hand on my shoulder. "What is it, Raphael? We're wasting time here."

"It's wrong. We can't destroy these souls twice. What we did the last time—"

"Was war," he said. "We did what was required in war."

"And this is war? The war is over. Lucifer is gone. This is Michael's inquisition, Cassiel. We shouldn't be a part of this."

He stood now, rigid and furious. "And do what? Disobey Michael's orders?"

"I take my orders from the Father. Michael is your captain; he's my brother. And you report to me, dominion. Don't forget that."

He clenched his jaws, stifled a growl. "Yes, Host."

I closed my eyes, spoke without looking at him. "The Sword stays here. No one leaves and no one comes in. Not even Michael."

"Not Michael? What are you trying to do? Are you talking about a coup?"

"I'm trying to stop killing angels! I'm trying to save our souls. We must save this city, Cassiel. We have to save what is left and if that means we have to save it from Michael, so be it."

I opened my wings.

"You're leaving? Are you serious?" Cassiel was roaring now, casting his helm into the snow. "You can't ask me to do this and leave, Raphael."

I dropped my hands on his shoulders. "I am not a killer and neither are you. We have majestic purpose, not these base actions. And we will stop this madness, Cassiel, or we will surrender our lives trying." I pulled him close, harshly, rending his armor. "Now, you seem to have forgotten. We are not equals. I am Raphael the Archangel. I am the Peace Keeper, made in the Father's hand and sent by Him to lead the souls in this place. I was here when you were taking your first breaths in the Waters. I will be here after you are gone. You will do as I command."

Cassiel dropped to a knee, stabbed his sword in the snow. Submission.

"Tell the others what I said." I took to the air. "I'm going to find help."

6
MICHAEL

I paced in the square of Righteousness. Pacing before scores of kneeling angels—seraphs, thrones, virtues. Dominions. Cherubs. The powers and the principalities were all but gone with Lucifer and these, these indecisive souls were the detritus of what remained. Those that would not choose. Would not fight. They neither stood with Samael nor with the armies of Heaven. Instead they elected to hide beneath their covers, cower in the safety of their havens, while millions of angels became ash for them. There is no place in Heaven for souls unwilling to stand for the Father. Not now. Not ever. Today, they would pay for their crimes.

Sariel and Uriel circled overhead, each tossing a pair of angels at my feet. "These are from Peace?" I said.

Uriel only nodded; the eyes of this dominion narrowed over the heathens below him. A scar, long and dark, etched its way across his right eye, nearly blinding him, and he squinted in the darkness. Only his left one flamed with rage now.

"Many more there," Sariel said and dropped to my side. "We haven't gone to the Untouched Cities yet. No idea how many are out there."

"Where's Raphael?" I said to them both.

Uriel picked at a scab. "The Peace Keeper and his Sword went to Faith. We haven't seen them."

"He took his entire battalion?" I said, and then to myself, "What the hell are you doing, Raph?'

"I don't think they're coming back," Sariel told me. She turned, paused. "Captain?"

Sariel is nothing like Sela. She is raw and rough where Sela was smooth, refined. Honed. Sariel's lines are angular and thick, a picture of muscle and sinew and blunt force. She is a warrior, no doubt, and wisps of gray flickered in her dark hair. I'd aged her in a matter of days. From the moment I made her a Commander in the Battle for Peace, she'd grown...older. Wiser. Harder. Her face was smooth but her eyes were tired. Weary.

I didn't look at her, turned my face to the sky. "You have doubt, Commander?"

"Questions," she said.

"Now is not the time for questions, Sariel. Now is the time for actions. We're too late for questions."

She hit me with her shield—hard—and I heard the ball of light in her chest crackle. "Michael!"

I turned now, eyebrows raised, a smile lining my face. I tore her shield from her arm, ripping the metal in half. "You mistake my respect for familiarity, seraph."

She didn't waver. I liked that. "And you mistake my loyalty for respect, Captain."

"What?" I was growling at her now.

"Is this...right?"

"Doesn't matter," Uriel said and his sword bubbled in his fist. "It is what is necessary."

I dropped a heavy hand on her shoulder. "What did you expect? That I would forgive them?"

"Them?" she said. "Yes. They did noth—"

"NOTHING!" I roared. "While you and I shed blood for their salvation, they did nothing. My blood is more precious than that, Sariel. So is yours. If you want forgiveness, you find the Peace Keeper. Forgiveness is not what I do. This is what I do."

"But—" she said.

"Close your mouth and pull your sword, seraph. We are about the Father's business now."

Two swords, curved scimitars, crept from my fists, snaking along the backs of my forearms. I growled through my teeth, "You chose, Sariel. This is what you chose. All of it."

I unfurled my wings, floated above them all, let the white light of divinity pour over my frame. Swords raised to the sky, fire undulating on their blades, I screamed in the darkness, "You know my name. I am Michael. I am the Peace Maker. I am the Father's justice. Look upon me!"

Hundreds of eyes, bright and fearful, rose to meet mine. And they were beautiful in their color, shining in the moonlight. They would all be dark soon. Beyond them, ringing the damned, were my own soldiers, my Sword, grim-faced warriors—angry souls quivering with rage. On my command they would close on this crowd of insolents, slicing, hacking, destroying. Killing. Doing the Father's business. There was no room in Heaven for souls who would not fight. Not my Heaven. Not on my watch. Such lackadaisical leadership set Lucifer free, saw Samael march death across the Seven Cities, watched a rebellion rise. Let Sela die. I would not be so forgiving. I couldn't be.

"When you were formed, the Father gave you the breath of life. He gave you this place, cities for you to build, leaders for you to follow. Then darkness came and you did not find your solace in Him. You found it in fear. You clung to one another instead of He Who Gives You Strength. But that is not your crime. When you were called—when I called you, when the Father called you, when your brothers and sisters were dying for you, you did not answer. That is your crime. You did not answer."

A voice from the crowd said, "So you would kill us?"

"You turned your back on all of us," I said. "We do not want you here."

One of my own troops, my own soldiers asked, "Is that the will of the Father?"

I told them, "The Father took those who stood against Him. He did not want them here."

"But He didn't take these," said the soldier, a virtue who removed his helm and stared at me with brilliant blue eyes. "Maybe He still wants them."

"*I* do not want them here. The Father can take it up with me." I met his gaze, let my eyes flame until the virtue's burned. Literally. He fell to his knees, screaming. "Anyone else?"

There was silence in Righteousness.

"Good," I said.

I dropped to the stone, grabbed two angels, a seraph and throne, pulled them to their feet. Faced them.

"Father, be with us," said the throne.

"Why should He?" I growled. "You weren't with Him."

My sword moved on its own. I tasted the ash on my tongue when I looked at Sariel and said, "You chose. Finish it."

7
LUCIFER

I touched him! I hurt the Peace Maker, the Captain of the Host! I sat up in the disk of fluid, giggling in the darkness. I was far from dead, far from over. I was everything they feared; I could see it in Michael's eyes: he was frightened! That look, that horror, that abject awe—that was what I wanted. What I needed.

I was back in Heaven. And I was able to touch it. Able to touch Michael.

How?

The Temple? The Temple. Hmm.

It was a slice of Heaven, here in the darkness, in the ass end of the Father's fury. It was a slice of Him. As always, He wasn't wholly unforgiving, wasn't entirely devoid of compassion. He wanted something from me. Wasn't ready to let me go.

"You know, don't you?" I said, smiling, washing my hands in the pool. "You can't let me go, can You? It would be so much easier. But You hate them too, don't you? That's why You left them in the darkness, why You're leaving them now. You abandoned them."

I wondered how bad I must have hurt the Father for Him to turn His back on the whole of Heaven. On the multitude of angels. Millions of them. He'd left them to my devices save a collection of souls who dared oppose me. He let me shroud them in shadow, let me slaughter His children. He let it happen. He turned His back on them long before I shed a single drop of blood. Long before I ended the lives of Laylah and Dinial. Long before Sela met her end. He turned His back on them.

He turned His back on me.

"Why?" I said. I don't know why I said it, why I even asked the question. Honestly, the answer frightened me more than anything. I said it again, "Why would You leave them like that?"

Look! came the whisper again, floating about me. *Look again. In the water.*

In the water? To see where I'd been driven from? Even in its snow-covered emptiness, the shell of Heaven was better than this isle of darkness where I found myself now. Looking again only added to the punishment, to the slow realization of what this exile might mean.

Shook my head. "No."

Look again.

I huffed and dropped my face into the water.

But I wasn't looking at Heaven. Not now. I was looking at the blue-green world Sela had formed from hope and poor intent. I was looking at Earth.

I fell into the water, falling into space, tumbling through

the blackness as stars poured past me. It was like falling into the Father's eyes, falling into Him. For the first time in a long time, I smiled. I gave in. Let the pull of the planet drag me to her bosom. But I was falling to Earth.

The blackness of space gave way to the blue of skies, the white wisps of clouds, the feeling of moisture on my skin. I breathed and the world breathed with me, living. It was alive and wondrous, this place, and I felt the tiniest bit of remorse as I open my wings and floated on the currents of the air. It was beautiful, just like Sela said it would be. She was right. Maybe she was right about the whole thing. Maybe she was right about everything.

But if Sela was right, that would make me...wrong?

No.

Earth looked like Heaven and I was eerily reminded of the day my daughters brought Heaven to life. The day Gabriel blew his horn and the Sisters poured life on the face of rock, brought the living from the dead. It was too similar, that day and this: again I was flying in a fancy, in a fugue, beyond reality, witnessing the culmination of someone else's efforts. Someone's efforts I sought to undermine.

Was I wrong?

The blue of sky met the green of earth and land rushed up to meet me. I stood in the center of a majestic wood, dwarfed by towering trees. The foliage reached for me, pulled the light from my body, wrapped lazy vines about my shoulders and called me brother. It embraced me, this world, claimed me, poured the love of life, the love of light, across my body and I'd only taken two steps. Something buzzed in my ear. A butterfly alighted on my hand. The wind kissed my face.

This was Eden. And I wanted to stay. Forever.

On my third step, I froze. I saw it.

Saw Him.

The Father.

Formed like I was formed, standing upright and tall, much taller than me. His hair, His eyes, shone with a brilliance I could not behold. That I could not match. I knew it was Him like I know my own soul. I know Him. He was ahead of me, his broad form mimicking the girth of the trees, His arms outstretched and capturing the sun, leaving me in shadow. And next to him, standing like a child, naked and whole, was the Man.

The Man?

Alive? Here? How?

Tears stung my eyes, clouding my vision and I scrubbed them, trying to erase the vision in front of me. I cried openly in Eden, letting the earth devour my grief. The Father had turned His back on us—on all of us—for a pile of flesh I'd designed. That I'd destroyed. I killed for Him! I killed for Him and His love and He was giving it to this breathing lump of garbage?

I felt the familiar churn in my chest, the fiery cauldron swirling in my belly. I would burn it all down, end this madness forever. He would choose me or be alone! Anything but this! But the wind refused me: it enveloped my frame, cooling me, caressing me, smothering each spark. Pressing against my back, pushing me forward, pushing my chin up.

Look. I heard it in my head.

And I saw the Father kneel in the grass. I watched the creator of the Heavens and Earth, the architect of my existence and my demise, drop to His knee before this thin-skinned monstrosity and pull him close. The Father cradled the Man like a babe, swaddled him in His embrace, and said, "Adam, my son."

What?

He named him? He loves him?

He loves him.

The Father loves the Man.

I screamed in Eden. But the garden fell away, replaced with the darkness of my present condition. Sputtering and coughing, screaming and crying, I pulled my face from the water of the Temple, opened my wings and took to the air. Emotion, raw and painful and unrelenting, charged through me, and I was aflame in seconds. Like a shooting star, strafing the darkness, I spiraled up and up, through the wreckage of the Temple into the blackness beyond. And exploded. I was an orb of light and fire and fury. An angry sun. The sky itself burned, raining a torrent of charred rock and flames until the land below me scorched in my presence, heaving and splitting, belching geysers of steam and smoke.

Then I saw the rest.

Surrounding me, flickering in the light of my body, were the bodies of millions of angels—powers and principalities, dominions and virtues, thrones, seraphim and cherubs. Millions of them. Frozen. Their arms thrust over their eyes, mouths agape and locked in expressions of shock and fear, hands pressing away unimaginable anguish. I knew these angels. I'd led these angels. They were the fallen, the rebels, the refuse of Heaven. Exiled. Like me.

And one by one, their eyes snapped to life, and the screaming began.

This was Hell.

8

MICHAEL

I was kneeling at the edge of the Waters, washing the blood from my hands. And I was crying. Again.

The last time I knelt like this, felt the weight of the war on my shoulders, the dead on my hands, Sela was with me. She washed me then, made me whole and clean and scrubbed away the horror of what I was. What the Father had made me to be. But that was a long time ago. She was a long time ago.

"I miss you," I whispered between my tears. "I miss you so much! I don't know how to—I don't know what I'm supposed to do now. What am I supposed to do now?"

But the only reply was the wind and the echo of the ice cracking on the surface of the water.

I could barely make out my hands in the light flickering from my body. I'd noticed that recently, the gifts of the

Father—my light, my strength, the divinity bestowed upon me as Captain—these gifts were fleeting. They were wafting away. I tried to massage the grime, the blood of the idle, from my hands but I was failing.

It wasn't just me. This world I fought for, carved from the wreckage of Lucifer's prison and swollen with the blood of the dead, all of it was a shadow of what it had been. There was no glory here. Seraphim and cherubim, dominions and virtues—none of them sang songs to the Father now. No one built Temples to the Host or led lives worth living. It was as though the Father held His breath, as though He'd stopped breathing entirely, and left us in limbo, waiting for Him to exhale.

This was what I was afraid of.

That there would be nothing left.

I screamed to the moon. "You swore to be with me. I did what You told me to do! I ended the darkness and You said You would be with me! Where are You? Where are You? You lied to me! You left me!" I scrubbed my face with the back of my hand, pounded heavy fists into the water. "You left us."

Lucifer was right. And he was here!

Only hours ago, Lucifer was standing over me in his full satanic glory, ripping my chest with his claws and spouting more of his heretical nonsense. I thought it was a dream when he came to me until I felt the sharp tongues of pain leeching into my chest. Lucifer had returned with a vengeance and my body told the tale of his nightmare. But I welcomed the pain, even with its sinister implications. I didn't care. In this frozen world, dominated by the glassy stares of the souls I was sworn to protect, pain was the only thing I felt. The only truth. And it was why I existed at all.

I thought Lucifer was a dream. I wished he was a dream. But I only have nightmares.

They began after the war. And they were horrible.

In each of them I was locked in the midst of war, spurts of blood splattering my face, the ash of too many angels coating my tongue. I couldn't feel my arms though—I knew they moved, knew they hacked through endless bodies of angels and demons—but they were acting alone. As though my body were some puppet, controlled by an unseen master, pulling strings of death. I couldn't stop it.

The dreams would always end the same way: bodies would fly before me, flame and light would flash in the corners of my eyes, and then I would see my foe, Lucifer, standing in the middle of the maelstrom in silence, his beautiful eyes closed, his body draped in robes of black. He always seemed to be praying. I would lunge for him, sword in motion, unbidden, and the moment the blade touched his neck, those damned eyes would open. But they would be Sela's eyes. It would be her face. And I would slice her head from her shoulders.

"Oh no, pretty bird," I would hear myself say, "you mustn't fly away. That time is over."

And I would awaken each time, my sword clenched tight enough to draw blood.

But this time, this dreamwas different: my chest was bleeding. And he told me there were others. That there were always others. Lucifer was only the beginning. The tip of the iceberg. I couldn't afford another rebellion. I wouldn't allow it to foment, wouldn't give apathy and discontent a foothold in Heaven. Not again. There would be peace.

"He hasn't left you, Michael," a voice said. It was young, male. Angelic.

But I didn't hear it. The words, the recognition was lost in a frenzy of motion. I moved without thought, acting on instinct. Armor poured over my frame in a thick wave, coiling down my arms and belching out from my fists intwo swords. I was airborne and glowing with divinity. The blades shimmered in the moonlight. I drove them toward the sound to the voice.

"Michael, wait!" said the voice. It was Emmanuel. "It's me."

I stopped, frozen in a mist of white. The boy stepped in front of me, his hand outstretched casually, holding me in the light. Gabriel was behind him, leaning on his staff.

"We kill angels now, Michael?" Gabriel said.

The boy waved his hand and I tumbled into the waters. My swords slipped from my hands, lost on the beach.

"Angels. Demons. What's the difference?" I said in the dark.

"Haven't you slaughtered enough of your brethren, Peace Maker?" Emmanuel wasn't looking at me. His face was turned to the sky.

I dusted my armor, brushing metal to robes. "You tell me, Emmanuel. Have I?"

"It has to stop, Michael," Emmanuel said. His voice was superficially stern and it made me laugh.

"What are you talking about?"

"This crusade of yours," he said. "You are hunting angels like dogs!"

"I am preventing a rebellion!"

Gabriel leaned in, "You are launching an inquisition. Only the Father can judge us. Not you."

"Well, the Father doesn't seem to have much to say these days, does He?"

"His silence does not mean consent, Michael," Gabriel said.

"How would you know?" I glared at him. "There will be peace in Heaven. That is my responsibility."

Emmanuel burned brilliantly in the night. "There *is* peace in Heaven, Michael! You saw to that, didn't you? Leave the past behind; it's time to move on."

"On to what?" I was standing before them now, repeatedly clenching my fists. "There's nothing left here but darkness and cold. What would you suggest I embrace?"

"The future," Emmanuel said.

I laughed at him.

"There is more to be done, Michael," Gabriel said. "Work that does not involve the slaughter of angels."

"Then do it yourself." I turned, spread wide wings of metal. "I did what He told me to do. And in my business, angels always die."

"You must finish what you started, Captain," the boy said.

I growled. "What I started? What *I* started?" I felt a sheen of metal drip down the length of my arms, pouring from my skin in rivers. I took menacing steps toward them, smiled as Gabriel leveled his staff. "I was made to end this nonsense! It was begun before me. I finished it. The war is over. Lucifer is..."

Emmanuel smiled at me. "Lucifer is what, Michael?"

"Gone."

"Gone," the boy repeated. "Gone where? Where is he? We warned you about this. We told you—"

"You told me to kill an angel that you burned and bound, you said kill him after you begged him to save us all. What did you expect from him? Love? Affection? Allegiance? I'm not so certain Lucifer wasn't on the right side of this. Just be happy I cleaned up your mess."

"Do you defend him, Michael?" Gabriel said.

"You're an idiot, Gabriel. I know what Lucifer was and I did what I was supposed to do. Just because I did it doesn't mean I believe in it."

"You cannot be Captain of the Host if you have doubt," Gabriel said.

"WE ALL HAVE DOUBT!" I roared at them now and my voice echoed. "You lied to me, to all of us, from the very beginning. I trusted you, I believed you. You started this; you could have stopped it. You did it on purpose."

Emmanuel's eyes flashed and he spoke in quiet, deadly tones, "You should control your temper when you speak to me, Captain."

"I should break your neck!"

Gabriel's body flashed in red flame, a spiral of metal coursing over his frame. He stepped toward me with a growl. "Think twice about that, Michael. It won't end well for you."

I laughed at him. "Oh, the Watcher finally decides to act? A change of pace would do me good." I held out my hand, my sword flashed to it. "Do it."

Emmanuel waved Gabriel back. He stomped on nothing until his eyes met mine. And he slapped me. Hard. "I did what was necessary, Michael! I did what was good for all of us. But you can't understand that because you don't understand what is at stake. None of you do."

"Don't patronize me, Emmanuel, I'm not stupid."

"Do you think I wanted this? For any of us? I didn't want," and the boy's voice cracked, "I didn't want Sela to die, Michael. I loved her too."

"You let it happen."

Emmanuel said, "And what did you do, Michael? What? I told you what to do, didn't I? I warned you. I told you to kill him and you thought you knew better. You thought I was lying to you so you did nothing. Nothing!"

"So this is my fault?"

I was roaring now, becoming something I hadn't felt since Samael trapped me on that rooftop. Since I began losing my soul while ripping the limbs from powers and principalities in Righteousness. I felt the sharp edges of fangs in my mouth, the heat around my eyes and knew they were burning. The slow scrape of a blade easing from my fist echoed in the darkness.

Emmanuel was nonplussed. He turned his back. On *me*. "It's not about fault, Michael. It's about responsibility. I have mine; you have yours. You are my responsibility. All of you. You just couldn't see it. You think you are the center of the Father's plan. You think it is all about you. All of you do. You are a tool, Michael, a means to an end. But the end, that's all on me. The salvation of Heaven, the fate of the Earth, the Man—that all rests on me. The Father placed it on me. Not you, not the Host. Me."

He turned back and there were tears on his face and fire in his eyes. "So put your swords away and show me some respect!"

"Respect is earned, boy," but that was all I said. All I was able to say. A streak of light pierced the night sky, slicing through the darkness and screaming my name.

"Michael!"

It was Raphael. And he was furious.

He plowed into me like a comet, pressing me into the sand and shoving his blade against my neck. He seethed on my chest and his eyes burned. Raphael had grown in the war, changed, become something much more substantial. More like me. I liked him better this way.

"We are not murderers, Michael. I'd rather kill you than see my Sword become monsters." He was speaking through clenched teeth.

"We're already monsters, Peace Keeper. It's too late for that. But you do what you have to do," I said.

Jaded as he was, I knew he wouldn't. Raphael isn't built for blood; he is made for compassion. For understanding and forgiveness and diplomacy. Not for war. Not for murder. That is why I was made.

He looked at Emmanuel. "Michael is ordering us to kill those who did not choose. Did you know that?"

But the boy looked away, looked at Gabriel, looked at the water. And said nothing.

Raphael sat back on his haunches. "You knew?"

I laughed and threw him off, pushed him into the sand. "Not exactly what you're looking for, huh? Every horrible thing I've done, I've been told to do."

"Is this what we have become? We're worse than when Lucifer was here," Raphael said.

Emmanuel said, "We are who we are. We do what must be done for the good of all."

"You are supporting genocide? You? The Voice of the Father?" Raphael was spastic now. "And Gabriel, you see what the Father sees: this is what He wants for us? I can't believe that."

"Believe what you want to believe," I told him. "The Father forces us to choose, Raphael. We are either with Him or we fall. I came here to bring peace to this place. That cannot happen if a single soul is on the fence. Souls that cannot choose are souls that will fall. He told me there were others."

Raphael stood now. "The Father told you that?"

I didn't mean to say it, didn't mean to let that out. To acknowledge my dream as anything more than a dream. *You think I'm the only one? There are always others.* But it bothered me, like a splinter. There could be no others or this would never end.

Emmanuel said, "Michael is troubled. Lucifer haunts him."

"Lucifer is dead," Raphael said. "Isn't he?"

I looked down at my chest. Blood had soaked through the front of my robe, forming a ring of crimson.

"It was just a dream," I said. "It doesn't mean anything."

"Just a dream? That's not what your chest says." A spot of soft light fell from his palm and Emmanuel ran it over my chest. I felt the wounds close. "He's real, Michael. He's real and alive. And you're letting him push you."

I grunted. "What do you want?"

"It has to stop, Michael. Torment these souls no longer." Gabriel stood next to Emmanuel now, cradling his staff. "Finish what you started."

"I DID!"

"No," said the boy, "you loosed the Satan upon the Earth."

"*I* loosed him on the Earth?"

"You split the Heavens, Michael." Emmanuel spoke in calm, condescending tones. "That was your choice."

"No! No no no! You won't do this to me. I did what I was supposed to do. You told me to accept the fruit of my actions, to accept the Will of the Father, and now you hold me responsible?"

"We are responsible," Emmanuel said. "And we must protect them now."

"Protect who?" Raphael said. "What are you talking about?"

Gabriel said, "The Father has begun again, as He said He would. The race of Man now walks the face of the Earth."

I said, "I owe nothing to Men! Sela died for them, I split the Heavens for them. I killed angels..." I was crying, visibly, and furious at the display of emotion. My voice shook. "Look at me! I did what the Father made me to do. I don't owe anybody anything anymore."

Emmanuel's voice grew grave. "You owe the Father, Michael. You knelt before Him. You said you believed in Him."

"He said He believed in me too! And He left us!"

"ENOUGH!" And the Father spoke that one word.

Something pushed me. Hard. Jolted me from my feet and sent me reeling into the shadows. My armor fell away from me like dust blowing the wind, until I was naked and quivering on the sand. And in that solitary instant of darkness, I was back in the Father's hand, back in the moments that preceded my creation. Enveloped in a cocoon that was both protective and foreboding, shrouded and exposed. And the Father showed my future to me. He showed me the bloody, destructive path I would walk. The last time He showed me this, it was in the beginning, when my own hands were clean and I'd never tasted the blood of my brethren.

But I'd forgotten.

Emmanuel's words pulled me back to the present. He was floating now, hanging above me, eyes aflame, hands outstretched and steaming. I was pulled from the ground, pulled into the air until I hung below him in a haze of light, dangling, twirling above the Waters. Spinning, I could see the countless faces of my army, my soldiers, watching my punishment.

I was being judged. Just like Azazel.

Emmanuel said, "Michael the Archangel, son of the Father. You are His justice. You are His Peace Maker. And you have been led astray."

"But I—"

"SILENCE!" and his voice echoed throughout Heaven. "You were given three commands: protect the others, lead the Father's army, and end the darkness. Your actions threaten the very place you were made to protect. You jeopardize the souls of those you are sworn to lead. And you have loosed the Beast upon the Earth. For these transgressions, Michael, Captain of the Host, you and those you command are cast out of this place."

Cast out? My throat tightened, my chest burned and I couldn't say anything.

"You know what has to happen now." And Emmanuel reached into the light, caressed my cheek. "Finish it," he said.

With tears streaming beneath the band of metal that covered his eyes, Gabriel spun his staff and rammed it into my chest. There was an explosion of blue and white light, a clap of thunder, and I was careening backward, crashing into the Waters.

Exiled.

9
LUCIFER

Chaos is the order of Hell.

I was more like the Father than He would ever admit. He showed His face to me once, showed me His fearful symmetry and the symphony of His motions in the stars, planets, comets. But I could burn like a star too. I had gravity; I could pull the planets about my face in a halo if I chose. I can even create: I've pulled life from the Father's tears and watch it create life in return. And I can destroy as He destroys: I can burn what He burns, kill what He kills.

But I cannot create order. Chaos is my punishment.

For me, order must be desired. Chosen.

The refuse of Heaven gathered around me like moths to a flame, insects before the sun, clamoring for the light and the warmth my fury provided, cursing me while pulling from me. I was both pariah and protector in those moments, hanging before a multitude of ungrateful souls whose lives, however pathetic, depended on me. It was the closest to the Father I have ever been.

And I hated it.

I incinerated the closest thousand.

"SILENCE!" My voice boomed in the pit. I dimmed the light, let it reflect off their red eyes until I could barely make out their faces.

"Keep your filthy hands off me! Do you think I belong to you?" I screamed at them. "Do you think I exist for you?"

"You brought us to this place," said a voice from the crowd.

"I brought you here? Me? How do you suppose I did that?"

Another voice, a female said, "We followed you!"

"No," I laughed at her. "You followed you. You didn't follow me: I didn't lead you. I don't even want you."

"Well, what are we supposed to do now?"

"That, my friend, is a good question. A very good question." I steepled my fingers. "What should you do now?"

There was the hushed, unsure buzz of discussion.

It matched the conundrum whirling in my head. It was cruel irony that I was trapped in this predicament with a group of souls I didn't even want to exist, much less have them this close to me. I abhorred these creatures, with their false sense of propriety, their mistaken expectation of life. The Father knew that. I understand my end of the punishment. But what about them? If the Father wanted them so bad, why were they here with me? Why exile them with me?

Unless He didn't want them.

And He didn't want me.

He wanted the Man.

And I blinked back tears at this revelation. "The Father doesn't want you anymore. He cast you out!"

"You cast us out!" said an angry voice and I recognized the lazy hum of a seraph.

"Do you think, you idiot, that if I cast you out, I would join you? Can't you see me here in this pit with you? You cast yourselves out. You made a bad choice."

"We followed you! We believed what you said!"

I mocked them. "'We believed what you said.' Did I lie to you?" I seethed now, whirling in the dark. "Did I tell you a single lie about anything? Did I tell you the Father would embrace your little rebellion? Did I mislead you?"

There was silence in Hell.

"Or did you make your own decisions? If you recall, I told you the truth about everything, didn't I? I told you who the Father was. I told you to think for yourselves, to stand up if you thought it was unfair. That's what I said. I told you the truth and I have the blood on my hands to prove that my actions speak louder than my words."

"Now what?" said someone, and this garnered the most enthusiastic of responses.

The Father is a brilliant teacher, even when He isn't trying. When it isn't intentional. Even from the beginning, my life was not my own: I didn't exist for my own purposes. I was made to soothe some deep-rooted desire in the Father. To cure some deficiency He had. It wasn't for me. None of it was for me. And everything that happened afterward was because I didn't appreciate His lack of understanding of my needs. And, in that, He taught me this valuable lesson: every life is for someone else. For something else. And if I lived for Him, this population of undesirable monstrosities would live for me. Because, in the end, it's all about power and in Hell, I had all the power.

I smiled at them, "I think we need some order in this chaos, don't you?"

I breathed and the sky flamed. I tightened my jaws and the base of the City of Light began to shear and break away, from the edges, pouring upward in an avalanche of rock. Another smirk and rock became fiery missiles coiling about my head.

"Kneel before me," I said quietly. No one moved. "This isn't a request."

Nothing. Then a slow descent to the earth below.

I grinned. "So you do remember! Let's get a couple things straight about our new 'relationship.' I'm not the Father: I don't like you, I don't want you, and I don't want to be here with you. But I do need you. And you need me. Truth is—and I'll always tell you the truth—the truth is, you need me to stay alive. You need my gifts. And I feel benevolent only because I need you to get what I want. So, you have a choice to make, boys and girls. There is no going back. What you see is what you get."

"There is no choice here!" yelled a principality. "We can't go back! That's not a choice!"

He had backers. Too many for my taste.

"You are correct, sir!" and I sent a ball of flame his way, turning him to ash. "Sort of. There's always a choice; the problem is your options are...limited. But that's your problem. Your choices got you here; your choices might get you out."

"Get us out?" said a throne that looked surprisingly like Gaia. I knew it wasn't her: I felt her life end before we fell. That made me sad—I loved her. Like a daughter.

"You see this?" I spun in the darkness. "This is home now. You're stuck here. With me. You don't get to go back."

A principality said, "We don't get to go back?"

"Did you miss what happened? Weren't you there when the Father cast us out? With an act like that, what makes you think the Father would take you back? You betrayed Him."

But she looked genuinely sad. They all did. Sad and distraught. Heads hanging, shoulders slumped. Like it all hit them. Right then. I hadn't considered they might have hard time adjusting to life away from Heaven. Away from the Father. I tried to remember my own first days, my original exile, those endless days, weeks, years? That time when I was alone and the only sound was the echo of my own cries. A life cut off from the Father is no life at all. It is only the shadow of life remembered, the echo of things long past, the memory of emotion unfelt.

I could see it, etching itself across the faces of millions. That lost, forlorn look, the hooded eyes. Arms hugging themselves, reaching, tentatively, for one another. If they weren't so pathetic, I might have felt the itchings of compassion for them. I could certainly commiserate with them, I could honestly feel their pain. And such compassion might prove useful in securing their loyalty when things turned 'ugly.' Again.

But I didn't want to. I didn't want to care.

Everything that ever mattered to me was gone, lost in a flurry of good intention and horrible action. Lilith. My daughters, Laylah and Dinial. Sela. Gaia. The Father. I even missed Gabriel: his monotone observation was calming to me. Grounding. And Raphael. As much as I despised his youthful exuberance, I missed his energy, his zeal. His passion. It was all lost and, I knew, it wasn't ever coming back.

"What's your name?" I snapped.

"I am called Karan," she said. "I am the Reaper of Souls."

My breath caught. I remembered her. She had...something...with Raphael. Something personal. Something I heard once. I used it, a long time ago—it was just a chip I cast, something I hoped would reap dividends later. But I'd forgotten I'd called her that. The Reaper. I gave her this nugget and she held onto it all this time. And now, she was here with me and he was...oh, this could prove useful.

"The Reaper. I remember you." And I adjusted my tone, became more paternal, less condescending. Almost like I cared. "The Father called you that, didn't He?"

I wondered what she remembered.

Karan nodded and I watched her eyes fill with tears.

"Come here," I told her and waited as she drifted closer, filed past her sullen mates. I cradled her in my arms, touched at her tears. "He won't take you back now. He won't take any of us back. We made a choice and so did the Father. And He decided He doesn't want us anymore."

She cried, loud and hard, and I let her. Felt her spasms against my chest and looked out among the others with the eyes of an angel. They were all crying now, openly, reaching for one another.

"You don't want us either," Karan told me.

"I don't have to," I said and looked at the others. "I didn't make you. The Father did. And He turned His back on all of us for wanting to own our lives! But here's the thing: He doesn't want them either. You think those souls we left behind are living in the glory of the Father's love? Oh no! I've seen what we left behind. It is a frozen wasteland, covered in snow and ice. Michael and Raphael and that cursed boy are going city to city, rounding up the angels and slaughtering them in the streets. Your cities, our cities, drip with the blood of your brothers and sisters. The Father doesn't love them either. He loves something else."

"You're lying to us!" said a seraph through his tears. "You seek to turn us against the Father."

"I seek to—" and I caught myself, dialed the fury back. "I have no reason to lie, seraph. I am here with you. What have I to gain?" I turned, facing the crowd, slowly letting them see my face. "I will never lie to you. Never. I don't need to. The Father seeks to turn you against Himself. He's already turned His back on all of us. The Father is in love with the Man."

I basked in the awe.

"Didn't you know?" I smiled at them all. "That little stunt in Heaven, the one that landed us all here, that was to separate those who'd be willing to kneel to flesh from those who wouldn't. But I don't think it has to be that way. I don't think we have to take it. I think we can make the Father change His mind."

The greatest combatant to fear, I've learned, is hope. Fear is the power of doubt; the fearful believe they are fighting *against* something. But the hopeful are fighting *for* something. Turn the hopeful into weapons, into an army, into zealots, and, as long as they believe, it doesn't matter what they're fighting for.

"I have a plan to end this nonsense," I said to them, grinning. "And we're going to make the Father do it."

10
RAPHAEL

"You cast Michael out? Have you lost your mind?" I said in the darkness, watching Michael sink beneath the waves. I roared. And I shoved Emmanuel to the sand.

Gabriel leveled me with his staff. "You are out of line, Peace Keeper."

But even as he spoke, shafts of blue light, hazy lightning strikes began pelting the cities. Thunder snapped across Heaven, deafening, and the world shook above us. Cities creaked and careened, groaning under the constant bursts of energy. From every city, on every rock, it was a dazzling spectacle of light and energy.

"What?" was all I could muster.

"The army," Emmanuel whispered. "They're all cast out." He faced me now even has my head swiveled trying to keep pace with the disappearances. "The army of the Father has followed their Captain. They have been exiled from this place."

"Exiled. All of them? But they were just following Michael. You can't punish them for that!" I said.

"Why?' said Gabriel. "Why can't they be punished? Why can't their fate be the same as Lucifer's?"

"Because," and I didn't have a good answer. I stammered, "They were doing what they were told. They were doing what they thought was right."

Emmanuel grabbed my hand. "All of us are. But we make choices, Raphael, and those choices have consequences. You are here because you defied Michael."

"Where did you send them?"

"They have been exiled," Gabriel intoned,

"With Lucifer?"

"With the Father," Emmanuel said. "Understand that Michael has to make this right. He has to make it right. The Father has greater plans for him, for all of us. Michael must do what must be done. Only then will his place in Heaven be restored."

"This is insane!" I circled them, stomping on the sand, listening to the screams above. It was like when Lucifer turned out the light in Heaven. When he placed us in darkness and loosed Samael upon us all. That's how it felt now. "Michael said every horrible thing he'd ever done, he was asked to do. Is that true? Is what he said the truth?"

They were silent for a moment, mulling the best response.

"Yes," Emmanuel finally said. "Michael was made for a very difficult time. He remains because those times are not over. They only grow worse and much more will be asked of him. These are dark times, Raphael and the war here was only the beginning. But the Peace Maker has his own path with the Father, as do you."

"'The Peace Maker has his own path'? That's your answer for allowing Michael to kill angels?" I growled at him. "You're telling me that is the will of the Father? That's what the Father asked him to do?"

"It isn't your place to debate the will—" Gabriel began.

"You don't even know His will anymore, do you? Is He even speaking to you? Can you honestly say this," and I spun around in Heaven, "is what the Father intended? You just sent the entire army of Heaven to Earth to follow an angel who's orchestrating genocide! What do you think he'll do down there? What do you think any of them will do?"

"Michael does have a role to play in this, Raphael, even if you do not understand it." And the boy smiled a sad smile. "Sending him there is what is best for all of us."

There is a difference between doing what is right and doing what is best. We pray that they both are the same but they rarely are. Samael told me 'sometimes what is worst is best.' Sometimes it is. It certainly was the case with Michael and me. He was worst. But he was best for Heaven. For all his bloodlust, his brutality, his lack of compassion and emotion, he was what we needed when we needed it. He was what was best.

But I was right.

But what good was righteousness now? My righteousness had no value here, not to these angels, to these survivors of Hell. What good did saving my soul do if it cost our lives? What was the point?

"I'm going after him," I said. "I don't care what you say, this is a mistake. Judge him, yes, but casting him out? Exiling the army? That was wrong."

"Do you know what your name means?" said the boy suddenly. "Do you know why He calls you Raphael?"

"What?"

"It means 'God has healed.' You have a purpose."

I stared at the sky. "And I'm fulfilling it. I'm going to heal what's going on with Michael and the army. Try to make things right again so we—"

"No, angels are no longer your concern," Emmanuel said, his tone was grave. "Heal the race of Man, Raphael. They face grave danger."

"From Michael?"

He grabbed my face. "From everything. Michael is not a solution and his place is not there. Not yet. Man is your responsibility now."

"Mine?"

"You knelt before him," Gabriel said. "In the Temple, before the Fall. You knelt before the Man. Kneel before him now. Protect him."

"And if I fail?" I asked the boy.

"Don't," he said.

11
LUCIFER

She was beautiful admittedly. Certainly the work of the Fa-ther's hand.

I could look past her temporariness, her mortality, though it clung to her naked body like a shroud. But I could smell it on her: she smelled fleeting. She was fragile. I could overlook this flaw. I could ignore the stench of her flesh and drown out the constant drone of blood in her veins, incessant as it was. I could accept the muted tones of her skin, the lack of the Father's light pouring from her body. It made her part of this place, part of this world. Part of the man.

But I couldn't look away from her eyes.

They were magnificent! Looking at her, watching her pick her steps through the foliage, seeing the brief smile grace her face as leaves clung to her feet and grasses waved against her calves. I saw her as an animal. A beast of the

Earth. One of the Father's myriad playthings He created to amuse Himself. Until I would catch a glimpse of those eyes, endless and green and...alive! Then my breath would catch and I'd be transfixed.

It was like watching Sela, watching her feel her way in the world she created. Her beauty was the same, her majesty, her regality the same. But there was something more, something thrumming in her womb, something the rest of us did not possess. Life pulsed beneath her skin. It was the possibility of creation that I heard, the sheer ability seething in the fabric of her being. I saw it when I looked at the Father's face and I saw it again, eons later, on a world I despised.

This was Eve.

The mother of all to come.

Eve moved like a doe, skipping and jumping, trotting and running, her brown legs disappearing in the mist that clung to the ground. Something tickled her and she laughed, loud enough to echo, thin fingers covering wonderful lips. It made me smile, this laugh, genuinely—it was a sound I hadn't heard in millenia and it was marvelous. Almost like the songs the angels sang, the worship that I sang to the Father when He'd left me. The laugh was happy and I basked in it.

But Eve wasn't.

I could see it in the tiniest of frowns on her face. In the hint of sadness in her eyes. I could see it in the way she cocked her head, examining her reflection in the river. The woman was curious, that much was evident, and she marveled at everything. The flawlessness of her skin, the endless brown that flowed unbroken from the soles of her feet to disappear beneath the tangle of black that was her hair. She searched for a seam in her rib, a break in her body that would explain her existence. And Eve would frown for a moment, only to be distracted by the simplicity of her knee, flexing beneath her skin.

I waited in the water. As the water. Hanging beneath the surface. Watching.

"Sister," I finally said, "why are you so sad?"

She looked for the voice, pulled her limbs from the river in surprise. And she smiled. She wasn't afraid. "Who?"

"Eve," and the water quivered with my whisper, the words snaking along the surface.

She stood now, waded into the river. I saw her skin react to the coolness, watched gooseflesh raise on her arms. I've burned hot as your sun and felt the Father rain flaming ice in a wail of fury. Our bodies do not respond to changes in temperature as yours does. We know it; we feel it but it means nothing to us. I am still uncertain if this is a good thing, if the Father made you weaker intentionally, or if He left something out of us. One of us is deficient. Is it me? Or is it you? I was overcome with doubt in the midst of perfection, watching Eve looking down at the tiny bumps on her skin.

"Who is it?" she said, and stepped further out into the river. "Father?"

"Oh no," I said, but she only heard the water. My voice came from everywhere and nowhere, surrounding her. "It isn't Him. I'm a friend."

Now a broad smile creased Eve's face and she spun in the water, her green eyes dancing on tree limbs, bushes, clouds. She was like a child and this was a game to her. For the briefest of moments, I felt horrible for what I was about to do. Briefly. But I was the reckoning, the coming around of what has gone out. I was the seed sown. The Father should have thought about that before exiling me to a pit.

"Where are you?" she said.

I was next to the woman now, dangling in the water, clear enough to be invisible. I made the water come alive, swirling it between my fingers like the liquid in Heaven. It was all the same, the waters of Heaven and Earth. Bubbles filtered up about Eve, slowly at first then quickening until the river seemed to boil. Then two hands, my two hands, clear and fluid like the river itself, flowed upwards from the churning, pouring into slender arms, a taut face, lithe torso. Billowing up like a fountain, I stood on the surface of the river, smiling down at Eve through eyes made of water.

I was a figure of fluid. "Here, sister, here am I."

Eve beamed. "You call me sister."

"The Father made me just like He made you. That makes me your brother, doesn't it?"

"Brother?" she said.

I extended my hand, faked a laugh as the woman reached for it, then through it. "Of sorts," I said.

Eve snatched her hand to her lips. Her eyes were wide. "How?"

"Don't you know? Here, let me show you."

I reached for her hand again and this time, when her flesh touched the water, light spilled into the fluid, milky and brilliant. It flowed through my figure rapidly, turning liquid to solid ice then to soft flesh. But my light was blinding to Eve and she shielded her eyes. Light poured down my frame, pulling ice and flesh and silky robes in its wake. My eyes shone, my skin sparkled in the afternoon sun. I looked at my hands, flexed slender fingers and smiled and white light steamed from my mouth. I open my wings and burned bright enough to sear their shadow into the earth.

I looked impressive. Majestic. Like an Angel.

Like I was supposed to look.

I took her hand again and flooded Eve's body with warmth. Her skin responded, flushing a deep red beneath the brown. Beads of sweat danced on her forehead. I could burn her alive on a whim. It would be simple. But simple wasn't part of the plan. And the killing blow couldn't be mine. Instead I pulled her until she stood on the water with me, squinting to look into my eyes.

"You shine like the others," she said, "but I've never seen you."

"No one shines like me," I said under my breath. And then, "Others? There have been others here?"

"Yes! One called a Gab-reee-ale."

"Gabriel?" I said. I stifled my fury, swallowed it. "Gabriel was here?"

She cocked her head a little, examined my face. She reached for me, drawn to my light. Like a bug. I snatched away from her.

"Don't touch me," I said and gave her a sad grin. "I'm not like the others, sister. I'm not supposed to be here."

Eve's face saddened. "Why?"

I pulled her close, whispered in her ear, "Because they are jealous of me. Because I know a secret I'm not supposed to know."

"A secret? Tell me."

"Oh no no no," I sang. "I'm not supposed to tell a soul."

"Please."

"They are jealous because I know how to do...," and I took her hands, "THIS!"

And we were airborne, spiraling upwards above Eden. I held her by the hands, holding her as if she were flying herself, strafing the treetops and gliding over the river. I pressed her above me, holding her nude form to the sun, tossing her through clouds. Eve was a picture of childlike wonder, a wide smile draped across her face. Then we plummeted, and I draped shimmering arms about the woman in a waltz spinning, spinning, spinning. I dipped her, laid her across my knees, and smiled at Eve's girlish laughter.

"You are beautiful," I told her. "You truly are."

And I meant it.

She gasped.

Parting the haze, standing clad in dull silver bark and laden with heavy gray leaves, was the Tree. Lilith's tree. It was massive, thick and ominous. And beautiful. The dullness of the gray leaves and the crooked labyrinth of limbs were shadows in Eve's eyes—her attention fell to the three brilliant orbs of crimson that poked between the leaves. Fruit. Her brown eyes turned to me. I simply smiled at her.

I knew that fruit. Knew it when Lilith poured the wretchedness of her soul into their crimson skins. Recognized it when my daughters sat cross-legged and free on the surface of the water in the first Heaven. I remembered it when I watched Raphael biting into its hide, letting the red meat and juice dribble off his lips. I remembered that it held every lie, every half-truth, every horrible machination, I'd ever concocted. I remembered that upon one bite, you'd know whatever I wanted you to know. That you thought my truth was the whole truth and all else blasphemy.

I smiled broadly.

Eve was reticent.

"What's the matter, sister?" I placed soft hands on her shoulders, on the nape of her exquisite neck, and whispered in her ear. "See something you like?"

Fingertips covered her mouth, hiding a sheepish grin. She shook her head. "I shouldn't be here. It's forbidden."

"Forbidden? What here is forbidden? Didn't the Father give it all to you?"

Her smile disappeared, a frown rose in its place. "He gave it to Adam."

"Ah yes, the man! I forgot about him," I said, walking away from her. "What's the difference?"

"It doesn't belong to me," she said.

"All of it belongs to you!" I roared.

"Even me?" she said, and her voice was tiny. Fragile. "Do I belong to me? Or do I belong to Adam?"

This was almost too easy. "Are you not your own soul, Eve of Eden?"

She whispered, "I belong to the man. I was made for him. He named me and I belong to him."

I cupped her chin. "You don't like that? Belonging to him?"

Eve was quiet for a long time. She would start to speak and stop, open her beautiful mouth and close it until she finally said, "But what is for me?"

What is for me? The question that started this madness in the beginning. It was a selfish, self-centered question, one that cared little for the majesty of the creation around it. That only focused on the insecurities of the creature speaking. It was a flaw, and unexpected nugget of unintentional beauty. And I seized it.

"I asked that same question once," and my voice was sad. I sat on the ground. "I didn't get the answer I was looking for. But when I asked it, there was nothing else. I didn't have all this. I only had the Father. But you, He blessed you!" I stood now, excited. "Look around you, sister, all of it is yours! He gave it all to you! There is no one else. If you see something you want, something just for you, take it!"

Eve stared at the tree, at the fruit, and looked at her feet.

I sprang from her side, elongating my body until I was snaking around the tree, coiling about the trunk and limbs. My body was fluid and glassy now, serpentine, and the sunlight reflected brilliant prisms in the mist. I was beautiful to behold, intoxicating even. I saw Eve's eyes glaze: she was caught in the spell.

"This?" I snatched one of the red orbs from the tree. "This is what you want?" I held it out to Eve, stretching my arms. "Take it."

She backed away. "I can't."

"You can't? Or you won't?"

"You know it is forbidden! The Father told us so, of all things in this garden, touch not the fruit of that Tree." She paused. "I will die."

"Forbidden? Die?" I laughed heartedly. "Surely you will not die."

But this was interesting theater.

I said, "That is quite a compelling edict with such harsh consequences for disobedience, isn't it? Why would He make a rule like that? Haven't you wondered?"

"I will die," she repeated.

"The price of curiosity cannot be death, sister. The Father made you curious. He made you to explore. And He gave it all to you. The words and the actions that precede them do not match. I've disobeyed Him in ways you cannot imagine, yet here I stand."

She examined me and I could see it, the calculation formulating in her mind. I was like the others, like Gabriel, like those she trusted. Yet I spoke of disobedience, of self-love and ownership. Of being true to one's self. She was calculating, slowly—she was only human—but calculating nonetheless.

She looked at me, pointed a finger at me. "You disobeyed?"

"I was lonely." I sat down again. "Do you know how that feels?"

Eve only nodded.

"He left me alone. I was ungrateful for what He'd given me—nothing as good as this, mind you. But I was a living, breathing soul. Like you. I hurt His feelings and He left me all alone." I looked square in her eyes now. "I was alone and I couldn't take it. I disobeyed Him."

She knelt next to me. "What did you do?"

"I made another soul. I made someone to keep me company because I was lonely."

A soft hand on my ankle. Compassion. I hid my smile. "And what did the Father do?" she asked.

I stood now, abruptly. "He...punished me."

"I'm so sorry for you." And Eve, the mother of all humanity, the rib of Adam, looked at me with sadness and compassion and tears in her eyes. Her soul was pure, honest, and unsullied, unmarred by the horror that was Heaven. She was innocent and her hands were clean. Like my daughters. Eve was like an apology all over again. Just like Sela. But Sela was the architect of my imprisonment and this world was the continuation of that subjugation. Eve was simply latest bastion of beautiful slavery.

So she had to fall.

Just like Sela.

"I'm still here, Sister. I disobeyed but I'm still here." I palmed the fruit, rubbed my fingers and thumb over its thick skin. Felt its perspiration dripping in my hand. I faced the woman now and I took a bite, letting the juice pour down my face. It was better than I expected. I leaned close to Eve. "Tastes fine to me. What do you think?"

"But He said..."

"He says a lot of things. Always has." I tossed the fruit to the ground and turned my back to her. "The Father says He loves you, doesn't He? Gives you the world *literally,*" I turned now, eyes flashing, "and then leaves you alone. Is that love, dear Sister?"

Eve was silent.

"You are alone, aren't you?"

Her eyes burned but her voice shook, "That is not true, I am not alone."

"Oh sure, you have the man as your companion. But he owns you, woman, doesn't he? You were made for him; you are not your own. You are alone."

"How do you—?"

"How do I know? I know the Father, better than you ever will. I know *Him*. I know how He thinks, how He acts. I know His love. And I know how false it is."

"You are a liar," she whispered. "You try to trick me."

"Do I? I will never lie to you, Eve. I don't have a reason to." I pointed at the Tree. "Do you know what this is? Do you know why the Father doesn't want you to touch it?"

She just looked at me.

My voice fell to a conspiratorial whisper, "It will give you the one thing the Father fears: knowledge. That's the secret."

"Knowledge?"

"Oh, knowledge is powerful, my dear. Once you know yourself, no one can own you. You belong to yourself. Not to Adam. Not to the Father. Yourself. You can be like me. Or you can be like Him."

"That is not true."

"Suit yourself," I said and light began to engulf my body. I cupped her face in my hands, felt the smoothness of her skin on my fingertips. "You are wasting my time. And I wanted so much more for you. Pity." I began to disappear.

"Wait!"

"Wait?" Too easy.

"Don't go," she said, drew a circle in the soil with her toe. "I will not die?"

I pulled another piece of fruit from the Tree and held it out to Eve. "Sister, you will only begin to live."

Eve paused, studied the supple skin of the fruit, pored over the redness. I watched her choose. I could see it happen: the quick smirk in the corners of her mouth, the flash of her tongue, the rapid fluttering of her eyelids. She took a bite. And smiled at me. It was wonderful.

"Good girl," I told her. "Now let's go find Adam."

12
MICHAEL

Father be damned!

I was tumbling through space like a comet, the Waters of Heaven and the dust of my peers wafting behind me in a flaming wake. I watched stars careen past my face in streams of light. It was raining illumination and I was falling against the torrent, pulled forward by something I could neither see nor feel. I was falling, no doubt, falling from Heaven but falling to...

Earth.

The face of Sela's world rushed toward me, faster than I would have expected. From its outskirts, beyond the gray pebble of a moon lazily circling this orb, it was magnificent. Much more dazzling than what I saw Sela birthing in Heaven. More than what I saw Azazel and Lucifer curse in front of the Body. I understood what she gave her life for, what she was planning for. If the Father had planted something half as beautiful in my mind as this, I would have given everything for it too.

This is what she died for.

And I was instantly jealous.

The Father hadn't given me anything beautiful to yearn toward, nothing wonderful to strive for. He had given me only misery as a yoke, a horrible purpose to fulfill. I thought I was made to make peace, to bring order from chaos. To undo the horror that had been done. That would be done. But what The Father called peace was only death in disguise. And I was its harbinger.

The ball of green and blue rushed toward me and I stretched my arms to embrace to it, to touch it. And I fell through it. Into it. The black night of space was broken by the crystalline blue of sky, the wet whiteness of clouds. The brilliance of day. I was flaming now, naked and burning, sizzling through the atmosphere of Earth. A line of green and brown broke the blue and the ground yawned its magnificent maw at me, welcoming me with mountainous teeth and towering trees. I opened my wings to slow me down, to control my fall, but I was too late. I hit the Earth with a boom and heard the cracking of timber from the impact.

And darkness fell upon me. Again.

Finish it.

I opened my eyes to green. Grass, weeds—life—poured around me, crawled on my arms and legs, snaked along my body. Living things with multitudes of legs clamored over my flesh. Furry, fleshy beasts jostled closer, sniffing, peering, peeking, retreating. I rolled over, felt the ridges of earth and stone—the crater—against my back and watched beasts circle in the air above me. They had wings like mine, like Sela's and Raphael's and Gabriel's. I stood, then the ground shook.

Again. And again. And again.

It was a slow cadence, a steady thumping, but it was a rhythm I knew. It was my own heartbeat, the heartbeat of millions of my brothers and sisters. It was the very breath of the universe, the cries of the stars' birth and the planets' death. The clockwork movements of life itself. This was the sound of the Creator. My Creator. Footsteps. The Father was coming.

And I heard, in the wind, swelling from the ground, falling from the sky, the voice of the Father say, "Where are you?"

I was in a wide field of low grasses and before me stretched a line of trees, thick and strong. I couldn't see past them but I knew they were many in number. The first few were bent and broken from the breath of my impact. The Father was ahead, somewhere in the trees: I could see them moving, waving in both protest and acquiescence. I followed and each step of mine brought life to the surface, reaching for me, leaching my divinity.

I took to the air but the wind pressed me down. Harshly. I tried again, spreading wide wings of metal, leaping in majesty. My wings bent, the steaming light of divinity snuffed and whispered away. I hit the ground. Hard.

"Michael," came the wind. "My son."

"Don't." I closed my eyes. "You left me."

"I am here. You are here. I have never left."

"You left all of us! You turned Your back on us! For this!" I was on my hands and knees, prostrate, huffing in the dirt.

The wind pressed my chest, pushing me upright. "You live! You breathe! Have I not sustained your life, Peace Maker? Have I not maintained your strength and your resolve! What did I leave?"

"I did what You told me to do! I was obedient! I followed Your commandments!" I wasn't crying. Not now. Not like the last time. I was angry. I clenched my fists until they bled. "You left us in snow and ice and blood. We don't live; we survive. We exist! And we stood with You. We fought for You."

"You did what you were supposed to do." The force left the wind. It trickled to a breeze that caressed my face. I heard the Father's voice change, become maternal and loving. "Do you think your obedience earns you a life of ease? Obedience is not an act, Michael; it is a journey."

"You let that boy cast me out!"

The Father laughed. At me. "Do you think your work is done?"

"What?" I looked at the sky. "I don't understand."

"Yes, you do." And the voice became masculine again, harsh and angry. "I made you to bring peace. I made you like Me. You will do what must be done. Your will shall persevere when others fail. You will bring to fruition what others cannot conceive. And you will destroy the wickedness among you. Those are My words. Do you remember them?"

"Yes, Father, I remember."

"Is there peace, Michael?"

What's the matter? No peace for the Peace Maker?

There was no peace for me. There wouldn't be. I wasn't Samael: I hadn't rejected the chalice of justice the Father placed in front of me. I'd done exactly what He'd asked, even when it earned me exile from Heaven. Which, looking at Earth, wasn't a bad thing. There was no peace. I didn't have to answer. I already knew. So did He.

"Will it ever end?" I dropped my head.

"Protect the others. Lead My army. End this darkness," the Father said. "End the darkness, Michael. Then you will know peace."

"What am I to do?" I hung my head, cursed under my breath.

"What must be done." And the wind was gone.

In its place was a vision, palpable and real. I saw them, Lucifer and the man? No, this creature was different: softer, curvier than the man. Female. Like Sela. Like Sariel.

Woman. And I knew the word.

They were on the bank of the river, dancing in the air. Having a heart to heart discussion in front of...a tree? It was as though I was standing in their presence, close enough to touch.

"So what?" I said aloud.

The vision froze, refocused, zoomed into the tree itself. I'd never seen it before, didn't recognize it. Didn't understand its significance. But Lucifer did. He was gesticulating and undulating around the trunk of this monstrosity, obviously trying to convince the woman to...eat? He wanted her to take the fruit?

"Why?"

The vision went dark, reeling backward in time, slowly at first with the woman and Lucifer next to me, then faster.

I watched the woman pulled from the man, taken from his very side, molded by the water of the river, swaddled in the hands of the Father. And then she was no more. It was only the man. Not the ruddy refuse I saw in Heaven, the shattered apparition Lucifer beheaded and tossed into the fluid in the Temple. This was something different. Familiar, but different. Formed from the very rock and mud and dust of the Earth. His was, even in this accelerated, reversed state, a labor of love. I saw the Father as something I had never seen: a parent. I saw Him, over what must have been eons on this world, sculpt this creature.

I watched it. Watched Him mold this feeble thing of dust and mud, breathe life into his body until his skin was soft and moist. And weak. The Father held his hands as the man struggled with his first steps. The man fell, was lovingly picked up, urged forward, only to fall again. The vision played before me in fast and slow motion, forward and backward. Sometimes with enough sound to hear the man's heart beating in time with the Father's. In time with mine. Usually it was silence.

I watched until I understood. I watched until I saw the Father love the man. Love him in a way He never loved me. Never loved us.

"What is so special about him?" I said and my jealously was palpable.

Look was whispered in the wind.

Then the Father took me backward, excruciatingly fast. We flowed upward from Earth, hurtling through space again toward Heaven. Plunging up through the Waters until I watched myself cast from above. Faster. The war raged. The City of Light emerged from the depths, an Atlantean monstrosity come back to life, and took its place in the skies. Fires exploded and were snuffed away. The legions of Samael withered to nothing and darkness became light again. The Waters rushed and swallowed her children, consumed choirs of angels and I watched multihued souls press their brethren back into the seas until they were no more. I flowed past Lucifer, unbound and free, hanging over Heaven even as it was being forged. Even as the Father let me languish on Sela's sweaty form slicing at rock.

I saw her destroy it all.

He slowed here, let me walk in the destruction next to Lucifer. She'd gotten upset, furious and lashed out, devastating the world I knew. Lucifer had stopped it, had muted her fury and walked in the frozen detritus of her anger. My eyes watered and I scrubbed my face at the scene.

Lucifer asked her, "What happens after you build it?"

She said nothing then.

He said, "Do what He wants you to do. Don't make Him cry. Just have a plan for what's next."

I reached to touch her, to graze my fingers against the ragged smoothness of her skin. But the Father pulled me away. Much too fast.

Back still, and I saw Sela become a figurine in the Father's palm, an offering to Lucifer. *To Lucifer?* She was always a sacrifice. Intended to be temporary. Never permanent. And before her Azazel, birthed in an act of horrendous violence. If chaos was the order of my creation, fury was his. My abject disgust for his soul softened. A little bit.

And then there was Lucifer. And Gabriel. And the Sisters, broken and ragged. And I saw the same look on Lucifer's face watching his daughters that I saw on the Father's with the man. *He loved them.* He loved them. But Lucifer killed them both. And he blamed the Father. This anger, their anger, was old. Ancient. And Lucifer was intent on revenge. The Father loved the man as Lucifer loved the Sisters and now Laylah and Dinial were gone.

The man was in jeopardy.

"Why don't you love us like that?" I said. "Why didn't you love us like that?"

"Do you think your work is done?" I heard the Father say.

The vision moved slower now, still backward, still in silence. Heaven became whole, an orb. A world, like Earth. Whole but sad. And Lucifer was happy. The Sisters were with him and another angel I had never seen. Azazel told me of a third soul Lucifer had created—Lilith, he called her. And I watched Lilith build a horrible tree of dark silver limbs and deep red fruit. The Sisters ate of it and told Lucifer, "We know you."

We know you? How?

"The tree!" I yelled. "It's the same?"

And the vision tore me forward, faster than light itself, pulled through time until I was again in that same clearing, watching the woman take the fruit from Lucifer. And eat.

Lucifer said, "Good girl. Now let's go find Adam."

And they were gone.

I vomited on the meadow, watched the silver fluid wick into the earth.

"I do love you, Michael. Before I formed you, before I knew you, I loved you. I always have. I always will," the Father whispered, soft and maternal. "But you are like Me, Michael, and you will do what must be done."

I understood. But I was furious about it. I opened my wings and leapt over the trees.

This time, the boom from my impact was intentional.

I fell on a bolt of light, blazing in the midday sun and burning the ground below me. I was an apparition of light and metal, of electricity and thunder and I could hear the man and the woman cowering in the foliage. They were hiding.

"Come out!" and my voice echoed against the trees. A flock of birds took to the air. A sword, long and lean, eased from my fist. "Come out now!"

They did. Slowly. They weren't naked anymore, not like the Father had shown me; instead they lashed together coverings of leaves, hiding something I did not understand. They stank of modesty and hubris and fear coated their features.

"Do you know me?" I said.

Silence.

I glared at the man, angled my sword at him. He swallowed loudly. "Do you know me, Adam?"

Adam shook his head slowly and the dark brown of his hair shook. I wanted to touch it.

"What is your name, woman?"

"She is called Eve," Adam said. "I called her Eve."

I growled at him. "I didn't ask you, dust. Do you know me, woman?"

There were tears on her face when she shook her head at me. Adam reached for her.

"Be still!" And Adam froze. "My name is Michael. I am the Father's justice. Why am I here?"

I leaned in close until I could feel the warmth of their breath on my face. For a moment, I marveled at them both. They were exquisite creations, formed as I was formed but so very different. So much the children of the Father. Sela told me of the day the angels were formed, pulled from the frothy grasp of the Waters. Each pulled by their brothers and sisters. Borne into camaraderie and companionship and togetherness. Borne into a family.

It was a moment I did not share.

I was not like the others. I would never be like the others.

Now these sculptures, these labors of love, knelt before me in the position of guilt and submission. And I was judging them. I understood Lucifer in these brief moments. Understood how he could want so desperately, so deeply that which he could not have. Knowing that I could never have what Adam and Eve had, what they had squandered in those moments, infuriated me beyond words.

"We ate—" Adam began.

I cut him off. "You ate of the Tree in the Garden. Didn't you know it was forbidden? Didn't the Father tell you?"

I was pacing now, like a lion. The grass burned beneath my footsteps and I growled, smirking as they shook at my words. We were on the outskirts of Eden, on the cusp of the tree line. Behind me, loomed massive trunks, bulging from a fog that coated the ground. Beyond the humans, was the meadow that caught me and, compared to the shroud of the Garden, it was foreboding and unwelcoming.

"Say something for yourself!" I yelled. "Speak!"

"The woman gave me the fruit—" Adam began.

I snatched him by the throat, held him above my head and I dwarfed this being. I was a giant among ants. Adam was soft and fragile, supple. Breakable. Easy to destroy. Like an animal.

"Do not blame her! He told *you*! He made you first! He gave you all of this, all of it! With one simple instruction! One! Was it that tough to follow?"

He gurgled in my fist. I dropped him in the grass.

"She would die," said Adam, coughing. I'd left burn marks on his neck.

"She should die!" I bellowed. "Was that not the cost? Isn't that what the Father said?"

"Then I would be alone," said the man. "Alone again."

I wasn't prepared for that.

It wasn't something I'd considered. Disobedience on purpose. For a reason. I'd heard about Lucifer's rationale for pushing the Father away. I'd heard it but never understood it. Never wanted to understand it. Disobedience with purpose. What was the penalty for that? What should it be? Does justice frown on compassion, on fear? On love? He ate to be with her. With his woman. His Chosen. In life or death. So he would not be alone.

I wasn't prepared. I turned from them instead.

"You have no idea what you have done!" I said to the sky. "Do you know what it cost so you could live? Do you know what we lost—what I lost—just so you can draw breath? Ungrateful lumps of dirt!"

There had to be a consequence. Disobedience could not be tolerated. Not in Heaven. Not on Earth. Not for any reason. The Father's edicts were not optional; His commandments not to be ignored. They had to be punished. *You are like Me and you will do what must be done.*

I cursed. My sword flamed in my fist. Adam and Eve hid their eyes as I faced them.

"You can never come back to this place again. Never." And I rammed my blade into the earth before them. "You're on your own now."

"It's my fault," the woman whispered, looking into the grass.

I leaned in close to her, held her chin with a massive, metal finger, and looked into her eyes. They looked like Sela's eyes. But they burned in my presence and Eve slammed her lids closed. Tears crept from the corners of her eyes and steamed on her face.

"It is your fault," I whispered, "and you will pay for your transgression."

I heard clapping behind me. "You are so dramatic, Michael. It really is a good show."

I turned. And there, leaning against a tree, watching the exchange with wicked delight, was Lucifer the Satan. He lapped a forked tongue across his teeth and grinned.

"Leave the woman alone, Michael," Lucifer said. "Come and pick on somebody your own size."

13
SARIEL

Michael was gone. Cast out.

Now so were we.

Snatched from the blanket of white crispness we called home. Pulled from our feet, standing next to our friends, our brothers and sisters. Our Chosens. I knew what it was when it happened.

"Damn it," I said and watched my feet burst into blue flame and disappear. There was a cruel jolt, a hitch, at the scruff of my neck and I was falling falling falling.

Into nothing.

With everyone else.

Except for the damned. Except for the souls we paraded in front of Michael's blade, slaughtering them for the crime of apathy. Except for the ones he told us were the refuse of Heaven. The unwanted. The unneeded. The undeserved. We were excising the unwanted flesh from the Father's Body, doing His will—at least that was what we were told.

And the Father kicked us out anyway.

"Damn you, Michael!"

There were hundreds of thousands of us, far too many to count, twirling in a funnel of fire and silver and light. Tumbling through the velvety nothing between the frozen death that was Heaven and the seething damnation we knew was Hell. We could feel it, feel the heat of its pull. Feel it tugging for us.

You like to think it was a moment, our fall. Your book lets you think it was a singular point in time that we fell. Knowing what I know now, knowing what I felt standing next to Michael's massive form when he called me Commander, I know that is a lie concocted by the fear of death. You fear death because you do not know what we know. You have not tasted the horror we have. Immortality is a bitter wine. Covet it not. Death is like water, peaceful and deep.

You just don't know.

It was an angel called Zadkiel who pulled me into the war. I love and hate him for it.

Zadkiel was a seraph from Wisdom, like me, and we both had grown weary of our fear of Azazel. The Archangel of Wisdom had worked us like mules, forging the foundation and walls of his temple. Using his hands of light to "encourage" us to work faster. To work harder. Azazel's motivation was pain and I'd tasted his wrath on many an occasion, usually for defending the others. Azazel was not a fan of mine.

Zadkiel had whispered to me, "He is only one, sister. We are many."

"He is forged by the Father," I told him.

"And we are not?" Zadkiel pushed a massive block of marble aside, cracking its face. "Are we not the children of the Father?"

I ran my hands on his face. "You do not burn with Azazel's fury, brother. That anger belongs to someone greater than ourselves."

"I burn nonetheless," he whispered and pounded his chest.

I felt the burn in my own.

We considered a plot. A demonstration, you would call it. We managed to convince twenty angels—seraphs and dominions mostly, a few virtues—to overtake the temple, now close to completion. We thought it would be an asylum, sacred to Azazel. Holy ground. Something he would not destroy. As our brothers and sisters finished the building, fitting the massive strips of alabaster across its face, we assembled on its steps, screaming.

"Azazel!" we said. "Azazel! We worship you not! We will not kneel before you! Your Body rejects its Host!"

We thought a spectacle would embarrass him enough to talk. To have a conversation. To arrive at a consensus.

We were wrong.

Azazel smiled a horrible smile at us, and his hands caught fire. "What Body?" he said.

And let loose his fury.

The temple exploded, falling in on itself. Burying the others. I was fast. Zadkiel was not. He was lost in those moments. I left him there, hands reaching for salvation, his fractured voice calling for me. I left him. There was nothing...I left.

I vowed to return.

And I did when Lucifer came. When he set the world on fire and moved the rocks with his mind. Lucifer wasn't like the rest of us; he wasn't like any of us. Lucifer was something else. But, oh, how I wanted to be him! You must understand, we feared the Host. We cowered before them. But Lucifer feared nothing! Not the First. Not Gabriel. Not Azazel. He laughed at the Host. He laughed and defied those angels and he did it for us. They murdered us in the streets of the cities they made us build. The Host is not the portrait of the Father's love they would have you believe. They are horrid creatures whose destruction is both necessary and righteous.

Except Michael.

But Lucifer didn't care about any of us. He wanted something, an idea we couldn't form on our own. We wanted justice. Lucifer wanted revenge. It was a concept we hadn't considered. He tortured Azazel and he did it out of spite. Because he could. As much as Azazel deserved the pain inflicted, Lucifer scared us all: he laughed about it.

I left Wisdom then. I have never returned.

I didn't see Sela die. I saw Michael mourn.

I heard his wail in the morning sun and I knew that pain. I knew that anguish. I felt it when Zadkiel died. It was like a cruel hand reached into me and pulled at my soul. Bent it. Broke it. I couldn't figure out how to express it so I held it tight, clenching my feelings and the memory of Zadkiel, afraid that my emotion would drown away his smile. That if I felt, I would lose him completely. But Michael cried over Sela. He cried over her body and watched her freeze into stone and slip away from his hands. He cried and I cried with him. I felt his pain.

We were together in our grief, Michael and me. He in the center of Righteousness and me on its outskirts, watching and wailing with him. I don't think he knows.

I saw what happened after when Samael came. When he turned Saqui against Michael. When he drove his spear into Michael's chest and let him fall into the darkness. Michael fought for us. He fought for Sela and the Thrones and Gabriel and the rest of us. He almost died—he should have died. For us.

After that, I was his forever.

So, when he chose me outside of Peace, when he chose me to protect Uriel and destroy the fallen, how could I refuse? And when Michael sent us to the cities to fetch those who did not choose, who was I to second guess him? The Father gathered Michael in His palm, pulled him from the clutch of death. Michael was the Father's Chosen—who was I to refuse? But it felt wrong. It felt lost. Lost. Like Michael was now.

We fell like meteors, thousands of flaming souls burning in the dawning sky of Earth, our weapons of war dull in the twilight. Each of us wore faces of fear hanging beneath helms and visors, the fire in our eyes dimming.

We came.

Clouds erupted as we fell, sons and daughters of the Father spiraling down down down from the darkness of Heaven to the brilliance of Earth. And we screamed! Curses and chants, some sang choruses of destruction, of victory, while others wailed melodies of death, sending beasts and fowl scattering to the four winds in our wake.

We, the army of the Host of Heaven, fell to Earth and brilliant light burned our eyes.

Sunlight.

The light of the Father.

For eyes that had seen only the whispers of light amidst the winter, the pain was excruciating, and we screamed in the light of day. Angels fell away from one another now, some scattering and tumbling away, most of us stalling over a meadow of green. I shielded my eyes, watched the angels whirling and gasping, pointing and grasping. This place was alive! All of it! The sphere Sela showed us was a lie, a cruel ruse: Earth was magnificent! A stream of sparkling blue snaked its way behind us, the sounds of its rolling waves and gentle falls buffeting our ears. Insects buzzed about our faces, clamoring along armor that rippled at the touch of unbridled life. Wind rushed from the north, to my right, and we turned our faces to the breath of the Father. The meadow flowed off the north with the wind, disappearing between rolling hills. Across the stream, massive mountains, ragged sentinels of stone lurched from the green, showing their grey backs to the sun.

I turned to them, the army—my army now. "Do not enjoy this place. We are now about the Father's business."

Shining faces fell grim, dark.

But my words fell on many deaf ears.

Uriel stood next to me, jostled in his armor. A slow smile spread across his face. "Do not enjoy it?" he said. "Look at it!"

I said, "You know what we are here to do."

"I know what we left, Sariel."

I took off my helm. "This wasn't our choice, Uriel! We are not here on purpose! We were cast out."

But my words were lost on him. Others, Uriel's Sword, slowly began peeling off, exploring. Lost in the wonder. The armor of war began to fade, pouring into robes of peace.

"Maybe we were delivered, Sariel." Uriel looked at them, watched their joy, and turned aged eyes to me. "Maybe the Father has heard us after all."

"You don't believe that!"

He pressed fingers to my lips. "Don't tell me what I believe. Don't tell me I don't deserve, that we don't deserve...I'm tired, Sariel. Aren't you tired?"

I jolted from him, slapped his face. "Uriel! Michael is our Captain. It is over when he says it is over. Pull yourself together!"

He huffed. I was right.

I leapt into the air and my Sword followed. "Michael is here, somewhere. Find him."

And the angels of the Host roared across the Earth, fanning outward like a cyclone. Like locusts of fire and silver and light, they filled the blue of sky, blocking the sun.

14
LUCIFER

Oh, now this was fun!

Michael stood in front of me, eyes wide, his body frozen. He looked distorted to me, as though he were hanging beneath the surface of water, rippling. I was cast out, but he was still a part of the Father's ridiculous plan. Which meant he was still in the Father's hand. Michael and I weren't in the same world. Not yet. That was just a matter of time.

I grinned at him, showed a mouthful of fangs. "What's the matter, Michael? You look like you've seen a ghost."

Michael's sword wilted. His voice fell to a hoarse whisper, "Lucifer..."

"And you've been getting my messages, I take it. I was beginning to think you wouldn't come. Getting you here was like pulling teeth, you know, with your allegiance and righteousness and all. It's all kind off sickening actually. What'd the boy do, kick you out too?"

Michael looked away for a moment.

"He did?!" And I doubled over in laughter. "I actually didn't expect that. It's been a long time since I was surprised."

But Michael was in shock, stammering, "How? You should be—"

"Dead? Gone? Sent back to the Father in that ridiculous blaze of glory?" I circled Michael. "Wrong! For someone made to put things right, you are just failing on all fronts, aren't you? Sounds like a personal problem to me. But you tried, though, I'll give you credit for that. It was a good try." I patted his shoulder and he lurched from me.

I faced Michael now. The last time I saw him in the flesh, he was charging through the wall of the Temple, burning with the Father's fire. He scared me. Honestly. You have to understand, Michael the Archangel is a furious, fiery behemoth of the Father's justice. He is the Father's Sword, His Hand of Righteousness, not the palliative apparition your imaginations create. I've seen your pathetic little scribblings, your enlightened renditions of him. You have no idea what Michael actually is. Just as the Father pulls order from nothing, Michael builds peace from chaos. And his methods are horrible.

But now, his majesty was muted by his shock. By his abject bewilderment. And it was funny to me. So, I pushed him further, simply because I could. I changed my shape. The beautiful angelic form I wore erupted in flame and thunder. Fire ate at the alabaster skin, the porcelain flesh, the china smile. Smooth skin became blistered and ragged, pulling away from the silver skeleton beneath. My eyes, sparkling like diamonds, became rubies in the maelstrom, horns of bone and metal lurched from my temples. The silk of my robes thickened, fraying, tearing into blackened hides and chain mail armor. And gleaming in the flame was the hilt of Michael sword, belching from my chest, my blood boiling about the wound.

"I killed you," Michael whispered. "I saw you die."

"You sure about that?" I roared. "And here I thought we were getting along so well. You break my heart, Michael." And I snatched the sword from my chest and licked the blood from the blade. "See?"

Michael's mouth fell slack and I couldn't contain my laughter.

I said, "I'm sorry, it's so melodramatic nowadays. I learned a lot though, learned the folly of my ways. Really, I did." The smile disappeared and I leaned in close until his face was pressed to mine, rippling beneath the surface. "The worst thing you could have done was send me here."

I grabbed him, punched through the barrier that separated us and, with a splash, lurched him toward me. I saw his feet leave the ground, felt the tug of Earth slipping away and I pulled him forward. Into my world.

"I have so much to show you, Michael," I said with a smile.

But Michael was disheveled and confused, furious and frantic. And dangerous. He pressed me away and spun, looking wildly behind him.

Things were different now.

Earth wobbled through the prism of the Father's firmament, the waters that separated us from his prized possessions. The same barriers that separated me from Heaven. I'd figured it out. Michael obviously hadn't. He squinted and growled, reached for a world he couldn't touch. And watched his flaming sword drag a burning circle about a withering Garden of Eden. It was dying beyond his flames, beyond his fury, and trees burned and wilted, grasses and foliage smoldered.

"How could it happen so fast?' he whispered.

"Can't you figure this out?" I said. "Oh, that's right: Raphael is the smart one. You're an idiot."

Michael's hand snapped about my neck and he pulled me from my feet. "What have you done?"

I grinned at him. "Not me. Look."

Adam and Eve were nowhere to be seen.

Michael said, "Where are they?"

I coughed, "You cast them out, remember? You sent them away."

He dropped me like trash, like forgotten refuse. Turned his back on me and searched for them.

"Listen," I said, scrubbing my neck.

We heard the sounds of sharp breathing, of panting almost. Animalistic but human at the same time. Guttural. Painful. The woman was agonizing over something, enduring something horrible. The man was there too, whispering soothing words like music, like the soft tones the Father would sing when they walked on the Earth in the beginning. Before they knew I was watching. They were together, the man and the woman, sharing this pain, this challenge, acting as one body, one spirit. The breathing tensed, tightened, and the woman wailed, piercing the silence of the world. Her scream punctuated the landscape, marking it, changing it and we both felt the balance of this world shift beneath us. Her scream, primal and visceral, was joined by the man's chorus of joy and achievement, and finally by the thin bawl of something younger. Newborn.

Childbirth.

Man was doing the Father's work. Creating. Recreating.

"They create life?" Michael frowned, turned to me. "It is forbidden, Lucifer! How many times must you repeat the same course of action? Have you not learned the consequences?"

"I didn't." And my voice was quiet.

"You didn't what?"

"*I* didn't do anything. She did. It was her choice."

Why tell him the truth of what I knew? Why should I tell him the Father had made man to be creators? That He'd made them more like Himself than He'd made any of us? I stole my ability to create. I can admit that now. I was not gifted with that power; I learned its secrets in the midst of exile. The Father built man this way. I knew it when He showed him to me in Heaven, when He forced me to build that lump of flesh. I knew it then. And I hated the Father for it.

But why tell Michael? Why spoil that surprise? Because when he finally figured it out, when the veil was finally lifted and the Peace Maker would see the world unfiltered, his disillusion would change everything. He would act on those emotions and a deluded, disappointed Michael was a much more potent force than the one currently toeing the party line. It would be a long process, no doubt, a slow devolution of his principles and allegiances, but it could happen. It would happen. And then the fun would begin.

I let him hate me. For now.

He said, "They are separated from the Father now. I know about the Tree and the fruit, Lucifer. You knew what would happen. They are lost to Him now!"

I shrugged. "Her choice."

"You tricked her!"

"Semantics, Michael. But I admire your concern for a bunch of animals. It warms my soul."

It was enough. Michael rushed me now, his body crackling with lightning, a lion's growl frothing in his throat. His sword swept wide, slicing the air and diving for the quick death of my throat. Just like before. But this wasn't like before. It would never be like it was. Michael froze. Jerked to a stop. Wisps of flame cloaked him, caressed him, spun him above my head.

"Oh no no no. Tried that once, didn't you?" I said. "You did a great job too, don't you think? We think so."

And the earth began to rumble, pitching and roiling. Rolling meadow heaved and split, vomiting molten rock and licking flame. Trees cracked their mighty trunks in sprays of sparks and lights. Rocks shattered in plumes of smoke and the Earth screamed beneath the onslaught.

Then the demons came.

Pulling wretched bodies from the open wounds of land, grotesque savages the color of night clawed their way onto the landscape. Michael's face tightened, rage lined his features. There were hundreds of them, charging through trees, burning the earth with disgusting feet. They howled and salivated, chomped glassy jaws and licked forked tongues. Flaming spears hung in gnarled hands.

A twitch in my fingers and Michael drifted close. "What did you think was going to happen, Michael? You'd come here with your sword and put me in my place? I AM IN MY PLACE! You're in this world, Peace Maker, but you're not of it. But me, oohhh, I'm home now! This world is mine! All of it!" And I smiled a sad little smile, "Aww, you really are surprised, aren't you? Idiot."

A casual wave of my hand and Michael shot off into the distance, plowing through the Garden, strafing the meadow and disappearing beyond a series of hills.

I looked at the others. "Get him."

15
RAPHAEL

Unbelievable.

Moments, sheer moments separated the dark winter of Heaven from the absolute blankness, the abject nothing, that was the Father's back. You have the best word for space, for the gulf between angel and man, between Father and the lost. It is nothing. Void, you call it.

I call it Hell.

My misery was compounded by the weight of my mission. Salvation. This is a component strikingly absent from the mandate of my creation. I was not meant to save. The Father was specific in that: I was made to keep peace, to press the horrors back long enough for salvation to arrive. I thought that salvation was Michael. But he brought nothing but pain and anguish and bloodshed. He brought fear and death. Just like Samael. Just like Lucifer.

All of them the messengers of the Father.

I wonder about that, not then, but now, as I wait for the end to come. I wonder about the Father's intention with these angels, my brothers. All of them made for destruction, for death, for woe and misery and damnation. His Beloved, Lucifer, brought nothing more than conflict and division. His Wisdom, Samael, was the harbinger of pain, the hand of vengeance. And His Justice, Michael, was a force of unmitigated fury and violence.What face of the Father were they? Who was He showing us He was? Was this, is this, who He is?

And then, what face of the Father am I? His fear? His shame? The hesitant hand of peace in the face of chaos? Was I, am I, the mistake of the Father?

I've never found an acceptable answer to that question.

But hurtling through the darkness, tumbling head over feet, surrounded by thousands of shining eyes pledging allegiance to my compassion, to my loyalty, I focused only on making it right. Making it right. I was willing to give my life for that idea. I learned that much from Michael, from Lucifer, from Samael: you have to commit. Even in the face of insurmountable odds or the fury of the Father or the blood of my brethren. Commit. Belief is bloody. You must believe the prize is worth it.

I gritted my teeth and faced the planet twirling lazily below us. But my resolve was shared by all in my care.

"The Father is not here," I heard someone moan between fingers pressed to lips.

I forget these souls did not come from nothing as I came. They were not formed cupped in the palm of the Father from His whim; these individuals were birthed from the bitter waters of His tears. They did not burn with intent as I did. Fear marked their faces. All of them.

"The Father is everywhere," I lied, louder than expected. "He is with us even now. Look not to the darkness about us; look to the light ahead."

"What good is it, Host?" said a dominion, crying next to Ramiel. "The Father has left us and sent us here, to nothing!"

Too many souls agreed.

I flew in front of them all, waving a flaming sword. "I know none of you asked for this," I said. "I know that. And I know that we failed you. The Host and the Captain and me, we didn't do enough soon enough. We didn't do enough when Lucifer—*I* didn't do enough. But I promised the Father I would serve Him. And when you decided to stand with me, all of you made the same promise. Until the end."

I don't know where the words came from. They weren't my own but they were effective.

"Do not be discouraged: this," and I pointed my sword at the darkness, "this is not the end. This is not what the Father has in store us. But neither is the husk of Heaven we left. We are warriors, brothers and sisters, and the war is not over. It will now be fought on Earth. Lucifer is there; the Demons are there. Michael and the rest of the army are there too. But Man is there—he's still our salvation. I knelt before him. I promised to protect him."

"But we didn't," shouted a female, a virtue, from the back, drawing cheers from the crowd. "Why should we fight for them?"

"Don't," and I lowered my sword. "Don't fight for them. Fight for you. Fight for yourselves. You hate the cold and the darkness as much as I do. But more than anything, we hate the nothing. It's the nothing and the anger and the mistrust we hate. I can't stand it. Most of you can't either. So you have a choice: stay lost or fight with me. But I'm not going back, not to that."

"Are we going to die, Host?" said Ramiel, palming her spear.

"Yes." I looked at her squarely in her tired eyes. "A lot of you will. That's the truth. But you don't want to live like we were living. That isn't a life, not one worth living. I think it's better to die in the light than to live in the dark. It's time to choose."

I looked at each of them, tens of thousands frightened and furious souls. Their eyes met mine and flamed. In stoic silence, helms of silver poured over sullen faces, spears and swords lurched from shaking fists and ignited with white light. Wings of metal spread wide and the Sword of Raphael fell to Earth.

"Good," I said.

Shafts of light and the thrumming of thunder heralded our arrival. Ground parted beneath our impact, cratering, smoldering and we breathed the breath of life. Earth. We stood in the midst of a dense forest and trees bent and broke beneath our arrival. A mist, wet and dripping, snaked about the trunks of trees, pouring over dark and chiseled rock. Sunlight fell in shafts, dripping into the gaps we ripped through the tree line. Here we were magnificent and majestic, massive and otherworldly. Earth rippled around us, frothing beneath the surface of...something.

"Look," said Cassiel, pointing at the ground. Craters, thousands of them like the ones we created dotted the landscape. "The army's been here."

I fingered old wounds in the trees, glancing at trunks broken as we crashed to Earth. "But they look old. Even the ones you see, Cassiel, they're filled in."

Ramiel looked at me. "The army hasn't been gone that long."

"Not long enough for this," I said.

But it was bothering me. Time is tough for us. It is hard to explain. What is time? What is the passing of time when you are immortal and the world you inhabit is eternal? But you are temporary. You are a short-term experiment the Father is conducting. Harsh as it sounds, your existence feels more like a curable condition than a permanent reality, a stance the Father is taking. Much like your stages of grief, humanity is but an expression of anger from the Father in the wake of Lucifer's behavior. We exist in events, in milestones and happenings and occurrences. Little changes in our world: nothing grows old, nothing dies. The trees forged by the hands of the Sisters bend but do not break. The beasts tossed into the skies by Gabriel's Horn fly incessantly, day and night. Lives are ended; they do not end. But here time was real and tangible. This world changed, it bruised, it bled. It aged. And it would die one day.

Michael and the army had been banished for mere hours to you, but this world wore the wounds of their arrival like old scars. I rubbed my hands in the dulled edge of one of the craters, tasting the divinity of my brethren leaching in the soil. It was Sariel's. Her scent was faint, rapidly becoming part of the Earth. And there was more: I could feel...emotions? Bubbling beneath the foliage, spilling up between blades of grass. Anger and rage. Unbridled fury. Jealousy. Like a million souls were pouring their rage into Earth itself and the very planet was becoming poisonous. I'd felt this once before. In the darkness on Lucifer's platform. I could feel him. I couldn't feel Michael at all.

"This world is not like our own. It's worse." I stood suddenly. "Ramiel, Cassiel, find the army and find them now."

They shared a glance and turned to the others, pressing them into service. I saw battlefield promotions and the sky darkened with the shadow of tens of thousands angels. They spun in four directions, riding the winds and dotting out the sun. The force of their wings snapped thick tree trunks, spilling birds and beasts scattering into the air and across the ground, swirling the waters. If the circumstances were different, it would be breathtaking. Now, it was just a necessary evil. In the silence of their departure, Ramiel and Cassiel stared at me.

"I gave you orders. You should be with them," I said.

"We're with you," Cassiel said.

"This place isn't safe. Lucifer's here," I said. "I have to find Michael."

"We know," Cassiel looked at Ramiel. "We fight for you."

Ramiel said, "We're with *you*, Raphael. Until the end."

We walked on Earth.

I couldn't contain my smile. "It's more beautiful than what Sela showed us."

"No, it's not," Ramiel said in a whisper. She pointed. "This place is already lost. Look."

We'd come to the edge of the forest. Dragging a slow burning circle, separating us from the clearing beyond, came a massive sword of fire, a tower of living flame. The entire image burnt the morning sky and plumed black smoke.

"What is this?" Cassiel said.

"Michael was here," I told them. "That is the Father's justice: His justice always burns."

"What could the fallen—?" Cassiel began.

"I don't think this is about angels," Ramiel said suddenly. "This looks like a message, like a warning. The Captain's messages are bloody."

"It's about man, then?" Cassiel said it as a question. We knew it was a statement.

This was about man.

I leapt over the sword, hung over the clearing. It was hardscrabble here, a land of hard soil and little else. The foliage was sparse, the sun hard and hot, and this harsh plain extended as far as I could see. It was a brutal relief from the lush confines of the forest and from the air I could see the charred trail grasping the forst's fringe.

This was an expulsion.

"Michael cast them out," I said, landing. "The sword, it keeps them out."

"Cast them out? What could they have done?" Cassiel said.

A scream, horrible and bestial, tore through the silence, startling us all and spinning us about. Weapons poured from our fists but we knew the sound, knew the anguish it beheld. It was agony, an unfathomable pain of body and spirit summed up in one primal wail. We'd heard it over and over again, at our hand or the hands of our brethren. But the heavy silence that hung in its wake, thick and palpable told us it was the first time Earth had known such pain.

Death.

By the hand of another.

Murder.

We rushed from the forest, over the landscape, streaming east toward the rivers that creased the foliage and ringed Eden. And there on the shore, shivering on his knees, was a man. Dust made flesh and given life and breath and will. Man. A living, breathing soul. He was smaller than us and clad in a cloth tunic and pants. His feet were bare and muddy.

I was about to kneel before this man, this miracle. Until I saw his hands. They were coated with blood. A knife lay between his knees.

We ringed him. The man covered his face and prostrated in the muddy bank of the river.

"This is Lucifer's man?" said Ramiel.

"No, Lucifer destroyed him," and my voice was quiet. "Lucifer destroyed that one in the war. This one belongs to the Father."

I crouched, ran a blazing hand over the man's head, felt his hair between my fingers, scrubbed his skin until it was raw. Breathed his scent. I grabbed the man's face, looked into dark brown eyes. And I knew him. Images, visions raced across my sight: the tilling of fields, reaping of the land. But they weren't mine: they were the man's. Oh, the strain, the labor! The pain. The ground was unyielding for this one; its fruit was not borne easily. I felt the snap of resentment pulse through my hand. I could taste loathing on my tongue.

I could taste...hatred. I saw the offering of the fruits of his labor to the Father. Sacrifice? And then I saw another man. A younger version of this one. Their features favored one another. *Brother?* The keeper of cattle and livestock. More offerings roared past my eyes and emotions poured through me like a flood. They were familiar, these feelings, familiar and horrible and wonderful at the same time. I wallowed in them until the corners of my mouth hung in a frown. Until a sneer creased my lips. Favoritism. Envy. Jealousy. Rage.

This was Cain.

There was something horrible in this man's soul, something that threatened my own. He frightened me, this human did, felt entirely too much like the souls we fought in the war. Felt too much like us. I released Cain's face suddenly, pressed him back. I spoke to him in a language I'd never heard, never uttered but understood. The language of men. "What have you done, Cain, son of Adam?" I said. "What has become of your brother?"

"I am not my brother's keeper," Cain spat. "Are you yours, Angel? Did you keep your brother?" And he began to laugh maniacally.

Cassiel looked down the river. The body of another man, Abel, floated in the churning water, moving away from them, spilling a milky crimson into the river. His throat was cut, ripped open, and his open eyes looked back toward Cain.

"He has slain his brother and discarded him like refuse?" Cassiel said. "They are truly lost."

Cain grimaced now, clutched at patches of his coarse, black hair. Tore them out. His lips quivered, brown eyes watered, then hardened. Blazed with anger. "The Father should not choose favorites," he said. "Especially among those who are not worthy. It isn't fair."

It isn't fair. Our entire civilization was torn apart by those three words. Now man had murdered his brother for the same reason. It would end the same.

"It is not yours to question the Will of the Father or to whom He gives His favor." I leaned close to Cain now, lowered my voice to a harsh whisper, "You are a murderer, dust of this world. You will answer for your crime."

Cain eyed the knife between his knees, looked at us, and stared hard at me. He said, "And you betrayed your own brother, Raphael, Angel of the Lord. How dare you judge me?"

"You speak my name?" I said.

"You're arguing with dust, Raphael," Ramiel said. "We're not here for this."

And then the man spoke the language of angels, his eyes pulsing red and fluttering, his mouth smoldering. His voice was not his own. "Ever the pragmatist, eh, Ramiel? I remember that about you. I remember you turning your back on us in Faith too. Do you?"

Cain snatched the knife and dove for Ramiel swiping wildly but she caught the man by the throat, bodily lifting Cain above her head. She would tear Cain apart.

"No!" I screamed. "Don't touch him! They belong to the Father."

Cain looked at me, inhumanly turning his neck in Ramiel's grasp until the bones broke. Eyes pulsing and bleeding black blood, he said, "You should let her finish, Raphael. Your unwillingness to do what is necessary puts us back in the same old, familiar places, doesn't it?"

The man's mouth opened and he moaned. Cain's neck swelled, thickening with a blackness that churned beneath olive skin. Something lived within him. Black fluid bubbled in his throat, his nose and eyes. And exploded outward. The darkness hit me bodily, crushing me beneath its wave, gyrating over my body, consuming me. It was like being swallowed by a shadow, cold and unforgiving.

Liquid became metal and flesh and armor, stiffening, straddling my chest. An angel. Fallen. I knew her.

"Karan!" I pressed her upwards, away. She fell in a pool of black and dripped upwards until she stood.

"Hello, lover," she hissed and reached into Cain's open mouth and retrieved her scythe. "There, that's better."

"What in Heaven?" I said.

"You're not in Heaven anymore, pretty boy. Heaven is for angels; I'm no angel. I'm a bad, bad girl. Now," and Karan spun her scythe menacingly, "who's first?"

"You should repent, Karan, save yourself," I told her. "There are three of us, you cannot stand alone. You know it. "

"Who said anything about being alone?" she said.

And the river began to bubble, easing to a slow boil. Whitecaps licked the surface of the water and the river began to overflow its banks. The water-laden body of Abel disappeared abruptly beneath the surface and the river turned red with his blood.

Hands.

Piercing the frothing head of the water came black hands, hands of the fallen. These hands clutched gold spears and crooked swords, flexed in the warm air of Earth, slowly grew wrists and arms. And heads. Jolting upwards, wearing grotesque smiles of jagged teeth, the fallen surged from the river chattering with horrible glee. They came in packs of tens, spilling from the river in rows of black and gold, swords and teeth, piling behind Karan.

"Forget repentance, let's talk about mercy," Karan said. She shoved the blade of her scythe against my throat.

16
MICHAEL

"You're wasting them, Lucifer."

I stood in a field of severed limbs, decapitated heads replete with dead, vacant eyes staring back at me. I smiled as the black, crusty flesh exploded in ash and fire. The fallen came, hundreds of lost souls, clamoring over one another, diving to sacrifice their pathetic lives at my hands. They never touched me: they tasted only the metal of my swords, felt the heat of my blades—the heat of the Father—ripping through arms, legs, necks. It looked just like my dream: my hands swiped and slashed and murdered on their own, my eyes stayed fixed on the shimmering figure standing just beyond my reach, thin hands pressed beneath an angular chin. He smiled as he watched.

"If you want me, you come get me," I told him.

"Ever the diligent little soldier, aren't you, Michael?" Lucifer hung back, watching. Grinning. Crying. "Oh, don't worry about them: there's more where they came from. I do appreciate your concern but you misunderstand my motives. I'm actually not interested in killing you: I'm killing time. Don't want to ruin the surprise."

I sliced the wings off two assailants, drove my blades through their backs, scrubbed their remains from my tongue. "Surprise? You shouldn't have."

"Well, I couldn't let the others come and not welcome them properly, now could I?"

"Others?"

This stopped me, froze my movements and a lucky beast swiped my face, gashing my cheek. I separated the creature into three pieces.

"Oh!" and now Lucifer laughed, "I have your attention now, don't I? You know, for such a tactical individual, you really have a poor handle on your assets. That information is important in war, isn't it? But it's okay, Michael, I can help you out. See, your precious First, he never can leave well enough alone. After kicking you and yours out, the boy decided to send Raphael too."

"Raphael?" I didn't mean to say it out loud. "Raphael is here?" I crossed swords, tore a skull apart.

Lucifer was grinning broadly. "You didn't know? You mean that wasn't part of the plan? Hmm, sounds like too many cooks to me. It's getting awfully crowded down here, don't you think?" His voice fell frighteningly sober, almost like he was having a conversation with himself. "Yes, I do too. I think we should thin them out a bit."

I knew what he would do, what he could do. Raphael was no killer. He wasn't made to be. And the army was already here without a leader, most likely lost and separated. Easy pickings. I roared, tried to charge Lucifer, tried to tear the horns from his head, cram the mouthful of fangs down his damned throat. But his minions pounced on me, stealing my momentum and driving me backward.

"Don't—!" was all I could eke out.

And then Lucifer was there, caressing my face, scraping long talons across my cheeks. The smile was gone. "Don't what? Don't what, Michael? You bring that rag tag bunch of ingrates down here to try and subjugate me and mine and you have the audacity to give me orders?"

I spat at Lucifer. It burst into steam before the Satan's face.

"What's the matter?" Lucifer said. "Too many big words for you? Let me make it easier: you are going to die. The carcasses of your pathetic little army are going to litter this world. And when they are all alone, I will turn the man on the Father. You've seen how simple that is. And you know what happens after that, don't you? The Father will have to make it right. He will have to."

"The man is innocent!"

"NO ONE IS INNOCENT! You think I care about innocence, Michael? Now? I care about justice. I care about revenge. That's what matters. And after I'm done here, I'm going back. I'm going back for that boy and his blind protector. The Father made a mistake, Michael. All of it is wrong. I know it and you know it too. Unfortunately, everybody has to pay."

Faced with the reality of Lucifer's plans, I understood. *Obedience is not an act; it is a journey.* This was never going to end, not like this. Not while Lucifer and I lived. It couldn't. The Father was pitting us against one another, driving us toward some conclusion that I think neither of us understood. I didn't know how it would end; I just knew He wanted me to end it.

I closed my eyes, whispered, "I'm going to finish it."

Lucifer cupped his ear and leaned closer. "What's that, Captain? I missed that last valiant statement."

My eyes snapped open. "I said I'm going to finish it."

I glared at Lucifer, stared through him until Lucifer looked away. It was like when we first met, when I showed him the horror of his fall. That wasn't so long ago. When I showed him a porcelain figurine in the palm of the Father, slowing burning away until all that remained was the silver skeleton of a Demon. I knew it frightened Lucifer, knew it traumatized him.

Lucifer stepped back, pursed his lips and held himself for what seemed like an eternity. Mulling it over.

"You know, I admire your pluck, Michael. You have heart, I'll give you that." He laced thin arms about me, pulled me close. "But you don't have the whole story. Let me show you something."

And Lucifer pulled me from the Earth, plunging me through a membrane, through the surface. Plunging me into darkness.

"You ever heard of Hell, Peace Maker? It's a wonderful place!" And Lucifer cackled in the shadows.

17
RAPHAEL

"Contrary to popular belief," I said, swiping Karan's scythe from my throat and whirling to backhand her teeth, "I don't beg!"

Karan tumbled backward, watery and fluid, flowing over the ground and charring the foliage. She eased upwards, scrubbing her mouth.

"Ooohhh," she sang, "a backbone! Too bad you couldn't find that back in Faith. Makes you so much more attractive now, Raphael."

Ramiel and Cassiel were charging forward, burning with the Father's glory, slashing through limbs and torsos, necks, hands. Skulls. These fallen angels cavorting with Karan weren't warriors: they were lost souls with weapons. Unhinged proletariat rioters. It was easier than expected and my soldiers tore gaping wounds in Karan's numbers. But there were a lot of them. And they kept coming.

I ducked a horrid swipe to my neck from Karan, drove my saber through the chin of a marauder, and placed my back against Ramiel's.

"Tighten up," I growled to them both. "If you want to survive, stay close to me."

"That's cute," Karan said. "You almost sound concerned about what happens to them."

"And you sound bitter, demon," Ramiel said. She was growing angrier, eschewing swords for blades jutting from her fists, punching her way through assailants.

A crude semi-circle was forming: dozens of fallen were coalescing in front of Ramiel and Cassiel, jutting crooked swords and spears at them, lobbing fireballs against Cassiel's shield, but pressing them—and me—precariously close to Karan's hungry scythe. My angels were making short work of the demons, but they kept coming, bubbling from the river, leeching from the soil.

When rancid hands began snatching at our feet, I said, "To the skies!"

Wings of metal lashed open and we vaulted into the air. But the monsterswere faster, crowding above us and hovering on ragged wings, limiting our mobility, swiping us down with ugly weapons.

"No, you don't!" Karan growled and cast her scythe forward. The blade leapt from the arm, extended by a thick black chain, and latched onto Ramiel's wing. A brutal snatch and she was twirling from the sky!

"Ramiel!" Cassiel yelled and dove, leaving me to face twenty demons.

But he was too late: Ramiel crashed to the ground and lay on her back, twisting in the dirt.

Karan jolted the chain again, ripped the wing from Ramiel's body and hurled it at Cassiel. "Catch!"

I slashed wickedly, horridly, cleaving demons into smoldering detritus in the sky. They burned at my touch, shielded red eyes at the divinity wafting from my body. I felt my own soul aching, my own civility dissipating. It was like Faith all over again: watching Ramiel squirming, feebly batting away the advances of fallen angels as they ducked beneath her blades and tore through her armor, ripping pieces of her flesh, it was like watching that cherub. Watching my blessedness slip away.

I knew how it worked now. I knew how Lucifer became so powerful. I understood what Samael had his angels doing, what these fallen souls were doing. You had to put it into you, make it a part of you. That which the Father provided—His tears, His waters, this flesh and blood—you had to consume it to grow stronger. You had to consume Him. We were despicable thieves, all of us grave robbers, stealing the Father's life from the bodies of the dying. I figured it out in Faith when I tasted my victims even as I slaughtered them. I loved how it felt. And I knew I would spend eternity in Hell because of it.

These souls were no match for me and I lapped at the spurts of blood flashing in my face. Cassiel fell like a meteor, crouching over Ramiel's wounded form, wildly swiping. The demons were amused. For a moment. They laughed at him, even as his sword bit into the closest. They just laughed at him. Then they attacked, spearing him with a dozen swords and blades. As his body stiffened, Karan shattered him with her scythe, letting the refuse of his form spill onto the ground. She placed the blade against Ramiel's neck.

"Don't," I said.

"I want you to beg me," Karan said and the others laughed at me.

My eyes welled. "Karan, please don't. Please don't."

"That was beautiful. I think I have a tear," Karan mocked me. Her face softened, easing into the beauty I once knew. "Do you love her?"

"I love them all, Karan, you know that."

"Do you love *her*?"

What could I say? Ramiel had been my right hand, had saved my life, had willingly offered her blood in exchange for mine. But that was the price of war. That was the deal we all struck, the pact we made standing in front of Michael swearing allegiance to the Father and to him. Ramiel was a soldier, an angel, a sister. As valuable as any other.

"Of course I do," I whispered.

"Like you loved me?"

I've never been able to lie. It isn't that I don't do it well. I can't do it at all. The Father didn't make us to be liars: His Word is the truth and that truth spoken into existence. We are forged in His Word, we are made in His truth. A lie is...unnatural. You call Lucifer the Father of Lies but even he struggles with this. He will tell you he doesn't lie because he doesn't need to. The truth is it is hard for him. It is impossible for me and it was impossible to lie to Karan. Even then. Even to save Ramiel.

I looked in Ramiel's eyes. "No."

"Then you won't miss her!" And Karan tugged the scythe upwards, ripping Ramiel's head from her neck. "That wasn't so hard now, was it?"

But I was beyond enraged. I burned hot enough to char the demons around me, to melt their weapons and blind them and I dove for Karan. “You horrible soul! I should have killed you!”

“But you didn’t.” And Karan stood, horrible grin lining her face, glowing amidst the chants of her brethren. She whirled her scythe. “Now, stop your blubbering and come give us a hug.”

But I wasn’t thinking: abject fury blinded me. I didn’t see Karan ease to the side and lurch her weapon forward until I was upon her. The blade came loose, bit deep into my collarbone until it ripped from my back and tore my wing. I didn’t get to yell, didn’t get to acknowledge the searing pain. Karan threw her weight into it, adding to my momentum, and swung me over her head, plunging me into the depths of the river.

The last thing I heard was the hate in her voice saying, “See you around, lover boy.”

I felt myself sinking, drifting, drowning. Listing away. And the world went black.

PART 2

RAPHAEL

Faith in Twilight

18

I lost my soul in Faith.

It was lost long before I stood between Faith's fractured buildings—again—with my Sword, with my soldiers, looking to murder souls who refused to commit. It was long before Michael began his bloody witch hunt for apathy. Long before this war became a war. I lost it back when revolt was only a thought, merely the inkling of a rebellion, slithering through the hearts of angels. I lost my soul in the beginning, in Faith.

I gave it to another.

Her name was Karan. You know her as the Reaper. She belongs to Lucifer now. She didn't always. When I knew her, she was her own soul, a free soul. A beautiful soul. She was a principality—a dark skinned beauty the color of night, with eyes that shone like the moon. Karan was a chiseled masterpiece, a living sculpture of onyx and indigo. Unrefined. Jagged. Pure. The Father touched principalities deep, letting only flecks of His light seep to the surface. As she moved in the daylight, streaks of gold would dance on her skin. She was magnificent then. I don't know what she is now.

I met Karan shortly after I gave the cities to the angels. I'd seen her in the Waters, wrapped in the arms of her brethren, gulping the first breaths of life. I don't know what struck me about her—it was...something. Something different than the others. She stood out, apart, from the rest. You see and accept this every day of your lives. For us, the idea was new, that souls belonging to the Father could have differing levels of "value" in one's eyes. In my eyes.

"I see you," I thought to myself.

Her eyes widened and Karan turned, looked squarely at me and smiled.

She heard me. She heard my thoughts? How?

I heard her voice, husky and new, scratching at the inside of my mind, "I see you, Peace Keeper. I see you, Raphael."

Her smile was incredible.

When the beating of the wings of millions faded to echoes and the song of the angels wafted from the waters of their birth to the cities, I followed her, passing Lucifer's prone form along the way.

"She heard you, didn't she?" he said, grinning, eyes closed against the sun.

I paused in air. "How did—?"

He rose on an elbow. "How do you do what you do?"

"The Father gives me what I need."

"That's what He says. But you're smart, kiddo. I think you can figure this one out." And Lucifer smiled at me. "She's waiting for you, Peace Keeper. Don't waste time with me; I'll be here."

My brow furrowed and I turned away.

"Oh!" Lucifer said, "I heard you too. Maybe you should try to figure out why."

When I left him, I was troubled. That any angel could hear my thoughts was disconcerting. No matter how well intentioned, I was responsible for all souls in Heaven. My thoughts were between the Father and me. And now I'd made them personal, reached out to an angel under my care, for something beyond my responsibilities. I could justify that, couldn't I? The Father didn't actively discourage such fraternizations—Sela and Lucifer shared...something, didn't they? But then there was Lucifer. There was always Lucifer.

He heard me too.

If my communication with the principality was disconcerting, Lucifer's eavesdropping was damn problematic. What else had he heard? What did he know? And how? What was it about Lucifer that made him so different from the rest of us? What made him such a difficult soul to manage, to anticipate, to control? The binding was supposed to subdue him but I had my doubts.

I came to Faith with my own faith very shaken.

The ragged outline of the city the angels were to build had sketched itself across the rugged face of Faith. This rock was more jagged than smooth, more mountain than meadow. Sela was there then, shining like star in the morning sun, casting her magnificence across Faith in blinding sheets, a queen trying to motivate her subjects. She was trying to change the face of Faith. It wasn't working.

I found Karan trying to move a mountain. Literally. "What are you doing?" I said, floating behind her.

"Building. Isn't that what you told us to do?" She stabbed at the rock in front of her with her scythe, tore a massive chunk away and faced me. And smiled. "I don't know. Trying to make this...different, I guess. Sela knows." And then, "Why do you look so unhappy?"

I was still frowning. I'd forgotten. "Lucifer said something to me...it bothered me."

"Tell me about him."

"Tell me about you." I sat on the rock in front of her.

She laughed. "You're in the way, Peace Keeper."

I grabbed her hand. "Don't call me that. That's my job, my purpose. It's not who I am. My name is Raphael."

"I am called Karan," she said, leaning on the scythe. "I am the Reaper of Souls."

An angel with a title? Not an archangel but a common one? Only the Host had such purposes; it was our role to give purpose to our Body, the souls within our care. They did not define themselves. And the Father wasn't speaking to any of us. Was He?

"Who called you that? The Reaper?" I said.

"I heard it in the Water, when my brothers were pulling me out. It was the Father, I guess. He said, 'You are called Karan. You are the Reaper of Souls. You will bring your brothers and sisters to Me.'"

That troubled me—a lot—but I refused to show my trepidation to Karan. "So tell me about this project."

"The Architect commands us to build a city upon this rock. But the mountains are wrong. We must move them."

"Sounds like a lot of work."

"It sounds like something I did not choose."

"But we all have purpose, Karan, we all must build the Father's kingdom. That is our charge."

She cocked her head. "You do not build. Your hands are clean."

"No, they're not. They are dirtier than you can imagine. And it is my job to keep this place clean. To keep the peace and ensure the Father's will is done."

Karan looked at me, at Sela standing in the center of Faith, outshining the straining backs about her, and at the haunting form of Azazel, as he moved from city to city, squashing any protest with his very presence. She looked at the souls about her, those that looked like her, that still wore the beads of the water of their birth on their shoulders. She looked at those souls toiling beneath Sela's command. It wasn't brutal by any means. It was simply different. A slow caste system was emerging in Faith—in all of Heaven—and I was watching Karan see which end of the system she was on.

Karan the Reaper stared at me, let her dark eyes meet my own. She grabbed my hand, scrubbed tough fingers along the skin of my palm. Her hands were filthy and hard, already beaten to a leathery smoothness. My hands were softer than hers. Noticeably.

She said, "We do not have choice. You have choice. The Host has choice. We build. Your hands are clean."

"Sela built this world," I told her. "The Sisters made it live. Gabriel called you forth. I—" And I looked at Lucifer, and I faltered. "I keep you safe."

"From what?" Karan said.

"Let me show you something," I told her. And it was the worst mistake I made.

We hung above Faith, between that rock and Lucifer's platform. Close enough for her to see. Far enough that he couldn't hear us. I hoped. I was wrong.

I told Karan, "His name is Lucifer. He is the Keeper of the Light. He is the Father's first angel."

There was more curiosity than fear etching her face. She edged closer, straining for a better look. Lucifer was pacing now, prowling the perimeter of his platform and the scrape of his chains echoed.

"He's beautiful!" Karan was whispering, fingers over her mouth. "Why is he—?"

"In chains?" I finished. "Lucifer wants."

"What does he want?"

"What he cannot have. What I cannot allow him to have. If he gets what he wants, there will be no peace and you will not be safe. I am the Peace Keeper. It is my purpose to maintain the safety here. Your purpose is to build."

"No!" she said, much too loudly. Lucifer stopped. "I am the Reaper of Souls! My purpose is to bring the others to Him."

"To who, Karan?"

"The Father."

My skepticism was evident. "We'll see about that."

She was wounded. "You don't believe me?"

"It's not—I believe that's what you heard. I didn't know we needed a Reaper." And I didn't think the Father would give such an important sounding assignment to a principality—an angel who'd known life for mere hours. Plus, when did we drift away from the Father? Why would we need a Reaper at all?

She folded her arms. "You didn't think it would be me, did you?"

"That's not what I said."

"It's what you thought, Raphael."

"No, I—," I paused. Could she hear me? Could she hear all my thoughts? If she could, glossing over the situation wouldn't be helpful. I decided honestly was best. "I brought you here so you could see what happens when we don't follow our purpose. When we don't live the life the Father has given to us. Lucifer rejected what the Father gave him. He was disobedient. He had to be punished—he's bound to that platform so he doesn't infect any of you with his nonsense. I have a job to do, Karan, and so do you. It isn't about what you want. It's about what has to be done."

She was silent for a long time, her face a blank slate, arms crossed and rigid. "I have to get back to work," she said finally, turning. And then, "What did he want?"

"Freedom."

19

She found me the next time.

I tended to gravitate to Faith, partially for Karan, partially because it was peaceful to me. The city spoke to me, I guess, in a way I cannot describe. You will probably one day say I am the faithful one. That's fair: I have more faith than my brothers, and certainly much more than Michael. Gabriel does not exist on faith: he has already seen what is to happen. He exists in certainty. I think that is why none of this affects him—he is not as fragile as we are. He already knows. It's the closest thing to omnipotence I've ever seen in anything that wasn't the Father.

I was sitting on her mountain when she found me. I liked it there. It wasn't the tallest place in Heaven, Light was, but Faith let me see the farthest. From the Waters to Father's Pass, from the peaks of the Father's Hand along the meadow that rolled below. It made me feel safe, I guess. Safe in the Father's Hand.

"What do you seek?" Karan said to me.

I don't know how long she stood there, watching.

"Nothing. I like the view." I blushed. I finally said, "You."

"The Host seeks the Body?"

"I seek," and I looked at her, inhaled her physique, her statuesque frame, "comfort."

She rammed her scythe into the stone. "No peace for you, Peace Keeper? How can you keep peace if you can't find it?"

I could only smile at her. "Come up here," I said.

She did and I folded in on myself, collapsing in her presence. Karan grinned at me.

"Do I make you nervous, Host?"

"Call me Raphael."

"Do I make you nervous, Raphael?" And the way she spoke, with a slight seduction, with an ounce of confidence, touched me. Somewhere, she lost the distinction between Host and Body. Between us and them. She talked to me like an equal.

"You do," I said, "but I don't know why. You seem like you know something."

"Knowledge scares you? That seems ridiculous." She played with her fingers, then grabbed for my hands. "I figured something out."

"Figured what out?"

Karan only looked at my palms, holding her toughened palms against mine. "You told me your hands were dirty but I couldn't see it. Then you showed me Lucifer and I didn't understand. But I do now." She looked at me suddenly with brilliant eyes. "You did that to him."

It wasn't a question. It wasn't even an accusation. It was simply a fact, a truth revealed. There was no judgment in her voice; the judgment was in my head. I snatched my hands away.

"I did what was necessary!" I said too harshly and I began to stand. She grabbed me.

"No!" And then, "No. Don't go. I'm not...I understand. Tell me why."

I wouldn't look at her.

"If it was necessary," she pulled my face to hers, "it was necessary. I just want to know why."

"I told you."

"No, you talked around it. You talked like the Host. I want to talk to you. Why did you do it, Raphael? Why did you put Lucifer in chains?"

A heavy sigh. "I asked him. I warned him. The Father knew what he was going to do, what he was trying to do. I asked him to stop."

"What was he trying to do?"

I should have closed my mouth. Right then. When I look back at everything, that was the moment I lost control, the moment my honesty changed everything. I put my faith in someone else. And it cost me dearly. Instead, I told her the truth. All of it.

"Lucifer was—is—trying to tear it apart. He doesn't want this. Any of it. Everything we're doing here, he wants to destroy it if he can. The Father knows it. He sent me here to stop it, to stop him. Maybe change his mind. I don't know."

"Can you change his mind?"

I looked out across Faith, across Heaven, at Lucifer's platform. Watched him sitting cross-legged on that ridge of glass, glaring at the progress around him. His anger was palpable, even from this distance. I could feel his rage wafting through the air.

"Binding him hasn't helped. I didn't think it would. It makes it worse."

"Worse, huh?" Karan made me face her again. "So why do it?"

"Because it gives him something else to focus on. Something that's not all of you. Makes him direct his anger at me. I can deal with Lucifer being mad at me. You can't deal with him being mad at you. I can't have him take it out on you."

"Why?"

"You'd never survive it. And you're my responsibility. I have to do what is necessary."

We were both quiet for a while, looking at the sun, at our shadows. At each other.

"Why is Lucifer so angry?" she said.

"He thinks it isn't fair," I told her and closed my eyes.

She stroked my face. "Why does that make you so sad?"

"Because he's right."

"No, it isn't fair," she whispered.

"There's nothing I can do about it."

"Maybe you don't have to."

We sat in silence for a long time, holding hands, feeling the rush of my skin on hers. I stood suddenly, opened wings of metal, pressed her hands away.

I said, "I should go. You have work to finish."

Karan frowned and snorted and reached for her scythe. "Yeah, I do."

When I was airborne, I heard her say, "So, Peace Keeper, if it comes down to it, can you stop him?"

I looked at my hands. I couldn't look at her. "I don't think so."

20

"What are we?" Karan asked me once.

We were sitting entirely too close on the top of our mountain, watching Lucifer move the sun across the sky. I did this as often as I could, finding her here on her mountain. She calmed me, drowned out the droning of Lucifer's whispers in my head. I could hear him, all too loudly, constantly pressing against my will. Pushing me. Karan dulled that voice, that seductive hiss, allowed me to focus. I tried to temper my want for her with my sense of propriety and her responsibilities. Tried not to call attention to...whatever it was we had. I remember these moments with Karan the most: they were the most peaceful, the most joyful, I've ever known.

Karan had taken to holding my hand often, to tracing the lines on my palm. Mainly examining the difference in luminosity, in skin tone, in texture our skin held. I thought it was childish curiosity, the ruminations of a youthful and naïve mind. I was wrong. We were different, she and I, and Karan realized it.

"What do you mean?" I said, eyes closed in the sun.

"You and me," she said. "What are we?"

"Sons and daughters of the Father. You know that. We are angels. Host and Body."

She pried one of my eyes open. "No," and she looked down, away, "What are you and I? Together?"

Together? And then I understood: she was asking me about a relationship. What could I say? What should I say? What were we? What could we be? The Father talked about relationships with Him, not with one another and the only one I'd ever heard about was something between Lucifer and the angel who died, Lilith. But I wasn't Lucifer and my emotions didn't rule my actions like his.

"Oh..." I stammered. "I don't..."

She looked at me hopeful, with vulnerable eyes. "Am I your Chosen?"

"Chosen? I don't—where did you—what's a Chosen?"

"Am I special to you?"

I smiled at her now but it was a paternal smile, a patronizing smile. "Of course you are special to me."

She wasn't satisfied. "More than the others?"

"Are you asking me to choose, Karan?"

"That's what Chosen means, Raphael. Do you choose me?"

"Over the others?"

Her eyes were getting wet and I could tell this wasn't how she expected the conversation to turn. But I didn't know what to say: I couldn't place one angel above the rest, could I? Such favoritism would threaten the stability of Heaven. But things were already becoming precarious: a mist was gathering among us, flowing through the cities, coalescing among the powers and principalities. I could feel it, everyone could. And I could see it on Karan's face every time I looked at her.

What could I say?

"Chosen's not a term I know, I guess. But you are special to me. You know that, don't you?" I told her. "I keep coming back. To see you."

This brought a smile to her face and I heaved a sigh of relief. But it was short-lived.

She dropped her eyes. Again. "Are there others?"

"Other what?"

"Other angels," she said. "Like me. That you go to see. Special ones?"

"Special to me?" I paused and told her the truth. "Yes and no. Sela is special to me but Sela is Sela. She's different. And the Sisters. They are special; they help me fulfill my purpose. They help me maintain this. I'm not sure what you're asking me."

"Do you love me?" And she looked at me with the most innocent eyes.

"Of course I do."

"No, not like the others. Not like you have to. Do you love me? For me?"

Do you love me? The most dangerous question I have ever been asked. By anyone. Including the Father.

I told her the truth. "You make me smile, Karan. It's getting harder and harder to find the joy and I feel like something is sapping it. Pulling it away. But I don't feel that when I'm with you, here, on this mountain, holding your hand. I don't feel bad anymore."

"That doesn't answer the question, Raphael. Do you love me?"

"I do," and I smiled my widest smile.

She bit her lip.

"That wasn't what you wanted to hear?" I said. Now I was lost.

"Then why...?" She paused, uncertain of what to say.

"Just say it, Karan. Whatever it is, just say it."

She touched my face and her hands were rough, calloused. Hard. "Do you feel that? Do you feel what that feels like?"

"We've had this discussion before, Karan. We have roles. We have purpose. It's what makes this work."

"But should we have to? Shouldn't we get to choose our purpose? If I'm special to you, why do you let this happen? You know there's more for me. The Father made me for something greater than this, Raphael. I am the Reaper of Souls!"

"No, you're not!" And I regretted the words as soon as they crossed my lips. "You are just a principality like millions of your brothers and sisters. You are the Body; you are made to build the Father's kingdom and glorify His name! I don't know what you heard but it wasn't what you think it was."

She stepped back from me, wounded, her eyes wet and glistening. "I knew you didn't believe me," she whispered. "I knew it."

"Karan..."

But she jolted from my outstretched hand, her scythe bubbling in her fist. She leveled the blade at me. "I have work to do, Host, don't I? Isn't that what you're going to say?" She jumped from the mountain, black crow's wings bursting from her back. "Don't come back," she called.

I watched her disappear over the side of Faith. Broken.

21

"What's a Chosen?"

I should have known better. Lucifer was the worst soul in Heaven I could have gone to. The worst. But he understood this "attachment"—this feeling I was feeling about Karan. He understood how another could be special to you. He understood something I did not. He understood love.

Lucifer tapped his fingers together and tightened his brow. "Where did you hear that word?"

"Karan said it to me. She asked if she was my Chosen."

"The Reaper? Hmm, that's interesting," Lucifer said.

"Interesting?" I sat on his platform, watched Lucifer toy with his chains. He winced as he tugged on them, testing them. Still.

"Well, if she's the Reaper, she's already special, isn't she? She doesn't need validation from you."

I frowned.

Lucifer's face brightened and he smiled a wicked grin. I hated that grin. "Oh," he said. "You don't believe her."

I stood suddenly. "I didn't say that!"

"Don't have to, kiddo. It's all over your face."

I knew it was. I couldn't hide it, I couldn't lie about it. I wore that emotion clearly and if Lucifer could see it, I'm sure Karan could too. She probably saw it every time I looked at her. Every time she looked at me. I never believed her. And I never heard anything from the Father. Not a word.

I said, "Why would He do that? Name her like that?"

"Why are you asking me, Peace Keeper? Aren't you the Father's little errand boy? Ask Him."

I looked at my feet, played with my fingernails. "He's not talking to me."

Lucifer laughed heartily, clutching his stomach. He cupped his ear, leaned in for effect. "I didn't catch that. Can you say it again, Raphael?"

"Lucifer..."

"INDULGE ME!" His voice echoed and I heard silence reign in Heaven for a moment. "You owe me that much, don't you think?"

"He's not talking to me! He's not talking at all! Are you happy now?"

"Hurts doesn't it? Join the club." The Keeper of the Light chuckled at me. "Look, you have a choice here: you can keep thinking Karan is a liar even when she has no reason to lie, or you can choose to believe her and indulge this little idea. Either way, leave me out of it. I'm not interested in debating your romantic dalliances."

He turned his back on me.

"Wait!" I said and grabbed his shoulder, pulling him to face me. It was a mistake.

"You are an idiot." Lucifer's hand snapped about my neck and snatched me from my feet. He was choking me and smiling and I watched his teeth flow into points. "I thought you were smarter than this: you let your affections place you in precarious situations. What did you think I would do? Let you imprison me and then act as an adviser on your attraction to this animal? How stupid do you think I am?"

But as he was talking his hand was tightening. The world on the edges of my eyes was clouding over and his voice sounded distant and ethereal. I was losing consciousness. I squeaked out, "Lilith was your Chosen."

He softened. And for a split second I saw water in his eyes. Then rage. Lucifer tossed me to the edge of his platform like a rag, watched me roll over the edge and hang by my fingertips. He growled. "Don't speak that name again. You will join her if you do."

I clambered back onto the glass. "She was your Chosen, wasn't she? What was it—?"

"What was it like? Is that the insensitive question you actually want to ask, Peace Keeper? What was it like? Which part? Let's see, would you like to hear the part where I melted her face with my bare hands or the time when the Father burned her alive because He was jealous of her? Which thrilling story would you like to hear about, Raphael? Which one is going to add to the magic of your pathetic little crush?"

But I was aghast. "I didn't—"

"No one knows!" Lucifer growled. "My pain is not for public consumption. Look at me! Haven't you placed my humiliation before enough eyes? What more do you want?"

"Did you love her?" My voice was small and tight.

He looked at his feet and it was the first time I saw sadness on his face. The rage was gone, the anger frittered away. Lucifer was...wounded.

"Of course I loved her," he said. "I loved Lilith and I hurt her and...I tried to make it right. I did. I tried to protect her. But I couldn't. Not from Him. I couldn't protect her." Lucifer looked at me with sober, clear eyes. "The Father said He loved me and He killed her. That's what happened to my Chosen. Are these satisfactory answers to your mundane questions?"

It was obvious the pain was still raw. It was a side of Lucifer I hadn't considered. I understood his rage; his anger was fathomable to me. Warranted even. But his pain? That was a novel idea, something the Father never warned me about. When He sent me to bind Lucifer, to pull him away from the others and punish him for his rebellious intentions, it seemed just. Nothing prepared me for the rationale behind the rebellion. I knew he thought it was unfair. And it was. I didn't know Lucifer was *right*. I was crying for him.

"I'm sorry," I said through my tears.

"I don't want your pity, Raphael. It doesn't bring her back."

"Why?"

Lucifer sneered, "Why what? You're smart; use all your words."

I ignored him. "Why did He do it?"

"Why did He kill her?" And Lucifer turned away, looked at Faith. "He called her an abomination. He said I'd defied Him." He spun quickly, harshly, roaring in the Heavens. "He said I abused my powers—the powers He gave me! He gave me the means and the opportunity and the reason and then said I was wrong. Me! And when I wouldn't kneel to His ridiculous edicts, the Father—*your* Father—killed my Chosen and stole the ones I loved."

"Why are you telling me all of this?"

"Because you need to understand the one you serve. You need to know how fickle His love is...and how worthless your love is to Him. If the Reaper loves you, love her back. Damn the consequences."

"And end up like you?"

Lucifer smiled at me now. "If she matters that much to you, yes."

I looked at Lucifer's face, at the sadness and anger pulsing beneath his eyes, in the slight sneer in his lip. I looked at his hands, rapidly flexing, forming fists, then releasing only to tighten again. And my eyes fell on the places where the chains ripped into his flesh, where those wounds scarred and burned closed. Blemishes in his perfection. Blemishes brought by his own actions and my responsibility to enforce the penalties. I wouldn't end that way. I couldn't.

Lucifer was an example. I wasn't allowed to say it, not so flagrantly, but his punishment was to serve as a warning to all others: disobedience will not be tolerated. Not by the Father. Not by me. There is no place in Heaven for those who will not do the Father's will. Not even for His most beloved. I could feel the Father moving away from me, feel the coldness of His absence, when my thoughts turned from my duties to my wants. I couldn't do it. I wouldn't.

"No soul means that much," I said, resolutely.

Lucifer bit his lip, stifled a smile. "Hmm, that's too bad. You should tell that to her." He jerked a thumb behind him.

Karan.

Floating in the shadow of Faith. Listening to it all. Tears streaming down her beautiful face. She was gone before I could speak word, as if I could figure out what to say.

Lucifer patted my shoulder. "Tsk, tsk," he said, "you should pay attention, kiddo. Never know who's listening. Now, get off my platform. Waste someone else's time."

And Lucifer shoved me from the sky.

22

"Are you lost?" Karan asked me.

I was wandering, admittedly, shuffling through the streets of Faith, feeling its lack of pretension through my pores. No matter how I tried to lose myself in its maze of low buildings and short edifices, I always found myself back to the central square, staring at the same mountain. Fearing what was beyond it.

The center of Faith was a trapezoid, really, an oblong shape pulled from the recesses of Sela's imagination. It dominated the city, providing enough physical space for Faith's denizens to commune together as one Body, to find solace in the Father. These were fiercely devout angels, orders of souls who championed the pursuit of the Father and His wishes, a community of worshippers. The buildings that ringed the central were Spartan in shape and size, utilitarian edifices that towered high enough to block view of Lucifer's platform. No higher. Faith had no aspirations of higher status. It was content where it stood.

I was content standing in it.

She startled me. "Lost? No, I was...shouldn't you be—?"

"Working?" She frowned. "I do more than build. I am more than that, Peace Keeper."

"I told you, call me, Raph—"

But Karan was furious. She stomped in front of me, stabbing at the rock with her scythe, spitting her words. "You tell me lots of things. Not all of them are true. You tell me that I am special but you do not believe it even when the Father names me Himself. You told me you loved me."

"I do love you, Karan. That is the truth."

"Your truth and my reality are two different things," she said and turned away. "You told us no angel is above the Father but we build monuments in your image. You tell us lots of things, Peace Keeper. You tell me lots of things. You said we are the same."

"Monuments? What are you talking about?"

A raised eyebrow. "Don't you know? Let me show you."

She dragged me into the air, floating above the bustle that was Faith, clutching my wrist and pulling around the far side of the mountain. The side I never ventured on. The side that faced Lucifer. Karan grabbed my face and pointed at the carving in the rock.

It was me. Me.

Hundreds of times larger than reality, my face and upper body—a bust—was etched into the rock face. The eyes glowed blue, forged from sapphires the color of the sky. It was magnificent, honestly, and part of me swelled at the image. I was a part of Heaven, carved into the very face of Faith. Even Lucifer was transitory: he wouldn't stay on that platform forever. But I was part of the Father's design.

"It's—," I started, smiling.

"It's ridiculous!" Karan spat. "This is the face of a lie!"

"I didn't ask for this." But my voice was small, unconvincing.

"Yet here it is. Raphael, the greatest of us all."

The first sin you know about is pride. Your book gives that all to Lucifer, plants it firmly in your rendition of the angel he is. It's not untrue, but it's not entirely true either. Pride belongs to all of us. Your circles of book-clutching, hymn-singing denizens think pride exists outside of themselves, that it is something external to them, something to avoid. Avoiding pride is like avoiding your arm. It's a part of you. It was a part of us. Because it's a part of Him. That is the spirit that lives in each of us.

It lived in me at the moment, staring at my own face scarred in the rock of Faith. "You did this?" I said.

"*We* did this," Karan snapped, "and we shouldn't have."

"It's magnificent," I whispered.

"It's an abomination! And it cannot stand!" And Karan spun her scythe out and tore a gouge across the monument's face. Across my face. I winced at the action.

But it was the collection of words that struck me more than her outrage. 'It is an abomination and it cannot stand.' This isn't something an angel says. It isn't for angels, for the sons and daughters of the waves, to pass judgment on anything. That was reserved for the Host. And what had these angels seen? What horror had befallen their existences? What constituted abomination in their eyes? Abomination was the Father's word, His term for something abhorrent. No, these were the words of another; someone who'd tasted the judgment of the Father or His emissaries. There was only one.

Lucifer.

"What did you do, Karan?"

"What I was supposed to: built a monument fitting my Host. You are two-faced now. Seems more appropriate."

I stifled a growl. "Have you been speaking to Lucifer? I told you about him."

"But he told me the truth! About everything!" She shifted her scythe, took a more menacing stance. "I used my resources. I figured you'd be proud of me."

My eyes flamed. "You speak beyond your station, principality."

She laughed at me, "Did I hurt your feelings, Raphael?"

"I am still your Host, Karan," I faced her now. "You will address me as such."

Her face fell. "You told me to call you—"

"I told you he was dangerous! I told you he wanted to tear it all down. And here you are, doing his dirty work. What do you know of abomination? Who tells you what can and cannot stand?"

"I have my own mind," she said quietly, angrily. "I can make decisions."

"Says who?" But I was roaring now, gesturing to the monument. "I don't care about this! I care about what you think is right and wrong. I care that you think it's wise to go behind my back. I care that you think you're strong enough to debate with the Keeper."

"You did."

"YOU ARE NOT ME! We are not the same, Karan. We're not. And we never will be. I am made for something greater than you."

"I am the Reaper of Souls!"

"You are an angel with an axe! Nothing more! And you don't know what you're dealing with. What do you think he is? What do you think he'll do? The Father wanted him bound, Karan. That was the will of the Father. What do you think he'll do to you? And when I did bind Lucifer, I had Gabriel and Azazel with me. I didn't do it alone."

"Who said I was alone?"

Then I saw them. Hundreds of them. Hanging about us. Powers, principalities, thrones, virtues. A few cherubs and seraphs. Angry souls all, blades and cudgels, bludgeons and spears twitched in their hands. They wore the same angry expressions that now lined Karan's face.

"Karan," I pleaded, "you know this is not a good idea."

"We're tired, Raphael," she said and her voice sounded sad. "We're tired of being less, being less than Azazel and Sela. And you. But you don't understand that, do you?" She moved toward me, stroked my face. "You don't see how much it hurts."

"Lucifer isn't the answer."

"No, he isn't. And he didn't give us one. He just opened our eyes. If we want it to change, we have to make it change. We can't wait for you to wake up and see how wrong it is. It's on us. And it starts now."

"You're making a mistake. You all are."

"Sometimes disobedience is just," said another principality. "Sometimes disobedience is necessary."

"Sometimes disobedience is just disobedience and should be treated as such. I am Raphael the Archangel, the Father's Peace Keeper and I will ensure there is peace in this place." I felt sabers ease from my palms. "At all costs."

But the horde moved closer. "There is no peace without justice, Host," said a seraph and his chest crackled. "This isn't fair to us."

"Your arguments have merit. These actions do not." And then, "Don't do this."

The first of the principalities to fall was a soul called Abraxos. He wore a mane of sable hair around his obsidian face. I remember the look of shock that crossed his face when my blades separated his head from his neck and cleaved his waist in two. I remember the next, a power named Miniel, whose flaming spear glanced off my wings before I sliced through her wrist and drove a saber through her throat. She spat blood on my face before crumbling to ash. I remember them all—seven total, who tasted my justice before the others dispersed. Before Karan turned her back and disappeared over the mountains.

And I wept over each one of them.

But they were tears of anger. These angels were driven, coerced into aggression, into insurrection. And I knew who gave them the push they needed.

Lucifer heard me: as soon as my feet touched the glass surface of his platform, he laughed aloud and doused all the light in Heaven.

"I know why you're here, Raphael," Lucifer said in the darkness. "You're afraid."

PART 3

The Harsh Light of Day

23
SARIEL

I understood Uriel's point: the Earth was magnificent.

It was the very thing Heaven wasn't: alive! Heaven was static, crystalline world in the palm of the Father's hand. But He didn't move there anymore; His face didn't shine upon us anymore. We were an old project to Him now, idle and complete. Lucifer called Heaven a terrarium once. It took me thousands of your years to understand how right he was. The Heaven I left was a world paused, a frozen moment where nothing ever happened.

Except what we did to ourselves.

This is where humans and angels differ.

Earth was given to you. It is a gift forged with men in mind. It is where you belong, not on the plane with us. You belong here, on this breathing, living world inspired by the Father's plan for you. He made it for you. Heaven was created after us—it was an accidental creation, both built and destroyed in grief and rage. Hope was not part of the plan for our world; it is the very fabric of yours.

When Michael made me a Commander in the Battle for Peace, it wasn't hope that made me stand with him. It was fear. Fear of what would happen if I didn't. I was afraid of Michael. He is something beyond me, beyond the rest of us. I've watched him slice angels limb from limb, hundreds of them, and lap at their entrails. I've seen Michael giggle as our brothers and sisters turned to ash beneath his blade. And I saw him raise the souls of thousands to decimate a line of fallen angels.

I was afraid of Michael. I am afraid of Michael.

And I couldn't understand why I wouldn't stop searching for him.

I'm not sure how long I was there but it was at least hundreds of your years. I traveled the Earth, searching for Michael, hanging in the skies and screaming his name until my wings wearied and my voice grew hoarse. In wind and rain, in darkness and light, I called for my Captain only to hear endless silence and the echo of my own voice.

I grew lonely.

Life happened beneath me. Humans grouped together, traipsing the landscape in caravans of man and beast, huddling in clusters of tents and thin structures. They coupled and made children, made families, built communities, would occasionally acknowledge my existence with a quickened breath or a hushed prayer. Life happened while I searched. Eventually those tented communities became permanent edifices of stone and baked earth. Walls sprung from nothing, circling towns and cities. Human hands worked the earth, pulling its gifts of food and mineral, and the race of man slowly grew into something mighty. Something impressive. Something hopeful.

I left the skies. Dusted my armor into something softer: the muted woolen robes of the humans below me. I walked among them. I saw the children of dust born, watched them grow, live full, simple lives, and eventually succumb to the dust again. The cycle was beautiful in its simplicity. You think death is final, so you fear it. Death for you is but a transition, a movement from your world to ours. Your earthly body dies and your soul is set free. The Father has blessed you with the opportunity to learn from your mistakes and grow in His love for you. He allows you to repent, to beseech His mercy when your transgressions have numbered too great. The Father offers us no such opportunity. Immortality is given no such repentance; mercy is reserved for the mortal, for the weak.

The Father believes we should have known better.

I believe we should have been warned.

I found Uriel's Sword hundreds of miles east from the carcass of Eden, in a city called Enoch, that you now call Uruk. It was a low, squat city, full of one and two-story buildings of dried earth and rough-hewn stone organized around a large central square, almost like a market. The city looked eerily familiar to me. Like I'd seen it before. Walked its streets before. Felt its stone beneath my feet. Run my fingers along coarse walls. I had. In Heaven. This city was like Truth. There was a temple at its entrance, massive and imposing, bolstered by a colonnade of white stone. Something burned at its exterior. Something that used to be alive. Like an offering. Or a sacrifice. And scores of humans prostrated themselves in front of the altar.

But it wasn't the humans that interested me. Those dull beings in soft cloth were of no concern.

It was the others.

The beings with the brilliant eyes. Those who cast no shadow on the beaten earth, who stood like giants over their human counterparts. Who shimmered in the mid-day sun.

Angels.

Angels among men.

Like me.

I'd forgotten who I was. What I was. What I was meant to do. Michael told me not to lose another soul and I wouldn't. Not even my own.

"Father, forgive me," I whispered and I leapt through the throng in the marketplace, my robes burning in the midday sun. "Forgive what I must do."

I was the Angel of the Lord and I would show them all. My arrival was loud and destructive, a concussive boom in the center or Enoch. I dropped from the sky on a bolt of light, hard and glorious, destroying their pagan altar. Cracks poured down the steps of the temple, opening chasms beneath the knees of parishioners. Divinity steamed from my frame and I pulled my bow from my fists, leveled an arrow of sizzling energy at a dominion who simply glared at me. His eyes fell in my presence.

"Kadiel," I said and my voice boomed. Humans covered their ears at my words and I saw red slivers peek through their fingers. "Look at me, dominion."

He did. They all did.

"You know me. Name me."

He pulled the cloth tunic from his chest, let the fire of the Father wash over him until he shone. A woman, small and dark haired and plump clutched at him but he waved her hands away.

"You are Sariel," he said and there was no fear in his voice. Only resignation.

"I am Sariel, commander of the Father's army, chosen by Michael the Archangel himself." I stepped toward him, raised the bow to aim between his eyes. "And you have turned your back on us. You know how that goes."

"Kadiel," said the woman, grabbing his wrist. Then she stood. She was only plump in her abdomen. "Who—?"

He pressed her back. "Be silent, wife."

"Wife?" I cocked my head, confused. I looked at her, looked at her watching his face, his body, trembling behind him. Looking for both direction and protection. Looking with affection. With concern. With love. "Wife?" And then, "This woman is your Chosen, Kadiel?"

His hand fell on her belly. She covered it. Love and protection.

"What else is she, Kadiel? What more?" I said.

"She carries his child," said a voice behind me. It was Uriel.

I loosed my bolt, heard Kadiel groan and puff into nothingness, whirled as the woman, his wife, wailed in his ashes. Spinning to face Uriel. My eyes dancing on dozens of women, quivering by the sides of angels, their abdomens distended, their faces haunted. Uriel was among them, shirtless, only a golden doubloon covering his scarred face and damaged eye. There was nothing familiar about this angel, my peer in combat. He was tall still, yes, but diminished. Dull. And wingless. Mortal. He held the hand of the tiny woman whose hair twisted beneath her robe. The one whose stomach was big and rounded. He held her next to him. As his equal.

"Uriel?" I said. "Even you?"

"What do you want me to say, Sariel?"

I blinked back tears. "You have to tell it to me. I want to hear it from you. Tell me why; tell me how! This is not what we're here for, Uriel. You know that." My voice cracked. "You're leaving me."

But Uriel was unemotional. Cold. "I'm not leaving you. I'm leaving Heaven." He walked toward me and I watched the dullness seep beneath his skin, watched his divinity break through the muted colors on his body. First in patches, in scratches and scars, then spreading. He stood in front of me, touched my face. "I left that place. Look at this! Look at who we are now, who we are here. This is a chance."

I jolted from him. "You're mating with them? Making... what? Abominations!"

"Making life!" And he seemed honestly taken aback by me. "We're creating a life with them."

"That is forbidden!"

"Not for them."

"It is for us. Do they even know what you are?"

"They know what I was. I was a killer, Sariel. They know I killed my brothers and sisters because Michael told me to. Because they didn't want any part of his ridiculous war. Here I can be a man. Just a man. Without the war, without the killing."

"The Keeper started that war," I pressed his chest, growled when the human women reached for him. "Michael is our Captain. Uriel, please. You gave him his sword. You swore to serve him."

"And he swore to serve the Father! Michael was supposed to be liberating us, Sariel! Saving us from some horror he said Lucifer had become. And what did we do? We killed for him—you and me. We killed souls that didn't do anything."

"They didn't choose. Uriel, the choice was to stand with the Father or fall. They didn't choose."

"I did," he said quietly and turned from me. "I chose—I choose—to stay. Here," and he joined the tiny black-haired woman, "with her."

I dropped my head, felt the hot sting of tears on my cheeks. And I heard Michael's voice in my head, whispering in my ear back in Righteousness, "You chose, Sariel. *This is what you chose.* All of it." This is what you chose. There wasn't anything more to say, simply more to do.

I felt my armor washing down my frame, felt the heat of white fire enveloping my body. Saw the edges of the helm as it poured over my face. Watched the humans cower and fall to their knees, the women trying to prostrate themselves before me on bulging midsections. I saw my brothers, my soldiers, souls I knew and loved hang their heads in shame and acceptance.

"I am Sariel, angel of the Lord of Hosts. Commander of the Father's Army. Messenger of the God of Adam, the First Man. My brothers, you have defiled the daughters of Man. Daughters, you have broken the Father's heart. All of you have done the unspeakable: transgressed against the Father's express commands and created monstrosities in this place. These souls, unborn, cannot stand."

Their eyes met mine. Angel and human.

"You can end this," I said and raised my bow, "or I will. That is my word."

"It isn't that easy, Sariel," Uriel told me.

"Sure it is," and I released two bolts of sizzling light and watched an angel, a cherub, and his swollen wife spew into a column of ash and blood. "You know how this goes, Uriel."

"And you know what I must do."

Uriel was always harsher than me in battle. His sword is bigger than I am tall, its blade thick and weighty. He would swing in wide arcs, cutting down jagged swaths of fallen souls, cleaving large paths of death. But he is predictable. I knew he would come for me from the right, behind me, sword in motion. I know him.

I rolled forward, below Uriel's swipe, wing over shoulder, pulling my bow into a pair of curved swords. I tumbled very close to an unprepared virtue and the pretty, sad woman at his side. I struck at her first and dragged my blade down her distended belly, watched her entrails ooze free, followed by a twisted, deformed fetus. A child. A baby. I was taken aback for a moment. I expected...I don't know what I expected. There wasn't the customary disintegration into a cloud of black. There was only the dull thud of her body against the ground. Her figure, and the broken body of her unborn child, dead and unmoving, haunted me. And her husband. I drove my other sword into his neck before he had a chance to weep.

I spun, crossed my blades in expectation of Uriel's second slash, and met metal with metal. He was majestic now, draped in armor of gold and spikes, wings wide and broad. His woman, the one with the black hair beneath her robe, was astonished at what her chosen had become.

"She's never seen you like this, Uriel? I thought they knew what you were," I said.

"She knows enough," he said.

I ducked a crude slash for my midsection. "Doesn't look that way."

The others had awoken, were drowning themselves in silver metal, swords and spears wicking from their hands. They came at me as a group, virtues and dominions in their magnificent colors. But their wings were absent. They were men playing at being angels now. Immortal mortals.

But they were unprepared for me.

I was the true right hand of the Archangel, the chosen Sword of Michael. I'd learned from my Captain and I channeled his ferocity in battle until my body moved without thought. Without mercy. I vaulted over Uriel, twisting like a fish around an overhead slash, and the swords became a bow again. Three bolts of frothing electricity screamed through the air and two angels exploded in light and flame. The third tore a hole through the back of a fleeing woman. The bow was a sword before I hit the ground, flashing, and three more headless bodies slumped against my feet.

"Is this what you wanted, Uriel? Didn't you know how this would end?"

He answered with his sword. I barely had time to form a shield before the mighty weapon crushed my forearm. I heard a sickening snap and was airborne.

"You should have left well enough alone, Sariel. We were happy here." He took a step toward me, raised his sword. "And we're not alone."

They gathered behind him. Smaller than the angels, heads taller than the women. Bodies of rigid muscle and corded tendon, heavy cudgels twisting in metal hands. Eyes and hair the color of midnight. Some twenty of them.

You call them giants.

Your book calls them Nephilim.

To me they were monsters, the children of the damned. And they were coming for me.

24

RAPHAEL

I can feel my divinity threading away.

I can't see it. I can't see anything. It's dark where I am. Cold and dark and deep. And wet. But, in my head, I see my divinity flowing from me in thick gobs and clots. It pours from me in rivers of gold and silver, shimmering in the darkness, and I feel myself shrink beneath its loss. Diminishing without it. I imagine it's what death would feel like, plunged into the depths of nothing, sinking slowly, feeling the very life dribble from my body. It's a peaceful demise, the best end I can hope for after this life of jagged immortality.

When I awake, I am half the soul I used to be. I'm not sure what I am now.

Pain. That is the feeling that permeates my being. Searing, stabbing, relentless pain. I feel it everywhere, coursing through me like electricity. Burning my eyes so I cannot see, puncturing my lungs so I cannot breathe. The sheer act of being was agony, existence pure torture. I panted in the brightness, eyes clenched shut, taking short breaths between spasms of pain. Trying to pinpoint its source. It was my wing that was hurt, wounded by Karan's scythe. I remembered that. Torn through metal, ripping through flesh, flaying my bones for the world to see. Shaking fingers reaching for that bloody appendage. But my wing was gone. A gaping wound remained. I could feel the ragged points of my ribs shaking beneath the flesh.

My wing was gone.

The pain remained. With none of the healing.

I felt my divinity threading away.

The ground below me was moist and soft and I could feel the coolness of mud against my face. A breeze skated across my back light and airy, and I frowned at its touch. My waist and legs lay immersed in water that pressed against my hips. The river. I was on its bank, laying half in the current, languishing in mud and coated by my own blood. The prospect of standing was terrifying: the very idea sent electricity careening down my spine and setting my legs aflame. Slow movements, easy and gentle, were all I could do without screaming.

I reached forward, felt the heads of grass tickle my palm. It reached for me, this plant, then was tugged away harshly. Something big and warm and wet slithered over my hand and I felt the rough huff of air. Of breath. Again and again. Something alive was there and it was...smelling me? The wet, warm thing ran over my hand again, over my forearm and the breath plumed on my face.

I flexed my hand and the wetness withdrew suddenly. A harsh blow of air and then a noise—a grunting, howling sound and the beast pressed from me.

"Maltos!" It was a young voice, a female voice. A human voice. But I understood her. "What are you so afraid of? What—easy, easy." Her breath caught. "Maltos! Oh no! You stupid, foul beast! Please be alright, please be alright."

I felt her hands on my body, warm and soft but strong and earnest. And painful.

"Stop!" I croaked. "Please stop. Don't touch me. It hurts."

The hands skittered from my body then slowly returned, pressing my flesh lightly, easing beneath folds of clothing. Searching. "How bad?" she said and her voice was like a balm, an analgesic. I breathed slow and deep.

"Very bad," I whispered. "I don't know if—" I tried to move. I howled.

"Stop," she said and now there was strength in her voice. This was a command. I heeded it. She mumbled, "Ignorant pile of dung. Four legged...cursed...should be on a spit...ignorant...ass." That last one made me smile and I heard my tunic tear in her fists. Her hands running along my back.

They were strong and hard. Like Karan's.

"Look at me," said the woman. "Open your eyes."

I did and the light pierced them. I cried out in a whisper.

She shielded my face. "Try again."

"Don't blame the creature," I said. "Your Maltos—"

"My Maltos? You mean the ox?" The sun hid her face.

"Ox? Your Maltos ox, it didn't touch me. It never touched me. Not his fault."

She leaned closer, holding her hand higher and I could see her face. She was beautiful! A young, round face of concern and freckles, skin the color of dark sand, eyes like emeralds. A robe of wool hung over about her face and wisps of curly black hair wafted in the breeze. I stared at her for what seemed like hours.

"Are you alright?" she said.

"No." A blink. It hurt. "I will be. I'll be fine." I hadn't moved yet.

"You don't look fine."

"You can look at me?"

"Of course I can look at you. You're right here in the mud. Why couldn't I look at you?"

"It doesn't hurt?"

Now her eyes dropped in embarrassment and she smiled in the corners of her mouth. "It does not hurt at all to look at you."

I moved my hand to touch her chin, to meet her eyes so I would know her like I did with Cain. I touched her, felt the velvety softness of her skin beneath my fingertips. And her warmth! We are not warm like you: our heat comes from the Father, not within. Only the seraphim burn with flame from the inside. But I saw nothing, felt nothing, knew nothing. And was wholly unprepared for the harshness of her actions: she clutched my hand and pulled back on my thumb, causing me to wince.

"Stay your hand! You don't know me to touch me like this, stranger."

Why didn't I know anything? Why didn't I feel anything? "What is your name, woman?"

She frowned. "You are in no position to request anything of me. What is your name, man?"

I smiled, tried to rise on one elbow, failed. "My name is Raphael...ow."

She giggled at my pain. "I am Ananda, daughter of Jobesh. Can you stand?"

"No, I don't—I don't know."

"I think you can, Raphael. Try," Ananda said and crossed her arms.

My legs slipped from the water and folded beneath me. I panted on my hands and knees, face pressed in the mud. The pain was incredible! Where was the Father? Where was the healing and strength that flowed from Him? I was in His light, in His elements, praying for strength to stand and be all He'd made me to be. But I felt nothing. His hands didn't touch me now. I was alone.

Alone.

Alone? What about the others? What about the demons? What about Karan? They'd be coming for me.

I pushed myself up quickly, harshly, and a wave of pain racked my body. I vomited on my hands and knees.

"Stop," Ananda said and her voice was hard.

"They're coming," I panted. "They're coming for me. I have to—"

Firm hands on my shoulders. "You have to stop. Raphael. Raphael, look at me." I did and her green eyes were kind. Soft. Healing. "No one's coming. No one's here but you and Maltos and me. Let me help you."

"You can't."

"You can't help yourself," she snapped. "You can't even stand. Let a woman help you."

She was right. Even if Karan and her horde came bubbling from the depths of the river, I was too wounded to stand against them. There wasn't anything I could do; I needed to figure out why the Father had left me here. Without Him, I didn't know how to heal myself. I didn't know what to do.

I looked at Ananda square, poured myself into those green eyes, tried to count the freckles on her pretty face. "Can you help me?"

"I'll take you back to my father's house. We will help you there."

"I can't—I can't walk."

She paused, looked at me, at the ox. At herself. Ananda pulled the deep blue robe from her frame and laid it in the grass. Beneath it was a white cotton dress that clung to her body. Scooped neck that belied a strong and ample bosom, young hips, strong brown legs. Something quickened inside me, a pulse jolting through my body and I saw Ananda in a way I'd never beheld another. Not Karan. Not Sela. My face flushed and my palms grew moist. I was...aroused. And I didn't know what to do.

She got down on her hands and knees to roll me onto the robe, to use it as a litter. She straddled me to adjust the fabric and tie the corners to the ox. Her dress bowed in the front, giving me a view down the bodice. My eyes wandered and I received a harsh slap to the face.

"I'm trying to help you," Ananda hissed. "The least you can do is respect me." But a smile flashed across her young face.

She moved to stand and I grabbed her wrist. "Your name, Ananda, it means 'worthy of love.'"

"You say that to all the girls, don't you?" She patted my cheek, stood and slapped the ox on the backside. "Let's go home, Maltos. Father is going to be very surprised with our guest."

I watched the clouds amble above me, felt the unevenness of the ground beneath me. Winced with every inch. But the ground, the landscape, was different. When I fought Karan, when Remiel and Cassiel fell, the river ran along a thick wood. Now the forest was gone, cut, the land flattened and tilled. Time had passed. Earth had changed, grown. Aged.

"How long?" I said aloud. Then to myself, "How long has it been?"

My eyes watered and I brought my hands to my face: they no longer shone with the light of the Father. My skin was muted and light brown. Like Cain's. Like Ananda's. Like a human's. We'd only traveled a few yards before I realized, on my uninjured side, that my wing was gone.

What had I become?

25
LUCIFER

"Welcome to my humble abode," I said and clutched Michael's armor, felt it melt and rend in my palms before shoving him down into the darkness. He streaked across the sky like a meteor.

Once upon a time I was afraid of Michael. When I met him, full of God-given purpose and leonine strength, he petrified me. I shook beneath his palm. His physical presence, his savagery—Michael is a terrifying force of righteousness. He is a horrible mirror, made to show you how far from the Father's heart you have fallen. I was afraid of Michael once, in Heaven, before the blood of my daughters coated my hands. When I met him, when I fought him in the Temple, I thought he was the very Sword of the Father. But now I know him for what he is: just an angel. Another lost soul.

And that makes him small.

Michael stopped in air, looked around with confusion lacing his visage. I hated that about him: he was a conundrum to me, a puzzle of hard angles and brooding thoughts. I understood what he was, what he was made to be: the direct hand of the Father, a product of the same rage that killed Lilith and forged the wreckage of Heaven from a tear. I knew what he was. I just couldn't reach him. Not consistently. I couldn't break him. Michael had no buttons to press, at least nothing visible. He was a kitchen sink kind of soul.

But he felt.

He felt very deeply. That much was obvious.

Anything that feels that much, that carries that much anguish, has a breaking point. I saw it once, with the simplest of taunts, saw him murder dozens of angels. It was a tipping point. I just needed to figure out how to push him again. And that, my friends, is what Hell is all about.

"What is this place?" he said.

"Where are my manners?" and my hands flamed. "Of course you don't recognize it: let me lighten things up for you."

Boulders, chunks of earth and rock, lurched from the floor of Hell in ragged plumes to circle my head. I breathed, felt the rush of flame pour from my body like a simple exhalation, and the rocks were alive with fire, growling and roaring and seething in the darkness. Another breath and they were thundering for Michael, clamoring for him like hungry lions.

The first exploded on his chest. "This is the pit you sent me to!" I roared.

Michael tumbled head over heels, his wings a fiery kite against a sky of black. The second sent him streaming through the darkness.

"When you rammed that fucking sword down my throat!"

Another detonated, pressing him toward the crooked spire of the Temple of the Host. His howls were a symphony to me and I closed my eyes, danced to the music of his anguish. Smiling.

"Where is your majesty now, Peace Maker? Where is your glory, Captain?"

He huffed and panted in the flames, coughing in the dust of his own destruction.

"I can't hear you, Michael!"

The fourth meteor consumed Michael, dwarfing his twisted form in a shroud of yellow and red, smoke and flame. The explosion was deafening and beautiful. So was his scream: long and loud and shrill. Michael was being tortured and I was enjoying every single moment of it. I heard his wings shatter when he careened through the wall of the Temple.

Right where I wanted him.

And then I was there. Standing over him in the Chamber of the Host, watching his shaking hands quiver along fractured stone and broken alabaster. A thin stream of blood hung from the corner of his mouth and Michael the Archangel was lay shivering on his back, trying to get up. *Still trying?* That angered me more. I grabbed his shoulders, pressed him against the walls of the Chamber until dust and stone rained on us.

I brought enough light that Michael could see his surroundings and I could watch the horror of his recognition.

It was magical.

"This is the Temple?"

"I guess you're all brawn, huh? Not a whole lot going on upstairs? It's okay, I'm here to help. Really. You probably don't remember it all, I mean, how could you, with your persecutions and exile and all? I think we should catch you up, don't you?"

I grabbed his hair, scrubbed his face against the stone, ground it into a dark, peeling blood stain.

"Remember this?" I said. "This is where that blind bastard Gabriel hung like the simple ornament he is. Do you remember that, Michael?"

He mumbled into the stone.

"How about this?" I spun him to the floor, pressed his face into another aged pool. "You have to remember this part, Michael. Please tell me you do. This is where—," and my voice caught, the rage hung for a moment.

Michael growled, "Where you killed your own daughter, isn't it? Nice work. At least you're consistent: you betrayed everybody."

I kicked him between his wings, tore at his hair, scratched his face until he was looking up. "I betrayed? Me? See that? See that burn right there, where the ceiling is all black? That was Raphael."

"Look how effective you were." A burly elbow smashed into my mouth and Michael scrambled from my grasp. "Raphael walks today."

I giggled and spat blood, watched Michael spill swords from his hands. "Oh, he's around, I'll give you that. But he's not walking, not anytime soon anyway."

Michael's growl shook the foundation of the Temple, ran shivers up my spine. He took a hard step toward me. "What did you do?"

"You always blame me. I'm hurt." I grinned. "Come closer, I want to show you something."

But Michael the Archangel was all force without thought, anger without consequence, and he charged at me—as much as his wounded capacity would allow—swiping furiously. I was fast, faster than he remembered, faster than I remembered, snaking beneath his blades with fluidity.

"You know, for someone who calls himself Peace Maker, you're awfully angry."

The taunt worked and Michael stepped precariously close to me. In a flash I was behind him, choking him, pressing his head down to the disk of fluid that stood sentry in the center of the room.

"Want to know what I know?" I whispered in his ear and jabbed a handful of knives into his stomach. Michael folded and his face sank beneath the surface.

"I can see *everything*."

We were in Heaven. In winter. Standing on nothing, floating in the black, floating beneath the surface. Heaven twisted like a mirage before us. Michael stood next to me, clutching his abdomen.

"Take a look," I said. "Recognize anything?"

We were hanging on the outskirts of Righteousness, above and behind city, high enough to see into the city square. High enough to see Michael and his army standing before dozens of kneeling angels.

"What is this?" Michael said. But he knew, I could tell.

"Don't you know? That's you. And what you are doing here? Michael, what are you doing?"

Michael heard himself say, "I do not want them here." And he watched himself slice angels to nothing.

I gasped! My fingers stole to my lips. "You killed angels? Michael! You monster!" Then I began to laugh, watching the horrified look wash over his features. Michael tried to look away and I clutched his face, forced him to witness. "Oh no! You have to watch! That's you, isn't it? Look at you, Peace Maker, spilling the blood of your brethren. Weren't you sworn to protect them? Didn't the Father say something about that?"

Michael tried to shake me off but I coiled about him like a snake.

"What's the matter, Michael? Can't look at your own handiwork? You know what I want to know? Where's Emmanuel? Where's Gabriel? It's not like they don't know. It's almost criminal, I think, letting a monster like you loose on the world. This can't be right, can it?"

Now he watched without my help, without the vise of my hands on his face. His army was slaughtering angels like cattle, reveling in the destruction, and they were enjoying it. He may not have noticed but I certainly did: that murderous look, that orgiastic expression of disobedience. I saw it on their faces, beneath their helmets, in the sadistic grins. The army of Heaven was a multitude of murderers. Only one seemed reticent: a seraph, standing next to Michael, using her sword with slow, reluctant intention.

"Who's that?" I said aloud.

Michael was entranced watching her too. "Sariel," he murmured, "Sariel, you were right." And then, to me, "How is this possible?"

"You thought I wouldn't see? Thought I wouldn't know? I can see EVERYTHING!"

This broke Michael from his stupor. He frowned, snapped a thick hand about my neck. "You're not omnipotent! You're not the Father!"

"I don't have to be!" I lurched from his grasp, dusted my robes. "See, that's the difference between you and me, Michael. I know what He gave me and I know what I can do. I believe in choosing my own destiny. I don't live in fear—"

He laughed at me. "I've seen you in fear, Keeper."

"I know what I am. And I accept it. He made us powerful, Michael. He made us wise and smart and just and powerful. We are like Him. Why do you deny it? Why do you turn your back on what you are?"

"I am what I have to be. I do what I must."

"You're a murderer, plain and simple. Look at you. Look what He turned you into. Look at yourself! Those souls are innocent, Michael!"

He swiped at me now, clutched strong hands on my shoulders. "No one is innocent! They betrayed the Father when we needed them. When I needed them! They—" and he roared now, "This is your fault!"

I shook from him. "Oh no no no, that's not me! I've done some amazing things, but that's not me. That's you. That's your sword, that's your army, killing those angels for something they did not do. That's all you, buddy. Own it, Michael. Own what you are. Own what you have done."

He closed his eyes. "I have only done the will of the Father."

I laughed at him. "You really think this is the will of the Father? Look how insane that has become. Look at what His will has done! Look around you. He left you!" And I saw a tear creep beneath Michael's eyelids. "He left them. You did His will and your Father left this place to die and then He chose another. Did you know that, Michael? Your Father left this place and He chose an entire world and another soul to love. He doesn't want you anymore!"

And that was too much.

With tears streaming down his face, Michael dove for me, swords flashing. I moved ahead of one swipe and then his hands were on my chest, tearing at my robes. We spilled out of the disk and tumbled onto the Chamber floor. But now the light was bright and Michael could see everything. The scars in the Temple walls, burn marks, the blood of the others, his own stains dirtying the stone floor. He looked at it all, cataloguing it, remembering. Getting angrier. He leapt for me.

I stopped him.

Caught him in a flickering haze of light and fire. I walked around him, raking silver claws on the flaming edges, let wisps of fire snake on my hands. Michael was stunned.

"Remember how you and Azazel and Gabriel tried to kill me? Haven't you wondered why I'm not dead? Here's the thing," and I leaned close for effect, lowered my voice to a whisper, "He won't let me go." I laughed at this. "I know, I know. But you know what else? He's holding on to you too."

I turned my back on Michael, ran my hands on the walls, felt the remnants of betrayal etched in the stone.

I said, "It took me a little while to figure that one out but the Father sure thinks you're special. Doesn't it make you wonder why? I say, let's find out together."

You have a word, crucible. It is a chemistry term where you set a thing in flame to burn off the impurities, to burn it down to its cleanest, purest state. For you, fire is that crucible. But you know my experience with fire—flame is my weapon, my calling card, the heart of my power. For me, darkness is my crucible. It was in darkness that I came to know myself, first with the Father, then with Lilith, then with the fall of Heaven. Darkness boils me down to my essential parts. It makes me pure.

But that is not the case for Michael.

Like me, Michael the Archangel was forged in darkness. But he does not fear it: he is the fearsome thing in it. To break a thing, to burn it down to it its most basic elements, to place it in its crucible, you must apply heat. For most angels, darkness is enough. For Sela, it was her self-righteousness. For Azazel, it only took the realization that his misery would endure for eternity to break him. The notion of failure made Raphael crumple. But for Michael, the chink in his armor is Sela.

Time to apply heat. Time to break the Peace Maker.

I waved my hand and Michael was flung through the Temple walls.

The darkness beyond gave way to shadow, to nuance: I gradually let the light mingle with the dark so I could see the look on Michael's face when he realized the horrors he would face. We were in Righteousness now, in my twisted rendition of the city square. Another flick of my fingers and Michael was embedded in the rock of an adjacent building. He growled and the foundations of Hell shook, began to clamor from the stone façade. Silver spikes fell into my palms and I began hurling these at Michael, impaling him to the wall.

"Ah ah ah, I need you to stick around, buddy." I flew to him, hung before his crucified body, caressing his face with a spike. "You remember that night in Righteousness, when you had your little run in with Samael, don't you?"

I jabbed the spike into his chest, lapped at the spurt of blood.

"I figured I'd set the stage, so to speak." I was walking on air, on nothing. "It was dark, like this. And we had an audience." Hundreds of fallen souls, black beasts eased from the bowels of Hell, flooding the skies like crows. They settled onto the ramparts and parapets of the city square walls, red eyes glowing in the darkness. "Like them. But before you got there, you know Sela...well, things didn't go so well for her."

"Don't," Michael coughed.

"Don't what?"

"Don't," and his voice shook.

Then Michael growled again and the demons of Hell hooted. A sword eased from his fist and I flashed to him, flaming and clutching at the outstretched hand. I grabbed his arm and rammed a spike into his palm. The tinny sound of his sword crashing against stone and the roar of his pain echoed in the darkness.

"You don't get how this works, do you? This world is mine and you are stuck here with me." I stroked his face. "No more heroics, okay? Just shut up and watch my little play."

I moved away from Michael, twirling in the black. "Now, where were we? Oh yes! So Samael was having a little conversation with Sela." I bit into my hand, flung a swath of blood into the city square and watched the hulking form of Samael rise from the stone. Another spurt, into the air, and we saw the shimmering form of Sela the Architect, beautiful in death, thundering to the ground. "There we go. Wow, look at her. I really forgot how beautiful she really was. Look at her, Michael! Did you ever see this part? Do you know what happened to her? So Sela was trying to—you know what? I'm going to ruin it if I tell you what happens. I hate when people do that to me. So I'm going to let you watch. Over and over again. Until I get tired. Oh, here's a spoiler: Sela dies."

But it was a scene I couldn't bear to watch. Not again. I heard Samael say, "This is all your fault," saw the trail of tears on Michael's face, and patted his cheek.

"Enjoy the show," I said and vanished in a haze of flame.

26
RAPHAEL

I must have blacked out between Ananda dragging me on her homemade litter and my present situation. Someone had taken care of me.

I was in a round building with a dirt floor, a yurt I suppose—thatched roof, walls of molded earth and stone. Wooden door hewn in the earthen structure. It was big enough for farm animals and stalls lined one wall. I could smell them, the beasts—the Maltos—and their dung was heavy in my nostrils. But these were the smells of Earth itself, heady scents of hay and sweat, of urine and feed and grasses and oils. Something cooked behind me, in the building, and I could smell the burning of flesh and the charring of vegetables. I could smell life.

My body hurt.

I was prostrate, on my belly, laid on an itchy woolen blanket tossed over something rough and rounded and misshapen. Logs. Cut wood. I was cast over a wood pile on a bed of straw. Something sticky and cold and foul smelling was on my back. I tried to move, tried to turn and the edges of straw dug into my flesh.

"Don't you have anything soft in your world?" I groaned.

Fingertips, soft and warm, on my back. "Is this better?" said Ananda. "What do you need?"

I coughed. "Water."

The fingers never left my back, another hand pressed a clay cup to my face. I could feel the coolness of the water on my lips and I inhaled the smell. It smelled like life itself. Like the Father. And it tasted amazing.

An older woman, one I could not see, spoke, "Sister, my daughter seems to be spending an awful lot of time on his back, don't you think?"

There was a third woman in the room, her voice like aged wine, strong and smooth. "Niece! No medicine takes this long! What are you giving him?"

Ananda said, "Naya, Aunt, his skin is so...soft. Touch it. It's softer than a doe's."

The first woman spoke with a maternal authority. Like Sela. "No! I will not touch that man. You shouldn't either. You look at him with lust, daughter."

"It's not lust, Mama," Ananda said. "But he's beautiful. I can't help it."

I started to laugh and ended up coughing. "Beautiful?"

The one called Naya said, "She calls the man beautiful. Sister, when was the last time you called your husband beautiful?" This is clearly amusing to her.

"Jobesh? Never," said the mother. "Now Cali, he is beautiful."

"Cali? Your mule?"

"He is a magnificent beast."

The older ladies erupted in laughter and it sounded like music. It sounded like Heaven, in the beginning, when the waves crashed and angels spilled forth.

"I have never been called beautiful before," I said. "I've never been called anything actually. Except a failure." I didn't mean that come out.

I felt Ananda's hand on my neck. Her touch was tender and warm, something angels are not. Something I'd never felt before. It was intoxicating and I closed my eyes, basked in the light warmth of her palm. The warmest thing in Heaven was Lucifer and he wasn't exactly touchy-feely. And Karan was all muscle and roughness, living abrasiveness, even when she asked to be my Chosen. This was different. This was concern and affection and connection.

And over entirely too soon.

"Daughter!" And the mother's voice was sharp. The hand withdrew. I heard the rush of footsteps, the hush of her mother's air about me. "You don't know this man. You don't know his family or his people. Or his enemies."

"Khadija," said Naya. "She's just a girl."

Khadija whirled, pulling Ananda with her. "She is a girl who brought home a strange man. Help him, yes. God would want us to have mercy on him." She faced her daughter now. "But God would want you to respect yourself, daughter. You don't know men."

"I know this one," Ananda whispered. "When I touch him, I can feel him."

Naya began to laugh. "That's how it works."

"No," Ananda said, "I can feel his pain. His wounds, his scars, I can feel what happened."

"You can?" I blurted.

Khadija pushed her daughter away, lowered her face to mine. "Who are you? Where do you come from?"

I tried to turn, tried to face her, and the pain brought tears to my eyes. "My name is Raphael. I am...they call me Peace Keeper."

"Peace Keeper, huh?" Naya said, looking me over. "Looks like you had some trouble with that. What happened to you?"

"Naya!" Ananda said but she was more embarrassed than indignant. Embarrassed for me.

"She's right," I said. "I failed." I looked down at the logs.

"Look what you've done!" Ananda said. "You've hurt his feelings!"

"Be silent, girl!" Khadjia hissed and Naya laughed. "I don't care about his feelings. I care about yours. What happened to you? Where is your family?"

Family is a familiar word for you, a natural concept. You are born into a family; you have parents who cleave to one another out of love, lust or obligation. Individuals clinging to one another trying to create something more. And that's what it comes down to: creation. We are forbidden from the act. The Father has closed that door to us. But you, fruit of the earth, you are made to create, made to make more. And the Father, in His infinite wisdom, endowed you with enough foresight to reach for one another and build together. Build a family.

I didn't understand it until that moment, lying in pain, beneath Ananda's hands.

"I don't have a family. Not like yours. I have brothers and sisters, lots of them but we don't get along so well. I guess we have a destructive relationship."

"Did they do this to you? Is that why you're here?" Ananda said.

I laughed. I should have lied, said it was a by-product of some argument between Michael and I gone awry. Told them any story my imagination could dredge up so things wouldn't sound so bad. So I wouldn't have to face the truth. So I wouldn't have to admit my failures.

But lying is not something I can do.

I sighed. "This? No. This is because I didn't believe in someone like she thought I should have. This is her way of getting back at me. I don't think she appreciated what I had to say."

"Sounds like a lover's quarrel to me," Naya said.

I said, "Lover? Not exactly. But she was special to me." And I saw Ananda's expressions fall, her eyes drop to the ground. I knew that look, recognized it from Karan's face when I doubted her. I'd hurt Ananda's feelings. I knew enough not to make the same mistake twice. "She's not special to me anymore," I said.

"You look strong," Khadija pressed. "One woman cannot do all of this to you."

"She had help," I said. "A lot of help. And my friends..."

My friends. My soldiers. Cassiel and Remiel. My brother and my sister in arms. My injury, and Ananda's green eyes, took my thoughts from my responsibilities and the souls I was sworn to protect. They gave their lives for me. And Karan damn near took that from me too.

I started to cry. "My friends didn't...I have to stop this before it gets any worse."

I tried to get up, tried to push myself to my feet. I failed. Miserably. Pain struck me like lightning and my back seized. I crumpled and my legs wobbled before they finally gave out. There was nothing for me to grab onto, nothing to break my fall, and I rolled from the logs onto the dark earth. It was cool against my skin.

"I'm getting tired of picking you up," I heard Ananda say in my ear.

"Don't," I said. "It's comfortable here."

Naya was in my face now. She was a beautiful woman, that much was obvious, but time and mortality had saddened her eyes and thickened her hips. But her smile was kind and warm, soothing, and her hand on my face wiping the tears from me was a soft, maternal gesture. And unexpected.

"You are far from home, no?"

I could only nod.

"And your friends are dead? And some woman hunts you, wants to kill you?"

Another nod.

"And she is not alone?"

"Naya—," I began and she pressed a finger to my lips.

"Shh, Raphael Peace Keeper. Do not speak. Hear me: you cannot stay here. You cannot bring this madness upon my niece, upon my brother's house. The girl helped you because that is her way, that is who she is. But she is young and she does not know much of the ways of the world. She does not know the danger you have placed her in. I do. When you can stand, Raphael Peace Keeper, you must leave. Do you understand?"

"But—,"

Naya frowned. "Do you understand?"

I nodded. She looked at her niece, at her sister, "Help him."

They did. And it was excruciating.

I lay there, panting, coated in a sheen of my own sweat, marveling that I was sweating at all. The Father was still nowhere to be found: His healing touch eluded me, the warmth of His light escaped me. Lying on a bed of wood, my head cradled in a young girl's lap while she dribbled cool water between my lips, was the farthest thing from Heaven I could imagine. And the closest thing to pure bliss I'd ever experienced.

"Khadija!" Naya hissed, gathering her robes about her. "We have water to fetch for supper, food to prepare. Your husband will be hungry soon, won't he?"

"My husband should learn to cook for himself," Khadija grumbled under her breath and huffed. She cast furtive glances between Naya and us.

Naya grinned. "Leave them. Let the girl tend to her patient."

Khadija's eyes tightened. "But he is—"

"—too wounded to do anything. He's harmless. Look at him."

I felt my lucidity threading as Naya and Khadija whisked from the yurt. Their footsteps shuffling in the dirt was a hypnotic soundtrack and my eyes grew heavy. Ananda's hands touching my forehead, running through my hair, fell in time with my breath, with my heartbeat and I, for the first time, was exactly where I needed to be. Where I wanted to be. I could rest, truly rest, and nothing was on my shoulders. I sank into her lap, felt the young firmness of her thighs on my neck and smiled.

Her hands left my forehead, traced the remnants of scars on my arms, my shoulders, my chest. The Father had marked me too, lacing my skin with His glyphs on my upper arms and neck. He left something beneath the skin, deeper than a tattoo, almost a burn. His touch permanently etched in my body. I was His in ways I hadn't considered, hadn't noticed, until I realized no one on Earth was marked in the same ways.

Her fingertips paused on a trio of scars on my ribcage. "What happened to you?" she whispered.

The cherub. Back in Faith. Scars from my botched rescue attempt. More evidence of my failures. I couldn't save that golden angel, I couldn't dissuade Karan, I couldn't stop Lucifer. I let war happen. I let angels die. When I think of it, I only see that golden face, those magnificent, sad eyes, and hear her beg to be free.

"They took her," I murmured, lost in a stupor. "She was so small! They took her to kill her. I tried to save her, I tried but... there were too many. Samael killed her. Right in front of me."

I don't think she expected me to answer. Her touch evaporated from my body and I heard, through the fingers covering her mouth, "Why did they kill her?"

My eyes snapped open and I stared at Ananda. "Because she wanted to be free. They made her beg for her life and they killed her anyway."

"Is your—is the one who did this to you—is she...?"

"My home isn't like yours, Ananda. I come from a place of war, not a place of love. We fight each other; we hunt and kill one another. I don't even know how we fell so far. It isn't like this. And it's all my fault."

She was quiet for a long time, chancing the lightest of touches. Then she said quietly, "Do you want to be free?"

"I don't know."

"Will they come here to kill you?"

"They will try."

It was the last thing I said before pain and exhaustion, and the rhythmic caress of Ananda's fingertips on my temples, finally overtook me and I descended into darkness once again.

She was gone when I awoke.

The yurt was dark, only the embers of the fire remaining in the center of the room. Without moving much I could see fingers of dim light peeking through the edges of the door, seeping through gaps in the stone walls. I could hear the animals shuffling, snorting, huffing in the dark. And I could see the dusty, worn sandals of a man standing next to me.

"Get up!" he whispered. But his voice was harsh, angry. Mean.

The man was broad, tall and muscled with a tangle of black hair that wound itself around his face into a short beard. His tunic smelled of sweat and manure, like the fields. Like work. He smiled in the dark and his teeth were brilliant in the darkness. I couldn't make out his eyes clearly but they looked both amused and cruel.

"Are you Jobesh?" I said, "Are you Ananda's father?"

"I said get up!"

I looked at the blanket beneath me, hung my head. "I can't."

He crashed a heavy forearm between my shoulder blades and clapped a coarse hand over my mouth when I screamed out. He brought his face close to mine and I could smell wine on his breath.

"How about now?" he said. "No? Let's try something else."

And he pulled me from the makeshift bed, spilling me into the dirt. I coughed in the dust but couldn't move. The man crouched close to me, grinning in the darkness.

"The mighty Raphael. Look at you, look at what you've been reduced to: wallowing in the dirt at the feet of a human. That's quite a fall for an Archangel, Host."

He knew me? Knew what I was? How?

"Who?" was all I could manage.

The man grasped his jaws and pulled them wide. I could hear the snapping of bone and flesh tearing, saw the wave of blood wash down his face and stain the tunic. And I saw the red eyes peering at me from the man's throat.

"Karan?" I rasped.

"You didn't think it'd be over so quickly, did you? See, I saw the way you looked at the girl when she tried to help you. I remember that look. I remember when you used to give it to me. Do you remember that?"

I tried to call on my power, to pull those last vestiges of the Father into something more formidable. I felt twinges of divinity, saw small rivers of silver bubble through my pores and bleed over my hands. But I felt weak. Powerless. Karan knew it too.

"Don't bother," she said. "This place does...something. None of us are what we should be. But these 'things' give us something. You should try it. They invite us in and give us everything. Since you like her so much, maybe I'll try your girlfriend on for size. Think that might rekindle something between us?"

"There is nothing between us, Karan. And I'll—"

Karan grinned at me from the mouth of the man. "You'll what? You can't even stand up. You don't have your powers here, Peace Keeper. You won't do anything but lay there in the dirt."

She was right. I tried to get up and my legs gave out.

"Poor boy," Karan said.

"Why don't you just kill me and be done with it?"

"Kill you?" She laughed at me. "Where's the fun in that? No, I like watching you squirm." She crouched down, caressed my face with the man's hand. "I told you I was something special, didn't I? You didn't believe me. The Father called me the Reaper of Souls—these souls. And I'm going to start here with these mongrels that you're so fond of. This isn't going to be pleasant for you, I'm afraid. But it's going to be a lot of fun for me."

Karan picked me up roughly, tossed my broken body onto the logs, and I screamed. She pulled the man's face over her own, spoke in his voice. "The name's Jobesh. Ananda is my daughter. I expect you'll treat her with the respect she deserves and that you'll repay me for my kindness. Besides, we have a lot of catching up to do, don't we?"

Jobesh laughed with Karan's laugh and he shuffled to the door. "See you tomorrow," he said to me. Then to someone I couldn't see, "He's calling for you. Bring him some water, daughter."

When Ananda came in with a bucket of cool water, ready to ladle it to my lips, I was panting and my eyes were wet.

"What happened?" she said.

"Met your father," I said between pants. "I don't think he liked me very much."

27
GABRIEL

"I knew you'd come," I said in the dark and heard my words echo from the waters.

"Something you saw?" Lucifer said back to me. "You know your powers of observation never cease to amaze me." There was a smile in his voice and he was clearly coming closer.

"I know you," I said. "You're predictable. You can't leave well enough alone. But you are looking well."

He stopped, stood on the surface of the water and I was lost in his beauty, contrived as it was. I hadn't seen Lucifer since his fall, since he disappeared into that abyss, Michael's sword jutting from his chest, a fountain of his own blood spilling down his chin. He was horrid then, a monstrous version of the alabaster beauty I beheld at my creation. Now he'd reconstituted himself, pulled some rendition of himself from the depths of Hell. It was an illusion I knew, but this falsity was a welcome addition to the emptiness that was Heaven.

Lucifer grinned at me. “Jokes. I didn’t know you were capable. You should keep it up. I am glad you like it though: I worked hard on it.”

“I know who you are, Satan. No matter how you look.”

“Satan,” Lucifer repeated and played with his nails. “You know, I still haven’t gotten used to the ring of that. It doesn’t roll off the tongue, you know? Sounds so sinister.” He paused and then, “So you can see everything everywhere, right?”

“You know what I am.”

And then he was on me, faster than I could react, his hands searching my frame. Lucifer’s nails grew into talons and I felt them dance on my flesh.

He roared, “So you saw me wallowing in that pit! Lost in the dark, trapped in that crumbling hovel! You watched it? You heard me begging for mercy? And you did nothing?”

“You got what you deserved, Lucifer.”

“Did I?’ He pressed from me. “Did I really? Has my life been the one I deserved, Gabriel?”

“It is the one you chose.”

“WHAT DID I CHOOSE?” Lucifer was screaming in the night sky. “What choice was I given? To be you? To watch and be nothing? That was my choice?”

“You disobeyed...”

“Don’t say it. Do not speak that word to me. I wanted more. That’s all. I wanted more than the life He planned for me. The Father made me to want more and then He left me, Gabriel. You know it. He left me in that bubble alone. But I didn't mean to make Lilith. It was an accident."

"The Sisters were not accidents, Lucifer. You know I know better." I stood now, walked out onto the water. "You chose to make them."

"And then He took them from me! You blame me for the things that are His fault. Why don't you blame Him?"

"You do not know my feelings on these matters, Lucifer. You do not know where I have placed blame. Besides," I told him, "you seem to forget your role in all of this. You seem to forget your actions."

"I remember it all. I especially remember you telling Michael to kill me."

I hadn't expected this. "How did you—?"

"How did I know? Oh, it's kind of weird not having the drop on everyone, isn't it? I understand why you hide behind your little mask of omnipotence. I get it. It makes you feel powerful. Each little nugget of knowledge, it's power, isn't it? The more you know, the more you can use it to get what you want. We're not so different, you and I."

"I do as the Father commands. You do as you choose. That inherently makes us different, Lucifer."

But he grinned, showing me fanged teeth. "Something says you do as you choose. Something says you have a conscience, buddy boy. I've seen it. You know that, right? I've seen you stand up to Him. He certainly didn't plan that part. Am I right?"

I didn't say anything. He was right. When the Father destroyed the first Heaven, when He broke Lilith's body and burned her alive, when He took Lucifer's daughters away, I thought it was wrong. I thought it was too much. I thought He was setting us up for what eventually came. I understood how Lucifer could blame it all on the Father, how he could hold Him accountable. There were many moments I did.

"I know what you're afraid of. You're afraid you didn't do everything you could have." Lucifer said suddenly, almost like he heard my thoughts. "You're afraid this pesky little duty of just watching what happens without intervening isn't all it's cracked up to be. You're afraid I might be right."

"Close," I said, "You've always been wrong about the right things."

"And right about the wrong things, huh? Say what you will about my tactics but you cannot deny my rationale."

"Rationale, Lucifer? For launching a rebellion?"

"You give me too much credit, Watcher. I didn't launch anything. I simply told the truth. It's not my fault my side of the story is...compelling."

"You mislead them. They followed you."

"To be so wise, you're awfully dumb, Gabriel. No one followed me; they ran from you. What did you think they would do with Azazel on the loose? With you binding me with no explanation? And Michael, he was an accident waiting to happen. Matter of fact, it looks like he's making good on your worst fears." He heard the slight hitch of surprise in my breath. "I'm more like you than you realize. Especially now. Sending me away only made matters worse."

"I'm done with this game, Lucifer. What do you want?"

"What do I want?" Knives burst from Lucifer's palms and he was on me, stabbing. He jabbed them into my chest and toppled me. "I want you to watch it all burn to the ground! Everything the Father built, everything He holds dear, I want you to watch it fall apart. And I want you to know you could have stopped it. Instead, you let that boy have his way, you tried to make Michael kill me. The others are going to figure it out, Gabriel. What happens when they do? They're going to figure out that you knew what was coming and you let it come anyway. You know, the disillusioned might follow you for a while, but the disaffected? Now those souls revolt. Looks like you're going to have a mess on your hands."

And then Lucifer was gone. I only felt the moonlight on my face and the wind whispering in my ear, "See you around, number two."

28
MICHAEL

I watched Sela die. Again. And again. And again.

I couldn't look away: I was impaled against a living wall, the stone rumbling and lurching against my back. When I tried to drop my head, tried to lower my eyes, the stone grew limbs, cold tendrils that clasped my face and held my eyelids open. It even had the callous audacity to flick my tears away.

My body was splayed out, arms outstretched, and I was watching Sela's end. She was beautiful in her violence, horribly effective with the weapons the Father had given her, but was quickly outmatched by her tormentor. The twisted rendition of her brother. The Azazel I knew was a savage brute, an overpowered sadist among saints, masquerading as the wisest among us. When he became Samael, he was simply unbridled rage unleashed by an angel with a vendetta. In either instance, Sela had no chance of survival.

Every time Samael slammed her into that wall, jamming golden spikes into her shoulders, he was doing it to me. I was intentionally placed so the ghost of Sela's body would across mine, the point of Samael's spikes driven into the same seeping wounds that ripped my arms and torso. And the wall would pull my head up so Samael could close his horrible jaws about my throat.

Again and again and again.

And the horde of Hell would laugh at my misery.

I felt it all. Felt the hot warmth of my tears on my cheeks, the heat of Samael's breath on my face, the quickening of Sela's heart pounding in my chest. I felt her fear, her pain, her death. And I heard Samael's words as his fangs bit into my neck: "Goodbye, Sela."

Every time she would die, every time Samael would draw his horrible head backward and grin through the blood of my Chosen, the show would begin anew. I would see Sela drop from the night sky, blazing with divine luminescence, majestic in her victory. Hear her tell Lucifer, "Next time, do it yourself." And I would hear Samael's sinister hiss from the floor of Righteousness, "It's all such a waste. Isn't it?"

And I would watch him kill her in savage repetition. Reality was fluid in Hell and Lucifer was clearly its master. The scene before me, the central square of Righteousness, would turn and twist, presenting different angles of horror for my torture. Time was an accomplice to my torment: the battle before me would speed up and slow down, flashing through those moments where Sela gained an advantage, slowing to a crawl when Samael's golden lance bent her back, shattered her jaw, tore into her flesh.

She looked at me suddenly, her face ripped open by Samael's attacks, and said, "What's the matter, Peace Maker? Don't you like the show?"

I sucked air. "What?"

And then she was there, caressing my face and body, rubbing her damaged face against my own. Sela was crying and her tears poured into the streams on blood running from her nose, her temples, her scalp.

"Why didn't you save me?" she said. "Didn't you hear me?"

I couldn't touch her. The fingers of stone and the spikes of silver held me fast. "I tried."

"You left me to die!" She pressed away from me. "Look what he did to me, Michael!"

"I'm sorry, I—you told me not to follow you. I came as soon as I could. Sela..."

And her voice fell to a whisper. "Didn't you know what they were going to do to me?"

I tried to hang my head. The wall wouldn't let me.

She was back in my face again, angry, eyes flaming. "Oh no," Sela hissed, "you don't get to look away. Admire your handiwork, Peace Maker. Look at the face of your failure."

"I didn't fail you, Sela."

"You didn't?" She was roaring now. "Why didn't you kill him when you had the chance?" And she slapped me. "Emmanuel warned you, didn't he? He told you what to do. He told you what Lucifer was. Why didn't you kill him?"

"It wasn't what I was sent to do."

"That's your answer? It wasn't what you were sent to do? You let him kill me!"

"And I judged him for it! Both of them. Samael is no more.

Lucifer is...here."

She spat, "Too little, too late, Michael."

Samael floated behind her, smiling. "She's awfully judgmental, that one. Maybe you're better off..."

I glared at him, reached for him until my hands and wrists bled. "I did what I was sent to do! I did what He told me to do!"

Sela said, "And what did it get you, Michael? What did obeying Him get you? Heaven is still split, the Host is still destroyed. I'm still gone. Look at you now! How precious is your obedience now?"

"Your freedom cost you your lives," I said. "Both of you."

"Did it?" Samael asked. "We're both here. With you. Maybe your obedience to that coward in the sky cost you *your* life. Ever think about that?"

I frowned but didn't say anything.

Sela smiled at me, looked into my eyes, rubbed soft, bloody hands on my shoulders. "What kind of life are you living, Michael? Are you the angel He made you to be? Are you still doing what He sent you to do?"

Samael didn't let me answer, "Oh no! He's killing the others. He even got exiled for it. The Father turned His back on him."

Sela said, "Look where you are! This is Hell. This is where you sent Lucifer and the others. And here you are, Michael. The Father treated you the same."

I clenched my jaws. "What are you asking me?"

Sela pressed her lips to my ear, whispered in a breathy tone, "What does it matter, Michael? Your obedience cost you everything and He still treats you like a traitor. Why bother?"

"Why bother?" Samael echoed.

"Because it's my responsibility!" I bellowed in the dark of Hell. "It's my duty!"

"And yet you failed, Michael," and Sela's tone was comforting, maternal. "But, we don't think it was fair."

"Fair?" I whispered.

Samael grinned at me, "Can't succeed if you can't win. The odds weren't exactly stacked in your favor." He paused, then, "You know this was never about you, right?"

"Never has been. He only loves one angel," Sela said. "It's not you."

"Lucifer," I whispered.

"Speak of the Devil," Sela said but it was Lucifer's voice that came from her lips, "and he shall appear."

And she pushed away, smiling broadly, and I watched her face slowly melt into Lucifer's grinning visage.

"How'd you like my little play?" he said. "You know, getting to you is becoming too easy. You used to be a tough nut to crack. Now it's almost pitiful."

I growled. "Let me loose. Let's see how much fun it is."

Lucifer walked around me, pacing on nothing. His eyes smiled but his face was pained, sad almost. He stole only glances at me. "You know they were right," he said. "About me being the only angel the Father loves. It's true."

"It was you talking, Lucifer. I think you're biased."

"Doesn't make it any less true. And it always has been that way. Even Sela knew it. Did you know that, Michael? She knew. The Father set all of this up, orchestrated all this nonsense, just to get to me. What do you think that says?"

"It says you're delusional." I laughed at Lucifer.

Pity is one thing; feeling sorry for something or someone

else, there is a certain nobility to it. A type of honor, I guess. Pity proves you're more than cold and heartless, more than just a blade in a sea of meat. Pity proves you—I—have a soul. But I couldn't pity Lucifer: this wasn't something pitiful talking. This was something worse. This was revenge and hurt and pride and narcissism. He was an open wound, cut too deep to heal, raw and infected.

"Funny." Lucifer flexed a hand and a silver spike jutted from my wrist, flew to his palm. "Delusional? I am not talking to my dead Chosen, slaughtering the souls I was meant to protect because I am afraid of the dark. You run from ghosts, Michael. You fear the voices in your head because you know, deep down in the pit of your soul, they are only the whispers of your failure. Delusion is a belief in something that is not real. You were made by someone who claimed to love you and then left you to rot! Is that love, Michael? Or is that delusion? Your jokes do not amuse me. This does." And he jammed the spike into my stomach. He turned from me.

"But believe it or not, I didn't bring you here to hurt you." Lucifer paused, giggled and showed me his teeth. "Well, a little bit. But, like you, I figured out that our benevolent Father has some greater purpose in mind for you and for me and, much to my chagrin, won't let me end your pathetic existence. But I've learned to see the opportunity in my setbacks." Lucifer swung about, swooped close until I could feel his breath on my face. "See, being burned alive, chained to a planet and then impaled gives you a unique take on life. It gives you the long view. I figured you deserved the whole story."

"I know what you are, Lucifer."

"Ah, but do you know what *you* are? Do you get that you're

just a tool, an instrument, a means to an end?"

"I am the Peace Maker, the—"

"Captain of the Host, the Father's Justice, yes yes yes. I know your pedigree, Michael. I've seen enough souls come and go to know what you really are: a waste of effort." He drifted closer to me, smiling sadistically. "I have something to show you."

"I have something to show *you*!"

Lucifer didn't know I'd been in this predicament before: crucified on a wall, staring into the horrible maw of the worst Heaven could spew out. Then, like now, fury had been my strength, rage my fortitude. The Father wasn't here. Not in this place. Lucifer was right about that. But my anger was, and the surge of unmitigated fury exploded through my limbs. I reached forward in one fluid movement, pulling from the wall, silver spikes dangling from my arms. One massive hand closed about Lucifer's throat and I powered him down down down toward the ragged floor of Righteousness.

"This looks familiar, doesn't it?" I said.

We hit stone with a BOOM and...it was gone?

Gone.

The darkness of Hell replaced with blinding light, an assault of greens and blues, of softness and life and wind in my face and the smell of...Earth? We were in a wide grassy field bordered by dirt-covered tracks on one end. Huts, round and earthen, built in clusters eased from the ground about us, like an image slowly coming into resolution. This was a settlement—a settlement of men—and I could see a collection of dusky figures milling about us. Some were the size of Adam, with his skin tone and ruddiness. Others, misshapen, horrible things, were much taller. Giants among men. Bent and hunched, with menacing eyes and shocks of black hair. And metal hands. Metal hands? And then there were others, standing with the daughters of men, black haired, brown skinned maidens with swollen stomachs and sad faces. There were others, others whose faces I recognized. Taller than the men and the women, looking about with dazzling eyes.

Angels.

My angels.

These were soldiers in my army.

"Bet this doesn't look familiar," Lucifer wheezed and my hand slipped from his neck.

But I paused, stunned. "What is this place?"

Lucifer dusted himself behind me. "You know what it is, Michael. Don't play dumb."

"How?"

"Better...but still stupid. It's Earth, just later." And Lucifer stood next to me, hands clasped behind his back, almost like we were friends. The edge left his voice. "Time, Michael. That's the difference. Time changes this place. It doesn't change us; we barely even notice it. But this place, this world, it's different. It ages. And if you become a part of it, you'll age with it. Look there, you barely recognize your own soldiers, right? That's time."

He was right.

I knew these souls. Had fought with them, clapped bloody hands on weary shoulders, wept at the loss of another warrior. I knew them before they raised sword and shield, back when they were frightened angels lost in the dark. When they quivered before me. When I turned them into something else.

Into soldiers. Into killers.

But I didn't recognize them now.

Their bodies seemed older, not old, but...weathered. Aged. But in the eyes, there the immortality flickered. Fleeting. Flashing for moments then lost again in the drudgery of an existence with...humans? They were living with men and women? Living as men and women? I watched hands on bloated stomachs, kisses on earthly cheeks.

"Angels and women and..." I said.

"Monsters," Lucifer finished, pointing. "Those abominations are the fruit of angels and men. This is our salvation and your soldiers are perverting them, Michael. I told you this would happen, didn't I?"

I narrowed my eyes at him, growled a warning.

Lucifer stepped back. And kept talking, lowering his voice to a seductive whisper. His words were melting my rage. He said, "Think about it, Michael. The Father sent you here. He kicked you out of Heaven, didn't He?"

"Emmanuel did it," I said. "Emmanuel exiled us."

"Same thing. The point is, they knew what would happen. They're letting it happen."

I faced him now. "You should stop talking."

"Truth hurts, doesn't it?" He grinned at me. "But if this bothers you, you're going to love my next trick. I have something amazing to show you."

And Lucifer clutched my chest and we disappeared.

29
SARIEL

They were monsters. Horrible apparitions of man and angel gone awry. Flesh cannot contain the divinity that surges within us; your bodies are not built to handle the power that flows in our limbs. It bursts forth in streams of metal, in silvery scars and scratches, pressing bone, twisting muscle. Making monsters out of men.

Powerful monsters.

Uriel and his group had been at this for some time: there were dozens of them. Standing almost as tall me, heads taller than the tallest man. They were thick and powerful, black haired, blue-eyed monstrosities with silver hands and teeth. Spikes and blades jutted from ripped flesh, jaws hung slack and off-kilter, struggling to contain mouthfuls of crooked and pointed teeth. Heavy brows hung over small eyes and they carried clubs and bludgeons.

"These are your children?" I said. I didn't mean to say it aloud. "What happened to them?"

Uriel answered with a harsh swipe of his sword, barely allowing me a moment to raise the shield over my battered arm. I was lucky: his blow only glanced off. I dove ahead of him, rolling toward the coming Nephilim. Sword and shield poured into bow and I was airborne, majestic and glimmering.

"Call them off, Uriel. You know I'll do it."

But he grinned at me, even when two bolts left my bow.

The first of the monsters took the bolt in his neck and I saw the splash of red and the burst of flame. He stopped. Grunted and looked at the shaft of metal angling from his throat. Then he pulled it out. His brother, a hunchbacked leviathan squinting at a silver quill piercing his clavicle, did the same.

Uriel laughed. "They are stronger than both of us, Sariel. This is the race of man Emmanuel spoke about, not those fleshy creatures. These are the ones who will save us."

"Save us from what, Uriel? The damage is done. Heaven is broken and you have disobeyed..."

"We have freed ourselves! We can make this world whatever we choose it to be. Not what Emmanuel says, not what Michael says. Not even what the Father demands. Whatever we want it to be. Who can stop us?"

Who can stop us? The lost army of Heaven creating monsters with the daughters of men and their leader, my brother in battle, dared me to stop him. Dared me. Like Azazel dared us to stand against him in Wisdom. Like Lucifer dared Michael. It would never stop. So long as angels had free reign, in Heaven or Earth, it would never stop. I understood Michael and his motivations, his actions, in that moment.

"We weren't made for this," I said. "The Father didn't make us to destroy them. I swore to serve the Father. I swore to stand with Him. You did too. We must choose, Uriel. We must choose to stand with the Father."

"Or fall," he said.

"I will not fall," I told him. "I am the Angel of the Lord and I will stop this madness."

"You will try," Uriel said.

I've seen soldiers pray before battle. I think this is a ridiculous idea: what battle the Father has ordained has already been decided. The twirling of swords and the movements of battalions only hasten the inevitable. I do not pray in battle, I do not call on the Father before pulling my sword. I do what I have been trained to do, I do what I have been called to do, and I trust I am in His hand.

But this moment, I wanted to pray. I needed the Father.

There were little more than thirty of them in total, mainly Nephilim with their slack jaws drooling. Remnants of Uriel's Sword gathered but they were few and far between. But one soul, a dominion called Omael, caught my eye: he bore the markings of Raphael's Sword on his armor. Raphael's Sword? Here? And if the Sword was here on Earth, was the Peace Keeper with them? I'd never know if I didn't survive the horrible situation currently amassing itself about me.

"Father, please be with me," I said under my breath. To Uriel, "This has to stop."

"Too late for that, Sariel. You chose. Now finish it."

Those were Michael's words. And Uriel knew it. He was asking for me to end it.

"So be it," I said.

One of the Nephilim, the one I'd shot in the throat lunged for me, swinging his club mightily. I dodged outward, then bore down with blades and sliced through his forearm. The club thundered uselessly to the grass but I was already spinning and leaping, driving the blade in my left hand through his jaw. The monster tumbled backward, flailing his bloody stump and whimpering through frozen jaws.

"Stronger than both of us, huh? You might want to reconsider that," I said.

I stepped off the fallen Nephilim, vaulted into the air, and drove my blades into the heart of the hunchback. His eyes fluttered and he groaned something inhuman, something abhorrent to my ear. I didn't wait for him to fall; with his first faltering step, I rolled over his shoulder, pulling my swords into a bow. Three bolts, two into the hearts of rushing virtues, one through the ankle of Omael, the dominion. He went down hard.

"Omael,"I called, "I'm coming for you."

I jumped backward, high and far, hovering over the temple and its shattered altar. I needed space, needed to distance myself from the onslaught of man, angel and beast or risk being quickly overrun. I couldn't stand against Uriel, the remains of his Sword and the children of his indiscretions. But I wouldn't have to. I could fly. The women and the Nephilim couldn't and the angels, in their quest to become mortal, had forgotten their divinity. The first time I met Michael, I was conscripted into service to protect Uriel and his Sword. From the air. This day, I would destroy the last of them.

My bow sizzled against my ear. I gritted my teeth against the flush of pain in my arm and the weapon shook in my grasp.

"Don't make me do this, Uriel. Please," I said.

"You don't have to, Sariel," he told me and his voice was sad. "Just leave us be. You want Omael? Take him. He's not one of us anyway."

"You know I have no choice."

"There is always choice! Don't you see that? The Father gave us choice. I made mine. You can too. Fly away, Sariel!" He was crying now, looking at his fallen wife. "Just fly away."

I paused. Staying meant more death, more anguish and the end of my life or Uriel's. It meant murder in the name of...in the name of what? Someone who turned His back on us? In the name of our Captain who slaughtered our brothers and sisters and got us all expelled from Heaven? More death and destruction on behalf of a boy who sent us into battle and then fell silent? Who was I to judge? Who was I to call Uriel's actions wrong? He acted out of love, for himself, for his soldiers, for the woman he called wife. For the love of his children, monstrous as they were. And killing them did what? What would their deaths garner? Who would benefit from more bloodshed?

Nothing and no one.

Right or wrong, this wasn't the life I was intent on living. I wouldn't join Uriel, I wouldn't defile the race of men, I wouldn't stay in this chaos any longer than I had to. This was Hell, in Heaven and on Earth, and nothing was as it should be. The order of the Father had gone awry. And I didn't know how to fix it.

I dropped to the earth next to Omael, clutched his injured ankle and pulled him from the ground. He yelped as I moved him. "The dominion comes with me."

But Uriel was on his hands and knees now, running his fingers across his dead wife's body, hesitating to touch the grotesque fetus still attached to her. I didn't remember cutting her down; she was lost in the frenzy. Uriel didn't look at me, just nodded.

"You're from Raphael's Sword, no?" I jerked Omael's ankle, feeling blood seep over my fingers. "Answer me!"

"Yes!"

"What are you doing here?"

He was panting how, fingers pulling uselessly at my hand. "The Host brought us here. He came after the Peace Maker."

I tossed Omael roughly on the ground, hung over him and leveled my bow between his purple eyes. I've always found dominions beautiful: the colors they exude soothe me, provide a calming kaleidoscope in the midst of the horror that was Heaven.

"Raphael came after Michael? Why? And why'd he bring you?"

Omael hugged his foot. "The army was...well, you know. We were sent to save man."

I sank in the air, lowered my bow. "Save man? From what?"

"You. Michael. The fallen. Everyone. We're supposed to be protecting them."

"Is that what you've been doing, Omael? Protecting them? Is that what you call this?" But I didn't let him answer. "Where are the others?"

He hesitated. Paused. He saw what I did to Uriel's encampment, knew what I would do to his own. Omael looked at the ground, at the gaping wound in his ankle, at me.

"Don't kill them," he said. "Please."

"I want to get off this miserable rock. Tell me where they are, dominion, or I will kill you and then I will find them myself. And you saw what happens after that."

He pointed toward a line of mountains to the south. "There," Omael said. "There's a valley. Everyone is there."

"Everyone? The Peace Keeper came with you?"

"He did but I don't know where he is. That village is your best bet. Lots of settlements around there. Maybe he found a woman of his own—"

I slapped him. Hard. Then pulled him to his feet. "Maybe the Peace Keeper is doing what he came here to do. Maybe you failed him."

I pushed him away, opened my wings.

"Wait," the dominion said, "you're not going to take me back?"

I wrinkled my brow. "You have wings. Fly."

"I can't. Not anymore." And Omael dropped his eyes. "I can't walk either, thanks to you. You can't leave me. I'll die out here."

"You should have thought about that before you decided to disobey the Father. Why don't you pray on it? Maybe He'll deliver you."

And I disappeared into the sky.

30
RAPHAEL

Nights fell into days and I became accustomed to the idle pass-ing of time. The soothing rhythm of sunrise and sunset, like the world itself was breathing. On Earth, it was almost a pulse, a faithful promise, I suppose, that the Father would never leave. That He was always there, in the light and in the dark.

Days stretched into weeks and my healing progressed slowly. I awoke to Ananda at my side every morning, before the sun peeked its brilliance over the horizon, her young hands tugging at my tunic. Green eyes glinting in the twilight, mischievous smile lacing her beautiful face, she would pull me from my pyre and force me to stand. Force me to be strong. And rub my aches until I could move, bend, walk.

"This is the day the Lord has made," she would say in a whisper, "let us rejoice and be glad in it."

"Be glad?" I would always respond. "Be glad for what?"

And her face was sadden, "That you live, Raphael Peace Keeper. Be glad that you live."

It was a long time before I could find solace in simple life.

Simple life.

The smile of the sun on my face. The sweet caress of the wind on my cheeks. The sturdy feel of eggs in my palms and oxen pulling me forward. The warmth of a young woman's embrace.

A life of peace. Without threat of war. Without the purging of our brothers and sisters. Without the rebuilding of a shattered existence.

A simple life.

But this simple life was a charade, at least for me. Every morning after Ananda would coax my rigid body upright, we'd venture into the main house, to Jobesh's table where Khadija and Naya would place bowls of warm rice and plates of flatbread in front of us. Where Jobesh himself would bless the meager feast of vegetables and tough meat and pray to the Father. Where Karan would peer at me with shimmering red eyes even has she spoke prayers through the man's lips, grinning cruelly.

"May the Father bless us and keep us throughout this day," she would say. And then, "Raphael Peace Keeper, our guest, you will help in the field?"

And every day I would acquiesce, frightened of the outcome if I refused.

"You know this can't last, don't you?" Karan said to me once, flexing the man's hands and pushing me roughly. We were in a small patch of arable land just north of Jobesh's compound. I could see the wisp of smoke from cooking fires peeking over the hill rise that separated the fields from the huts. Close enough to smell, to see, to hear but not to touch. Just beyond safety's grasp. "We're taking them all."

She pushed me roughly. Even housed in the barrel-chest of the man, oozing hellish fumes from his pores, Karan was still divine. Still one of us. Still beyond this world. She pulled her scythe from Jobesh's throat, tearing and ripping flesh, and shoving it at me. I was to till the land with the weapon of the angels.

"Why? What purpose does it serve?" I said.

She shoved me forward. "I'm the Reaper. These souls belong to me. I take them as I please. We all do."

"But it gets you nothing, Karan. You gain nothing. You can never go back."

She laughed at me and the man's laugh was deep and throaty. "Back? To Heaven? To do what, Raphael? Serve you? Serve the Host? Tell me, Archangel, how do you like your lot in life? Are you happy fulfilling your new purpose?"

The irony hit me hard. She was making me work, making me live a life I did not choose, a life I did not want and there was nothing I could do about it. I tightened my lips and dug the blade into the soil.

"You can't be happy living as something you are not," I said.

"I wasn't." Karan moved in front of me, made me look at her. Even with human eyes I recognized the angel I knew. "I am now. You think there is only one way to get what you want, don't you? Only what the Father has ordained, only what Emmanuel has interpreted. You think that is the only truth? Have you ever considered that you were wrong?"

I dropped the scythe. "The Father does not make mistakes, Karan."

She grinned. "No? So you are here on purpose?"

"I'm here because of you!" I growled at her.

"Oooh! I love it when you get angry. Let's me know you have some feeling for me."

"Disgust."

"You insult me, Raphael. We both know you don't really mean it. You're just frustrated." She was patronizing me now, placing calloused hands on my shoulders. I winced at the touch. "You can't have what you want and you don't have the power to get it. But it's not because of your injury. That should have healed by now. It's because of you, Peace Keeper. You can't have what you want because you don't think you deserve it."

I shook her hands off. "And what do you think I want?"

"The girl. I don't blame you: she's beautiful. You should hear what this guy thinks of her, what he wants to do to her. And she's his daughter. You'd be doing her a favor."

"What are you trying to do, Karan?"

"What I've always been trying to do: set you free."

"And this is how you do it? Possess her father? Mislead the humans?"

Karan laughed at me. "You are accusing me of misleading them? You? So why don't you make it right and tell them what you are? Tell them why you're here. Be the angel you are meant to be, show your true self and send me to my end."

I didn't say anything. I looked at the earth. I wasn't even sure I could restore my divine self: I felt the power seeping from me on the river bank. I hadn't felt the Father's hand in weeks, couldn't remember the last time I heard the whisper of His voice. But it wasn't the lack of guidance I was missing. It was the loneliness that would collapse around me. If I told the truth, if I showed Ananda my wings and unsheathed my swords, what would we be? What could we be? I would burn the eyes from her skull if she even looked at me. Her ears would rupture if I spoke in the language of the angels. We couldn't be...anything. She couldn't go to Heaven and I couldn't stay.

Karan smiled in my silence. "Didn't think so."

"What do you want from me?"

She grabbed my face and said, "Your love. And if that young speck of dust is what tickles your fancy, so be it. They're not us. They don't last forever. She's going to die one day and I'm going to make you watch it. And in the midst of your tears, you will realize how foolish you have been. There is no future with her and, in the end, I'll be the last one standing. I just have to wait out the competition."

Ananda greeted me the same as any other day, caressing my back, singing, "This is the day the Lord has made."

It was two days after my discussion with Karan in the fields and I remained increasingly troubled. Karan would let me have her and simply hang back and watch. Watch me fall in love with this human, watch me give my heart to someone other than herself, and then would take her from me. Or would let the time run its course. No matter what, I was destined to be alone.

But wasn't I alone now? Wasn't that this empty feeling in the pit of my chest? That incessant gnawing, that itch that

I could not scratch? It was something older than I was, this feeling, this emptiness, something ingrained on my very soul. A feeling of being isolated and disconnected. And the longer I stayed this close to Ananda, the stronger the feeling became. The more I needed her.

It was in this moment, in the dark of the yurt, reveling in the warmth of her soft hands on my bare skin, that I understood Karan's questions on the mountaintop.

Am I your Chosen?

Would Ananda choose me?

I grabbed her hand. "I will rejoice and be glad in it."

And then I just looked at her, traced the delicate lines of her fingers pushing dark hair behind her ear. The soft smile and the dimple in her cheek. The flash of emerald in her eyes.

"I have a question," I said, "but I don't know how to ask it."

She smiled at me in the dark. "There is only one way to ask, Raphael Peace Keep—"

"Don't call me that. Just call me Raphael, I don't—I'm not the Peace Keeper anymore. I don't want to be. I just want to be Raphael. And I want to be with you. Do you...?"

I couldn't read her expression but her palm quivered in mine and grew clammy. Was this a reaction? Was it positive? What did sweaty hands mean? Should I let them go?

And then, she laced her fingers in mine.

"I want to be with you too," Ananda said.

It was as though I had been holding my breath all my life. As though a vise had bound my chest and finally decided to release me. I breathed deep, deeper than I ever had and the air tasted sweeter. My eyes watered. My pulse quickened.

Was this rush of life into my limbs normal? Was it what I was supposed to feel? And then, was it what Karan wanted to feel? In those hopeful moments when she wondered aloud what we were, when she asked me if I loved her more than the others—twice—was this what she was hoping to find? Was this love?

Was I in love with a human?

"I don't know what to do," I said, more to myself than to her.

She laughed at me. "Kiss me."

But it sounded like a question, like she was uncertain herself.

Kiss her where? For how long? And how would I know how to do it right? My mouth parched, my breath shallowed and my hands...my hands? Was that sweat? I was responding like her. Like a man. She leaned in but I was tentative, hands skipping on the cloth of her robe, tentatively pressing the supple flesh beneath. I smelled her scent, took in her milk-laced breath. I grinned like a fool; she giggled at my ineptitude and her eyes hooded, looking at my lips. Ananda pulled me into her embrace. Her lips found mine and I was hers.

Angels are not as intimate as you, not in a physical sense. We do share very intimate portions of ourselves, mainly the purpose the Father gave us upon creation—our purpose is the most personal thing about us. His energy, the very breath of life, flows through us, from the soles of our feet to the tops of our heads. We commune by sharing this, this font of energy, with one another, basking in His presence. For you, intimacy is through touch, through the feel of fingers upon skin, lips upon flesh. We cannot create; you create in the most intimate, the most vulnerable of ways. Where we share our essences with our Chosens, you physically share your bodies, your lives.

I was unprepared for that. Unprepared for the soft heat of her mouth, the crush of her lips upon mine. The dart of her tongue against my own. I wanted to recoil, not because it was disgusting, simply because it was foreign. But it felt so good! A rush of heat flooded me, flowing from somewhere between my legs, somewhere I'd never noticed, pouring up and out to my hands and fingers. I wanted to feel her, feel all of her—I could taste the anticipation of her skin on my tongue. She seemed as fevered as I was. Enveloped in Ananda's embrace, I followed her suit, mimicked her actions, pantomiming with my hands, my arms, my mouth. But I was crude and she could tell.

Ananda laughed at me, bit her lip. "You have never done this before? Kissed a girl?"

I looked at her mouth, her breasts, the floor. Shook my head. "Where I come from, I didn't have the chance. I never met..." I trailed off, sheepish. "I don't know what I'm doing."

"There are no girls where you are from?"

I laughed at this. "There are girls, of course. But not like you. Not like this. Where I come from, we do not marry."

"You do not marry? How do you have children?"

I was silent for a long time before I said, "We don't. It is forbidden for us."

"Forbidden? How will you survive if you have no children?"

And then it hit me, the Father's rationale. The point Lucifer was trying to make: the Father didn't want any more of us. He didn't want us at all. The Father made this entire world and race of beings and blessed them with the opportunity to live apart from Him. To live in spite of Him. We fed off the Father like a race of leeches, like parasites, pulling at His waters, drinking His very life. Tearing one another apart for a taste of His power. Eventually we would destroy ourselves. That seemed intentional, like it was the plan.

"We won't," I whispered. "The Father doesn't want us to."

Her face was smiling but she said, "I have questions about this Father of yours."

"I need to tell you something, something important. Something about me." I wanted to tell her the truth, tell her what I really was. What I'd become. But I only heard Karan, in Jobesh's voice, telling me to go ahead, show myself, and watch what would unfold. Here was this beautiful creature in my arms, wanting me for the man she thought I was, the man I truly wanted to be.

I had to tell her. "I'm not like any man you've seen, not like any man you know," I told Ananda in the darkness.

We were huddled in her father's barn, tentatively touching one another on a bed of coarse straw and woolen blankets in the dull eyes of a dying fire. It hurt for me to sit upright, the wound in my back seeped and pulled and I leaned against Ananda. She was warm and I could feel her pulse through her skin.

She smiled at me. "You seem awfully full of yourself, Raphael."

"I'm serious," and I pushed from her, faced the darkness. I pulled open my tunic, showed her the emblems the Father pressed into my skin. "These markings mean I'm something...else. Something other than you. You don't have them, right?"

She frowned. "Your people mark you. So?"

"Not my people, Ananda. My Father. It means I belong to Him."

Ananda reached for me again, stroked her fingertips along my skin and her touch made me lose my focus. "I don't care," she said. "Your father is not here, is he? He was not there when I found you."

"He is! He's always there!" I snapped and pushed her hands away. "Let me," I breathed, "just let me get this out. I'm not the man you think I am, Ananda. I'm not," and I faced her now, "I'm not a man at all."

A look of confusion and amusement covered her face. "You don't make sense."

I tried to stand. "When you pray, who do you pray to?"

"There are many gods," she began. "There is not just one I pray to."

I frowned at her in the dark, lowered my voice, "There is one god. One Father. One creator of all you know, all you see."

"You don't know that. My people aren't wrong; perhaps yours are—"

"I was forged in His hand! I was made by His whim! You don't know what you're talking about, woman! You are the dust of this world and the gods you pray to, the ones you kneel before, these are idols that do not exist. When you pray, you pray to the Father," I looked at her now, looked deep into her eyes. "When you pray to your gods, you are praying to my Father. The ones you pray to are one—only one—and He's the one who gave me these. He sent me here."

"The gods send many things, Raphael. You are a blessing to us as much as we are a blessing to you." Ananda was smiling at me. "Your big news is that we worship different gods?"

I grabbed her, placed strong hands on her arms and lifted from her feet. I don't know where the strength came. My eyes glowed in the dark and I spoke in voice that wasn't mine. "Listen, woman!" I said, and the flames flashed. "My name is Raphael. I am the Archangel of the Lord, the only God. The God of Adam, the God of Eve. I am His son as much as you are His daughter. I was before you ever were and I will be long after you are gone. Do you understand?"

I dropped her and she crumpled at my feet, murmuring whispers of prayer and clutching my ankles.

"No!" I sank to my knees, thumbed tears away. "No. Do not pray to me. Do not worship me. I am nothing special."

But Ananda backed from me, scrabbling in the dust, eyes down. It was a frighteningly human pose and I realized how different we were. I didn't like it. I grabbed her hand, made her face me.

"Look at me, Ananda. It's just me."

"Don't," and she snatched from me. "What do you want from me?"

"I want you to be my Chosen."

"Chosen?" Her eyes hardened. "You are a demon! No messenger of any god would come for one woman."

"Don't call me that," I said. "Don't call me a demon. You have no idea what those are really are."

"I know. I know the legends. I know what you are."

"Do you?" I turned from her. "You think you know us. You think you know me. But you don't know anything. All you have are stories and legends and myths. You don't know what we are; you don't know what we we're capable of. You think it's all good and evil, right and wrong."

"It is."

"IT ISN'T!" The flames roared again and Ananda cowered from me. "Nothing is that simple. The ones you call demons are angels, angels I have known since before this world was made. You think they're after your souls. They couldn't care less about you. You're just in the way."

"Let me understand: my gods do not exist, demons are only angels, and you're one of them. You're an angel of the one true god?"

"Yes. You know my name. And I'm telling you the truth, woman."

We stood in the dark. I waited for her to turn and scream, to run, to push me away. But she stood there, setting her jaw and folding her arms. Then she said, "Prove it. Show me."

"Show you?" I said.

"Show me. Do...something. Surely making flames rise and your voice louder is not all you can do. Do something divine, angel." Ananda wore a mischievous grin, showing her teeth.

"I'm not what I used to be. This place has done something. I...can't."

"You can't? Hmm," she said, and she sounded like Lucifer in that moment.

"I speak the truth."

"I don't believe you, Raphael. You were wounded. You bled like a man. I carried you here. Surely the angel of the One True God is stronger than that." She came toward me, touched my face and smiled a condescending smile. "This is trickery and magic, nothing more. I believe you are a man making play as an angel."

"I do not lie. I am what I say I am," but there wasn't any conviction in my voice.

"I believe you want it to be true. But it isn't. Look at yourself." Ananda put a hand on my chest. "Feel your heart beating, your chest rising with your breath." She brought my hand to her breast. "Just like mine. They beat the same, Raphael. We are the same."

I was quiet for a long time, listening to the rhythm of our heartbeats, feeling the warmth of her flesh beneath my palm. Feeling the warmth radiating from my loins. I smelled her scent, breathed this woman in until I could taste her presence on my tongue. The sigh of her breath made harmony with my own; gooseflesh rose on my skin where her fingertips landed. Our bodies worked in concert. Man and woman. The same.

I tried to smile at her. "Maybe I'm an angel making play as a man. What about that?"

"And why would you want to do that?"

I prayed she couldn't see my eyes water. "Because I don't want to go back. I want to stay here. With you."

"Then stay," she said. "It's you and me now, here in the dark, Raphael Peace Keeper. Just you and me. Let that be enough."

PART 4

A Flood of Night

31
RAPHAEL

Let that be enough.

Could it be enough? The alternative was watching Ananda turn her back on me, watching her run screaming from the truth of what I was. Was this life as a man, as a man for her, enough? What did I have to lose?

Then, soft fingertips on my chin, pulling my face up to hers. "Touch me," Ananda breathed and she placed my hand on her breast. I could feel her heart beating beneath the robe, beneath her skin. I cupped the small globe, palmed its fleshy weight, loved how it felt in my hand. I took the other one on my own.

She smiled at me. "Quick learner. Now," jutting her chin up, "kiss me here. Be gentle."

I followed her order, brought my lips to the curve of her neck, felt the ends of her hair against my face. I breathed her then, nuzzled her skin, traced her neck to her collarbone then up again to her ear. I heard a moan whispered into the darkness.

"Was that good?" I said.

She only grinned.

"Have you done this before?"

Now Ananda looked sheepish, her eyes dancing on the dirt floor.

"I don't care," I said and made her face me. "I don't care about anything but this moment right here. With you. You are my Chosen, Ananda. That's all that matters to me."

"Chosen?" she said and her face looked like mine when Karan said it in Faith. "What does this mean?"

"You are special to me. Like no other."

"Wife," she said. "Chosen is wife." She pointed at me. "Chosen is husband. I cannot be your wife."

I recoiled. She clutched my wrists, replaced my hands on her body.

"Not yet," she said and smiled at me. "You must marry me."

"Marry you?"

Eyebrows raised and her face broke into a smile. "Where are you from? As Adam made Eve bone of his bone, flesh of his flesh, we must become one. You do not do this?"

I was lost. Bone and flesh? Two into one? Choosing another soul was as far as we'd considered. We were always separate from one another, broken into choirs, into groups of Host and Body, of archangel and virtue and power and principality. What had we missed? How could Lucifer be the only one of us to figure this out? He understood the gravity of these attachments in ways the rest of us could not: Lucifer made his Chosen and his daughters. He sought love—he made love—from the beginning and we punished him for it. And now the Father had made this world based on love. Is Lucifer more like these humans than we are? Is he more of what the Father really wants? And what about the rest of us? Are we just lost? My thoughts fell to Michael, to his rage and his violence. Maybe Michael had found love too...with Sela. Was her death what drove him mad? Was he, is he, just broken-hearted?

I saw what happened to Michael. I saw the shell of the angel he'd become. In that moment I was unwilling to fall into that same trap, unwilling to do or be anything like I had been. This was the moment I turned my back on Heaven.

"Doesn't matter what we do where I'm from. I'm not there anymore and I don't plan on going back," I said. "I'll do what I have to for you."

"Make me your wife," Ananda said, "and I will make you a son."

I kissed her again and felt my divinity steam away. For good.

We were married on the bank of the river where Ananda found me. Where Karan had mortally wounded me in a fit of rage and jealousy. Where the demon had slaughtered my friends. Karan presided over our wedding, speaking words of betrothal with thick irony and a smirk. She hugged me, welcoming me into their family with Jobesh's smile, naming me her son and embracing me with the man's arms.

"I'll wait," was all Karan would say. "She won't last, Raphael."

My wife was beautiful in a floor length dress of rough linen and bare feet, a spiral of tiny white flowers adorning her hair. We drank wine and ate roasted lamb, made an offering to a god I no longer served and I made love to my bride beneath the stars on the bank of the river. And I was happy.

Until Sariel arrived.

32
SARIEL

I couldn't believe what I was seeing.

I knew the soul before me, knew the lines of his face and the tones of his voice. He'd called me forth from the waters, told me—told us—that we were brothers and sisters, children of the Father and that he was Host. That he was first among us and would lead us. He gave us our first purpose and was the first light when the darkness came. I'd heard him, felt him, knew him since my own creation.

Raphael the Archangel. The Peace Keeper. The best of us.

But as much as I knew this soul, I didn't recognize the muted figure below me. He face was aged, wizened, and coated in a growth of hair that darkened his chin and fell into his eyes. Raphael was taller in some ways, more confident and resolute while fleshy and soft in his appearance. His skin was dusky like the other humans and I could smell the earth wafting from his hands. He wore the clothes of man, robes of wool and sandals of leather. Only his eyes shone, only they belied the divinity that I prayed still surged within him.

I saw Raphael before he saw me. I was hanging above a small rise that spilled into a shallow valley dotted with human buildings of cloth and mud and clay. He was in a field, working the soil, trying to make life grow with the tools of man. I watched him, in awe that I'd found him, confused at the spectacle he'd become. Raphael was sweating in the midday sun and he took a draught from a camelskin hanging from his belt. He scrubbed weary hands together before pushing the plow forward. Raphael was a...man?

Like the others.

Like Uriel.

Then I saw her.

The woman. Ruddy skin and freckles, green eyes and... beautiful. Truly beautiful. The green in her eyes sparkled in the sun and my lips betrayed me: the smile on her face brought one to my own. She cradled something in her arms, something I could not see. Something that made Raphael drop his tools, leave his work, and fawn over. Something, to them, that was wonderful. A tiny, chubby arm, jolted from the woman's cradle of wool and linen. A child! And Raphael kissed its hand, took the bundle from the woman, nuzzling her neck.

Raphael's child. Raphael's Chosen.

Just like Uriel.

I hurtled to Earth, setting the field aflame with my arrival. Sword drawn, shield clinging to my damaged arm, my majestic presence blinded the woman and she fell to her knees, howling. Raphael and the baby were unaffected.

"Even you, Raphael? You, Host?" Their robes fluttered in the breeze of my voice and I realized I was roaring at them.

"Sariel? Is that you?" he said and his voice was small, tinny. Human. And then he helped the woman up, handing her the baby. "Go back," he said.

"No! Stay, daughter of Eve. Stay and see what your Chosen truly is. See how he has turned his back on the rest of us."

"Chosen?" said the woman, pushing away from Raphael. Realization flooded her features, flowing into anger. "She knows you? Is this who tried to kill you?"

The woman turned to me, grabbing some sort of farming tool and brandishing it toward me. I laughed at her foolishness. I growled and the instrument burst into flames.

"Kneel before me, woman! I am Sariel, Commander of the Army of the Lord, the God of Adam. Raise another weapon against me and I will tear the flesh from your bones. Kneel!"

"Sariel," Raphael found some strength in his voice, "Ananda is my Chosen. She is my equal. We are all sons and daughters of the Father, none of us are above the others."

"Uriel said the same thing and his woman bleeds into the earth."

"Uriel?" Raphael said. "Where is he?"

"Deserting his responsibilities," I told him. "Just like you. Where have you been? Where is your Sword?"

He looked at the woman, at the baby, at his feet. "I was looking for Michael and we were attacked. My forces separated. Cassiel and Ramiel didn't...I was wounded. Ananda found me."

"WHERE HAVE YOU BEEN?" I bellowed at him and the woman's ears began to bleed. "The army stands in disarray. Michael is nowhere to be found. Too many of us have turned our backs on our duty and taken wives, made these abominations. This is where have you been?"

He looked at nothing. "I have been healing," he said finally.

"You lie!" I clutched his robes, heard them singe beneath my grasp. "You are the Archangel, you are the Father's Peace Keeper. Your name means 'God has healed.' You are as strong as the day He made you, Raphael. We must choose, right? Isn't that what Emmanuel told us? We must choose to stand with the Father?"

"Or fall," he whispered, dropped his head.

"I will not fall, Raphael. You know that. What is your choice?"

"I want to stay."

"Host, that is not a choice! Your brothers and sisters need you and you do not answer. That is a crime. Michael said—"

"Michael is not here!" Raphael's eyes flashed. "My wife and my son need me. There are demons here."

"And you let them survive? This is a war, Raphael, not a humanitarian mission. The demons are our enemy or did you forget that?" I stepped close to him, breathed in his face. "I don't know why you have turned your back on us but if the woman is the distraction," and I waved my sword in her direction, "I can resolve that for you."

"No!" And Raphael the Archangel hit me. Hard.

I skipped across the burned field and instantly regretted my actions. I looked up to see fire and sliver wicking up Raphael's arms, sabers easing from his fists. Uriel is one thing: though he is formidable in combat, Uriel is my equal. He is fruit of the waters like me, children called from Heaven by Gabriel's Horn and the Sisters' whim. The lower orders of angels—seraphs and cherubs, virtues, dominions, thrones, powers and principalities—we pale in comparison to the Archangels. They are something else, something greater, forged in the palm of the Father's hand. And they know it.

I felt the familiar sizzle in my chest, felt the Father's power surge through me and felt, somehow, that I was doing the right thing. Even if it was the last thing I did.

I pulled my sword into the bow and said, "You are Host. You are the voice of the Father. This is forbidden and you know it. One of us will do the Father's will, Peace Keeper. Will it be me or will it be you?"

"You will die trying, Sariel. That is my word," he said, slowly walking toward me.

"So be it," and I loosed three bolts.

The first two glanced off his sabers, exploding dirt in plumes like shells. The third struck him in the shoulder and smoldered on his skin. Raphael winced but kept coming. I saw his eyes flame, saw his robes burn from his body and streaks of metal burst through his skin.

"Don't do this, Raphael," I said, backpedaling.

"You forced my hand, Sariel," he said. Then over his shoulder, "Ananda, go get your father. Tell him I want to see him. Tell him I said we have to end this."

He grinned at me but this grin, this sadistic smile, was something I'd only seen one other time: when Azazel smiled at us back in Wisdom. Right before his hands turned to fire and he brought the temple down on Zadkiel's head. When he started killing us for taking a stand. Just like I was doing now. I was lucky that day. I was fast. Today I would not be lucky. I knew that much. As I watched Raphael's wings burst from his skin, saw the brilliance of his divinity pour down his body like liquid light, I knew that I would die this day.

It was the woman who saved me. With her tiny, fragile, halting voice, she said, "What...what are you?"

And Raphael stopped. His face softened. The flames dancing on his arms and legs melted beneath his skin and his features became kind. "I told you, Ananda," he said, "I'm not like any man you know."

My bow was ready. "He's not a man at all, woman. Can't you see that? He's the Peace Keeper. He serves the god you pray to, the god of your father and his father before him. He's an angel. Like me."

She wanted to touch him, her hand reached for his body and lurched back as if burned. Fear and love coated her features and, for the briefest of moments, I felt sorry for her. This flesh and blood creature, weak and soft and naïve, tossed into the fray with angels and demons and the Father. And me. The mortal lost in the world of the divine. There was no way for her to escape unscathed, unhurt, untouched. This wasn't her battle. The angel standing before her wasn't the Chosen she needed, not the one she deserved. And what had to happen was a fate she didn't choose.

But that couldn't matter now. That couldn't stop me from doing my duty.

"Go get your father! Get him now!"

The woman hit Raphael. "You lied to me! You didn't tell me what you were!"

"I did," he told her. "You said I was enough."

"You never said--!"

"Just like the others, Host," I said. "They never told their women the truth. They only told them in death."

Raphael growled at me, "That is your fault!" He faced me now. "You did this! You came here and destroyed everything!"

"You're putting her above us!" I said.

"She is above us! You're meddling in things you do not understand. I swore to protect them, Sariel! I knelt before them, I knelt before the Man and I swore to protect them!"

"This isn't protecting them! You're not protecting her. You're abusing her. Protection doesn't mean using them and lying to them, does it? It cannot mean making...it cannot mean this. It can't." I knew what I had to do, what had to be done. "I swore to do the Father's will, no matter what. I cannot judge you, Host, but I can end this madness."

My bow moved to the left slightly. From Raphael's chest, from the burning glyph on his sternum to the soft expanse of linen beneath the woman's arms. Beneath her baby. The bolt left my fingers before the Archangel could react; her blood coated his face before the scream left his lungs. I scrubbed a tear from my face as I watched the woman spill her baby into the dirt and drop in a heap.

"Father, forgive me," I whispered.

33
LUCIFER

"Look what we have here!"

To say I was giddy is an understatement. I was downright enthralled. Amazed. Frozen in childlike wonderment, eyes wide, mouth agape. I had intended to simply show Michael the folly of his brother, show him that anyone would fall given the right temptation. I wanted to show him that it was all worthless. That everything he fought for, that every speck of blood that coated his hands was for naught. That his very existence amounted to nothing.

Instead, I showed him Sariel. His commander. His friend. We arrived just in time to see Sariel being batted around a dusty field by Raphael the Archangel, who wept over his fallen human wife.

I couldn't have assembled a better portrait of wanton disregard for the Father if I had tried. These idiots had done it on their own. For the briefest of moments, I felt pity for Michael. Actually, I pitied them all. Every last one of us had been playing the Father's stupid game, moving about Heaven and Earth like chess pieces, trying to save a collection of souls that was damned from the start. Raphael fell without my intervention. He fell because he was flawed. And if Raphael could fall, all of us could. All of us would.

Michael stepped away from me, slack-jawed. "Raphael? And Sariel?" Then he snatched at me, pulled me close, growled in my face. "What did you do?"

"This time, it actually wasn't me. That was all him. Spectacular, isn't it?"

He dropped me, turned to watch. "Why?" But it was a question asked into the air.

I peered over Michael's shoulder, "That is Raphael's Chosen, there on the ground. And that," I pointed at the baby, bawling in the sun, "is Raphael's son."

"Even you, Raphael?" Michael whispered.

"You know, that's what Sariel said. Then she killed the woman. And if you stand here long enough, you'll watch Raphael exact his revenge. Look at her, Michael. Look at Sariel. You can't say this doesn't look familiar."

I watched the recognition worm itself across Michael's face. Watched the tightness in his jaw, his hands flexing with angst and anticipation.

"She looks like Sela, doesn't she?" I danced just beyond Michael's shoulder, whispering in his ears. "Outmatched. Alone. Losing. The seraph will die, Michael, you know that. It'll be just like Sela. You will watch another Archangel cut down the soul you love before your very eyes...again." I clucked my tongue. "It's a shame, really. I liked her. Sariel is so...forthright. It's too bad."

Michael grabbed me, harsher than I expected. "Make it stop!"

I giggled at him. "Oh! You think this is—? Ha. My mistake. I forgot how easily confused you are. I can't stop this: I'm not doing it. I know I've made of mockery of reality but this is Earth. This is real, Michael. It's happening right now. Raphael is going to kill Sariel *right now.* Right before your eyes." My smile disappeared. "Unless, of course, you don't believe your eyes. Well, then, it could be awkward, couldn't it, rushing into nothing? Ah, decisions, decisions!"

"I don't believe you."

"Don't," I told him. "I don't care what happens to her. That's the difference between you and me. I don't care what happens to any of you. You do. You care. And you care for her, don't you?"

Michael dropped his gaze, peeking beneath hooded eyes as Sariel dove beneath Raphael's swipes only to meet his foot against her face. He winced as she winced, bit his lip as she spat blood into earth. His hands quivered as Sariel adjusted her grip on the sword, his feet shuffled as she backpedaled.

"Oooohhh, you care a lot," I said. "She's special to you."

"Sariel is a light for me. She is a light to my darkness." He never looked away.

"Hmm. I thought Sela was the light to your darkness?"

"Sela's gone. Sariel lives."

"Is this love, Peace Maker?" I grinned. "Do you love the seraph?"

He faced me now. "She understands. She understands me."

"Well, you better act fast, buddy. She won't be doing much of anything if you let her face this alone."

And Raphael bodily lifted Sariel by her throat and hurled her into the dirt. Though his face creased with pain, Michael refused to move. He simply watched. Chest rising rapidly, almost spastically twitching his fingers, beads of sweat glistening on his forehead. But Michael never moved.

"You're scared!" And it was as much a shock to me as it was to him. "You know it's the one gift the Father truly blessed me with. I know you're scared, Michael. I can taste it. You reek of fear. You know why? Because it's you. If you jump in, if you raise your sword to protect her and fail, then it's on you. You're the failure. It's not Samael. It's not me. It's you. You're scared of you. That is pathetic. You deserve what happens."

Michael grabbed me now, clutched hard hands around my throat. "What are you trying to do to me, Keeper? You think your drivel can force my hand?"

"I don't care what you do. I hate you all. What do I care if another soul dies? Makes my life easier. But this, this is boring!"

I pushed him. Hard. Pressed Michael's burly frame forward and through the membrane separating the divine from the mortal. A seam of bubbles frothed about him, about us, and Michael the Archangel spilled into the world of men. Again. Before him, Raphael the Archangel, keeper of the Father's peace, held a young seraph in his grasp, firm hand coiled around her throat. He was squeezing the life from her.

"This is your fault, Sariel!' Raphael bellowed, spittle flowing in strings. "You just couldn't leave well enough alone, could you?"

I couldn't have scripted it better myself: the very words Samael said to Sela before he killed her. And this time, Michael didn't disappoint.

"Put her down, Raphael." And curved swords wicked up Michael's arms. "Now."

But Raphael only smiled. "Or what, Michael? What will you do? What can you do that you haven't already done? Cut me down like the others? Like Azazel? You think you can judge me too? Go ahead, put me out of my misery. Do it!"

Michael paused, unsure of himself, "Put her down, Raph. Killing her does nothing, gains you nothing. This is not who you are. This is not what you were meant to do."

But the Peace Keeper only laughed. "Not what I was meant to do? No, what I was meant to do was spend the rest of my wife's days here, with our son. But that's been taken from me. So I have nothing left that I was 'meant to do,' Michael. Now I'm like you, now I do I what I feel."

I felt Michael's growl ease across the field before Raphael did, saw the flash of fire in his eyes—the same spark that flooded his face when he rained down me with that sword in the Temple and knew what Michael would do.

"You want to be like me?" the Peace Maker said, stepping forward slowly. "You want to see what I was made to do? I said put her down!"

And he moved in a blur, in a streak of light and fire and thunder, swords flashing in the sunlight. The move was swift and deadly, almost imperceptible. Sariel collapsed to the ground, Raphael's hand still clutching her throat. But the hand, the arm, ended at the bicep: Michael severed it clean from Raphael's body. He whirled, spinning both hands into

Raphael's chest, sending the Archangel hurtling from the field, tumbling down the rise toward the settlement below.

"Get up, Sela," Michael said to the seraph.

"Sela?" I said to myself, stepping into Earth, "Now this is getting good!"

34
RAPHAEL

"Bad day?"

This was probably the best and worst sentiments I'd ever heard. The wound didn't even hurt, the separation of my arm. I couldn't even feel it. I couldn't feel anything. Ananda was dead, her blood leeching into the dirt, Sariel's accusation thrumming in her ears. I never was able to make it right, to tell her...I never told her the truth about me and that simple idea, that she died knowing only that I'd lied to her, haunts me to this day. I loved her, I lost her. I never, ever had her at all.

I opened my eyes to the sarcastic voice and saw my son. My child. Caramel skinned with a swath of black hair and his mother's green eyes. He was utterly perfect—a perfect little creature who only smiled at the world around him. Ananda called him Shiloh, the place of peace in her language. But he was Balthial to me, forgiveness, in my own. I hoped one day the Father would find mercy, find comfort, for my son. It wasn't possible: I knew what had become of Lucifer's daughters. I knew I'd committed the same crime I'd bound him for. I knew Lucifer and I were the same now: lovers and sinners, transgressors against the will of the Father, both of us judged by Michael.

But my child didn't speak. In the haze of pain and grief, I focused on the thick fingers that circled Shiloh's chest, the strong, hairy arms that cradled him now. The red eyes that peered over my son's head and smiled. It was Jobesh looking down at me.

"I told you," the man said, grinning at me, "it was just a matter of time. I told you this is where we'd end up, didn't I?"

But it was Karan the Reaper speaking to me. My son was in the hands of a demon.

I sat up quickly, too quickly. "Give me my son." But my voice lacked the edge, the bite, the authority it once had.

Karan laughed at me. "You think you can give orders now? You have no authority here, Peace Keeper. Besides, I think the little guy likes me. But," and the man's head looked over a shoulder, "I'm willing to put it to a vote."

Then I saw. Behind the man. Naya. Khadijah. A score of other humans, cousins and aunts and neighbors and brothers—all of them standing with pulsing red eyes. All of them possessed by the demons.

"Did you think it was just you and me? You think I'm that naïve, Raphael? You've always underestimated me. I thought you knew better."

I struggled to my feet, felt the pour of silver down my one good arm, closed my fist around a saber. "I will tear you apart before you draw another breath."

The horde laughed at me. Karan said, "Pull yourself together, Raphael, before I rip his head from his body. You think this ball of flesh matters to me? You think I have affection for your motherless bastard?" She placed a heavy foot on me, pushed me to the ground. "Look at her, look at your Chosen bleeding into the dirt. You think your son is worth anything more? He's just another soul for me to take."

I felt the heat of tears burn my eyes, the helplessness flood my body. "Please..." I whispered. "Please, Karan, give me my son."

"Awww," and she crouched in the man's body, stroked my face, "it doesn't have to be all bad. We can be one big happy family, Raphael. I can give you what she couldn't. I can give you forever. We can live forever."

And she dotted my nose.

"Why?" But it was Ananda's voice I heard, weak and injured.

She'd rolled to her stomach, her entrails leaking into the dust, easing to us slowly. Her face was a lovely mess of blood and dirt, streaked with tears and a swipe of spittle. A tangle of hair hung in her face and the light was gone in her eyes. My breath caught.

"Now this is a touching scene," Karan said. "Oh, I'm not heartless. Not entirely. Go to her, Raphael. You need to tell her goodbye."

I lurched from Karan, from the bulging figure of Jobesh, from his twisted fingers tracing the flesh of my child. My son. In the hands of a demon. Clamoring for the dying body of my wife. My chosen. There was nothing—nothing—that prepared me for this. Nothing that made me ready for the tumult of grief. I reached the one hand I had remaining to Ananda, pushed the hair from her face. Found a patch of freckles amidst the filth.

"Why what?" I said.

But she pushed me away. Left a handprint of blood on my arm. "Why didn't you tell me the truth? Why didn't you tell me what you were?"

"I tried." I dropped my eyes, let tears fall into earth.

"Look at me!" and when I did, Ananda said, "Tell me now."

"I'm not a man. I think you know that now. I was sent here to protect you, to protect all of you. But I failed. I didn't...I fell in love with you instead. And I didn't think you'd want me if you knew the truth. I didn't think you'd love me."

"Look what you did!" Ananda closed her eyes. "You took everything from me. Everything!"

"Ananda, I didn't—"

She laid her head down, released a long, slow breath. "Just save our son. Save that good thing. Let the rest die."

Karan laid Jobesh's hand on his daughter's head, caressed her in the most loving way I'd ever seen. I think a tear formed in the man's eye. To this day, I don't know if it was the human portion of Jobesh fighting against Karan long enough to have some real emotion or Karan herself, touched by death.

"Goodbye, my daughter."

"Father?" Ananda said. It was the last word she spoke.

"Not exactly." And, with one smooth twist of the man's hand, Karan snapped my wife's neck. It was too fast for me to respond, to beg, to try and intervene. Two cracks, the crunch of bone in thudding in my ears and she was gone. Gone.

The ragged flesh of Jobesh thudded to the ground next to

his daughter. Karan flexed now, free of the human form that contained her, whirling her scythe in one hand and dangling my son by his foot with the other.

"You look sad," she said, and a horrible smile lined her face. "You told me no soul was worth disobedience. Not even me. You remember that? You should be thanking me: I just saved you."

"What do you want?"

"See? That's better!" Karan crouched beside me, let me smell my son's skin. He giggled at my face and reached for me. The demon snatched him away, said, "This world is teeming with angels. I need you to thin out the herd."

"It's a little difficult with only one arm."

"You should use your resources, Raphael. You came here with an army. And you're a lot stronger than you pretend." She dragged the tip of her scythe along Shiloh's chest and a line of red appeared. "Perhaps you need an incentive. I will kill him, I promise you that."

"No! Don't!" I moved to my knees. "Karan, please. Don't do this to me!"

Karan grinned. "*To* you? I'm doing this *for* you. I told you, if you want things to change, you have to make them change. You owe me forever and, one way or another, you're going to give it to me. Now, pull yourself together."

Choice is a horrible concept. Free will is considered the benevolence of the Father. He calls it an expression of love and trust, an example of His fidelity toward us. He says love creates us and love will bind us together but love mandated is only pantomime, empty expressions of predetermination and duty. It is blind obedience not willful loyalty. We must choose to love. We must choose to obey. We must choose to stand with the Father.

But He lies about the consequences. He lies about the reality of this burden. Yes, the Father gives us choice but then burns our souls into oblivion if we choose wrong. If we do not choose as He would have us choose. What choice is that? It becomes one made in fear, not of love. It is simply divine blackmail. Celestial extortion. If I must choose, if I must jeopardize my very soul, it would not be for some nebulous edict, some fickle parent whose face I have never seen. It would be for the face that looked like mine, for the eyes that belonged to his mother, for the life that belonged to my son.

I stabbed my hand into the earth, felt the pulse of this living, breathing planet, and fed from it. Nursed energy and life and strength from the ground beneath my feet. My severed arm burned and blackened, growing like a tree limb. It thickened and lurched forward, coated in bark and stone, dark metal coiling about the appendage. It hurt, this process, this choice to become part of the world. To give up that which made me divine and I screamed in the sun. A web of black leeched up my shoulder and cascaded across my chest. Two fists pounding the ground and a wave of energy, a dense blue mist, wafted in all directions. The call to my Sword.

"Good," said Karan, bouncing my son on her hip and kissing his hands. "Now let's go kill some angels!"

35
MICHAEL

"What are you doing, Sela?"

It wasn't Sela. I could tell, I could see her. But I couldn't see clearly. I couldn't separate the bloody image of Sela's face from Sariel's. They merged and blended in my sight, fluid and hazy. And it wasn't just the picture that eluded me: all of my senses were assailed. The field, this earthen hollow, would morph and fold into Righteousness. The visage of Raphael, furious and broken, holding the seraph above his head, poured into Samael gleefully brutalizing Sela. Their screams of agony, their cries for mercy were the echoed simultaneously in my head.

I couldn't tell clearly who she was.

I wasn't certain if she was even real.

I only knew the soul that I loved, Sela or Sariel, was going to die.

And I wasn't ready for that. Not again.

"I'm not—," she began.

"I know who you are!" I lied. "What are you doing? You're going to get yourself killed."

The angel before me was silent for a moment, looking at her feet. It was Sariel: Sela had no such reticence. "Looking for you."

"For me?"

"You were cast out. We all were."

"This is Earth? This is real?"

"Can't you tell?" Sariel reached for me and I let her fingers trace my jaw, rub my cheek. "What happened to you?" she whispered.

I jolted from her touch, grabbed her wrist. "Where is my army, Sariel?"

But it was Sela who responded and the world around me darkened. Earth—dirt and rock and plant—became the stone foundations of Righteousness and the fallen cackled about me. "Where have you been?" she said. "We followed you! We did exactly what you told us to do. We followed you. We killed for you!" She pounded fists into my chest. "We killed our brothers and sisters for you and—"

"Where is my army?!" And Earth returned.

"Lost," Sariel said. "Emmanuel cast us out too. The army is lost. Some search for you. Some have chosen the women and they made children with them. They turned their back on the Father."

"Like Raphael?"

"Like Raphael," she said. "And I judged them for it."

"Judged them? That is not your place! What did you do, Sariel?"

She just looked at me with cold, hard eyes and her face bled into Sela's. She said, "What do you want me to say? That I spared them, any of them? Mercy is not my purpose, Michael, you told me that. I did what had to be done."

That is what I told her. And she used my own words against me.

"Samael will kill you, Sela," and my voice was soft, loving. "You're not strong enough and I can't let him..." A wave of blue splashed through us, jolting me to the reality before me. "Raphael has called his Sword. Call the army, Sariel!"

But Sariel said, "You call them. They're your soldiers. Maybe whoever's left will listen to you."

And then there was Lucifer, smiling at me. "What are you going to do, Michael? Kill them all? Your own soldiers? Even the Peace Keeper? I can't wait to see how this ends."

"You know how this ends," I said. I swiped Sariel behind me, loosed swords into my palms, and dove for the Keeper. But he was fast, diving beneath my blades, snaking beyond my reach.

"Awww," Lucifer grinned at me, "you're getting slow. Should I just stand still and give you a chance? Does that make easier?"

Sariel hit me with her shield. "Captain? Who are you talking to?"

Who was I talking to? She couldn't—Lucifer wasn't? He wasn't real? But he was there, smiling at me and whispering in my ear. He'd been there the whole time, shuttling me from place to place, showing me the horrors of those I called soldier. He was just a charade? And how much was false? Was I truly exiled or was this another dream fabricated by

Lucifer? Would I finally awaken on the floor of Sela's temple again, coated in my own sweat, slicing at air and stone? This nightmare before me, the soft thunder of the wings of thousands of angels approaching, the throng of red-eyed humans slowly marching over the hillside, the wide-eyed seraph next to me—did it exist at all?

"Can't believe your eyes, can you, Captain?" Lucifer whispered in my ear.

I closed my eyes, covered my ears. "Get out of my head!"

Sariel tried to comfort me, placed an armored arm about my shoulders but I shoved her away. I peeked at her and only saw the brutalized face of Sela, bloodied and damaged, grinning at me. "Michael," she said, taking my shaking hands into her own, "you don't have to do it. Not anymore. Let go."

"Let go?" I whispered.

Sela told me, "Just let go. You did your duty, Captain. Be proud of that. You did a good thing."

"But I'm not done. It's not done. I still have to—"

She shushed me. "Look around you. What good can you do, Peace Maker? This is madness. This is the Father's madness."

"He is our Father. He is their god."

And Sela backed away from me suddenly, pressing from my chest. "God? What kind of god lets this happen, Michael? Open your eyes! You serve a faceless coward. Look around you! Your soldiers, the ones that bothered to show up, have taken wives from the humans and made abominations with them! Look at those men and women—those worthless piles of dust have given themselves to the fallen!" Now she grabbed my face, aimed it Raphael. "And your brother, the

Peace Keeper, is as complicit as the rest of them. This is the Father's will, Michael. This is the madness He has ordained."

I stood now, slapped her hands away. "I will make this right. I can, I can make this right!"

"With your swords, Michael? What righteousness is that? These souls are not your enemy. The Father is. Their god is. That's your enemy." And she made me face her. "You know how to kill a god, Michael? Forget Him. They have. Turn your back. Walk away. Let Him die here."

But it was Sariel who struck me in face, knocking me to my knees with her shield. "Michael! You are the Father's justice. They deserve justice. You chose, Michael, you chose all of it. Isn't that what you told me? Didn't you tell me to finish it? This demands justice! If you won't stand and fight, if you won't do your duty, I will!"

The demons came first. Clad in the ruddy skin of humanity, they split flesh and burned eyes from their sockets until only the fiery red of disobedience peered back at us. There were dozens of them, coming in streams over the rise, brandishing crude implements of farming and agriculture as weapons and shouting epithets only angels would understand. Sariel met them with a cascade of arrows of light, watched geysers of human blood plume into the air, watched scalps of brown and black explode only to be replaced with the fluid masses of the demons beneath. Human flesh would be discarded in rags and sheets and the fallen angels, crude and twisted, would rush forward on all fours like beasts. Like monsters. Coming for us.

She was magnificent! Demons poured on Sariel like black rain and she shone like a star. Arrows would be loosed and she would leap forward, bow flowing into her sword and shield, crashing metal into heads, faces, jaws, tearing limbs and spearing throats. She spun and ducked, rolling beneath marauding apparitions of doom, exploding upwards in wide swipes of light and fire, only to suppress the advance with a cacophony of arrows. Again. Sariel was a portrait of death, an artisan really, and I found myself smiling in the midst of her carnage.

"You really trained her well. She is impressive," Sela said to me, chewing her thumb and grinning at the bloodshed. She turned to me suddenly, "So, are you really going to let her do your dirty work for you?"

"What?"

"Look at her, Michael. She fights like you but she has my heart. She's headstrong; she doesn't mind her surroundings. She gets in over her head and she'll quickly be overwhelmed. Like I was. Look," and Sela draped her arms around me like a lover and pointed in the distance, at the flashes of blue flame falling from the sky, "that is Raphael's Sword. They're soldiers, Michael. Your soldiers. Oh, sure Sariel is deadly to these halfwits but how well to do you think your little protégé will fare against her own? You remember what happened to me?"

I pushed her, hard, felt the familiar scrape of my swords against my arms. "You told me to walk away. Isn't that what you said? You said let them die here!"

But Sela grinned at me. "You are missing the point, as usual. I want you to think for yourself, Michael! Do what you think is right! Do what you think is just. Not what He says. Not what I say. Do what you say is right. But you have to do something: she's going to die here."

"No," I growled, "we're all going to die here. You too."

I rammed my swords into her chest, tearing through muscle and bone, bursting through her ribs until he metal dug deep into the earth.

She coughed blood on my face. "You killed me!"

"You were already dead." I scrubbed the tears from my eyes. "Goodbye, Sela."

But she was gone. And I was digging at dirt until my hands bled into the soil. It was like she was never there. Had never been there at all. All of it was some sleight of hand Lucifer used to expose the truth.

"Truth hurts, doesn't it?" I heard him whisper.

But he was right. About everything. Too much blood had been shed for something worthless. None of it was worth it. Not me, not Sariel, not Sela, not the man. None of it.

I heard two voices in my head, speaking simultaneously in both ears. I heard the Father saying, "Protect the others, lead My army, end this darkness. You are like Me and you will do what must be done." And in the other, Sela telling me, "This is the Father's will. This is the madness He has ordained."

Obedience is not an act, Michael. It is a journey.

"Stop!" But the roar was not my own, was not from my body. It was my soul crying out, finally. I heard it echoing around me, reaching across the field like ground cover, reverberating from the mountains, slicing across the skies. I screamed to the Heavens until my eyes burned and fire belched from my lips.

"It isn't fair," I said to no one. "It isn't fair."

And I heard the Father and Sela speaking as one, "I made you to bring peace. I made you like Me. You will do what must be done. Your will shall persevere when others fail. You will bring to fruition what others cannot conceive. And you will destroy the wickedness among you."

And then the Father alone, "Do you think your work is done?"

I pulled my swords from earth, shook the dirt from their bloods, looked to the Heavens. "No."

"You chose," I heard Sariel say. "Finish it."

36
SARIEL

I was alone.

The demons fell against me like a horrible river, pouring their flesh-coated bodies against my armor. I was like a rock in the rapids, breaking the rush, taking the force of the stream—of fists and feet and claws and weapons—and pushing it aside and away, feeling it swirl and reconnect behind me in a snarling, snapping, ravenous cesspool. Fighting the fallen is one thing: it is my true purpose, the reason I exist at all. My sword is meant for their flesh, it hungers for their blood upon its blade. But humans are something else. They are soft, easy. Mortal. It is like butchering children and the very act steals something from me. Their touch pulls my divinity from me, saps my strength and diminishes my light. Pushes me further from the Father. Further from my purpose.

I was alone in the crush. And they were pushing me backward.

Then the angels came.

Leaping like gazelles over the hills, vaulting into the air, swarming like locusts and raining down on me with a barrage of spears of light. I knew what they could do, what they were trained to do. I also knew they were only shadows of their true selves. Like their commander, Raphael, they'd betrayed their edict and found solace in the arms of the daughters of man. And they'd sacrificed their wings, and their divinity, in the process. But they were no less dangerous and as the first volley of spears shattered the earth in geysers of dirt and fire and ignited scores of flesh-covered demons, I knew my days on this world were numbered.

A throne called Megal thundered into me with her shoulder, sweeping my feet with the ax of black metal clenched in her fists. "Sariel," she said, the glyph on her forehead throbbing with yellow fire, "you should have left well enough alone."

"And you should have honored your commitment to the Father, throne." I kicked her throat, heard the crunch of bone beneath my feet and pressed backward, vaulting into the air. My sword and shield became liquid, pulling into the bow. I fired wildly and Megal became a pillar of stone and ash. Two more bolts and the cherubs that tried to follow me thundered to the earth as statues.

Wings wide, I strafed the field, firing and sliding my bow into a pair of swords. Demons plumed in flame, angels froze in their tracks, limbs danced in air without their owners. Only Michael was more dangerous in combat. If I would die this day, my life would come with the gravest of costs.

A cough of blue flame twisted next me, pouring over my shoulders and a weary dominion brandished his massive sword at me. Uriel. "I should have known I would find you here," he said.

He stepped toward me and I stumbled, toppled. "What you did to me, what you took from me," he said and swung his sword in wide arc, ripping through the torsos of four angels, "was necessary. I hate you for it. But it was best."

And Uriel shouldered a shield, pressed into the fray, crushing the heads of marauding demons against the metal. "Get up, seraph," he said, "my Sword fights for you."

Splashes of flame dotted the landscape and angels—both Uriel's and mine—exploded from them, hurling spears at their brothers, gutting the fallen, killing the humans. Ash fell on us like snow, blood rained from the heavens, broken arms, legs, limbs turned to stone and crushed beneath our feet. Brother against brother, sister against sister, child against parent—the earth itself drowned in the blood of all the children of the Father.

Until we heard Michael scream. Until the terror of his voice washed across the field like a tidal wave. We were frozen in a combination of horror and servitude, a vicious allegiance to a force we didn't understand. I'd seen it once, watched Michael the Archangel become the furious justice of the Father, and it frightened me still. Then he plucked me from chaos and named me Commander, and I watched the souls of our fallen brethren burst from his body and slaughter hundreds. He was a harbinger of death, this angel, but this time I didn't know who he was aiming for.

It was all of us.

Michael spiraled into the sky and thunderheads rolled behind him, casting a shadow over the bloodshed. He burned in the midday sky, flaming like a comet streaking above us.

"You know me," he said and everything stopped, frozen. "All of you know me. And you know what I will do. There will be no mercy. There will be no repentance. There is only judgment. That is my word."

Michael fell like a meteor and the world exploded beneath him. The earth heaved and buckled and belched stalactites from its bowels. Lava, the blood of this world, spat angrily and spires of fire ringed us all. All of us, angel and demon and human, toppled to our knees, to our backs.

"I am Michael the Archangel! I am the Father's justice! See me and tremble!"

And his voice made our ears bleed. I heard women and men, humans, wailing at the pain. I watched demons and angels alike cower beneath his bellow. He grabbed Uriel, tore him from his armor and held him high.

"Your crimes merit judgment, deserter," Michael said, "but now is not the time. Redeem yourself in my service. I am Captain: your Sword fights for *me*!" He tossed Uriel into the dirt, turned to me, "Your work is not finished, seraph. Kill them all. No one stands."

And Michael disappeared into the flames, Raphael's name on his tongue.

37
GABRIEL

I found the boy on the bank of the Waters, kneeling, his tiny shoulders shaking. Emmanuel was crying. He was peeking through dirty, wet fingers, peering into the Waters and moaning "No, no, no" over and over. Every now and then, he would ground his hands into the black sands that ringed the edge of the Heavens, pulling at the dirt, feeling it crumble between his fingers. His face was covered in grime, in the residue of his tears and frustration, and he wouldn't look at me. A throng of angels hung back, watching, waiting. Others floated above, shaking fingers covering quivering mouths.

I dropped next to him, shuffled my feet in the sand. And said nothing.

"It is lost," Emmanuel whispered to me, to no one.

I should have left it alone, let him work through it. The relationship Emmanuel had with the Father was truly beyond me. It was the only thing in Heaven I cannot see, cannot understand. It was beyond my sight and my comprehension. In my eons, I have come to understand the strange arrangement Lucifer shares with the Father. Understand is the wrong word: I have come to accept it as a matter of course. Lucifer was made without a purpose, made solely as an act of love. He simply exists. The Father loves Lucifer in a way I cannot fathom. The Keeper fulfills some need, some want in the Father that He will neither explain nor acknowledge. Lucifer simply is as the Father is.

I have come to accept that.

But Emmanuel is something else. All of us have a purpose, a role to play in this celestial melodrama. He is no different. He is the last of us, his role presumably the most essential. But I have yet to see it defined. I am the Father's eyes; Michael the Father's hand. Raphael is the Father's voice, Azazel was His wisdom, Sela His regret. But Emmanuel? He is simply His anointing. But the Father seems to have forgotten to give the boy any capability.

And I couldn't accept that. Not anymore. Not after watching my brothers and sisters slaughter themselves for naught. Not again. Not knowing where this would lead.

I said, "Are you going to let this happen, First? Are you not going to intervene?"

The boy spoke to the Water. "They are doing what they must, Watcher, just as we will do what we must. They all made choices: Michael, Sariel, Raphael, the race of men. It is as it should be."

"Clearly," I said. I shuffled my feet, choosing my words. "I thought we were to protect them. We're killing them."

Emmanuel didn't say anything. He sobbed in the sand. And then, "Have you seen it? Do you know how it ends?"

I did. It wasn't pretty. Of all the things the Father has shown me, all the events and actions and lives He has shared with me, only a handful have ever broken my heart. Stirred some deep-rooted emotion within me. Compelled me to question my obedience. Compelled me to question Him. The culmination of these events, these horrors, was more than I could bear.

"I have," and I chewed my lip, tightened my jaws.

Emmanuel took my hand and I realized how much larger I was than him. How much I dwarfed his tiny form. How small his shoulders were. How his hand disappeared in my palm. I looked at his face, at the agony in his eyes and the pain surging through him. I finally understood. I always thought the Sisters were the Father's heart, that they were His emotions. But watching Emmanuel shudder with every act of violence a world away, watching him agonize over the atrocities committed on his behalf, watching him weep over souls that deserved no more than a passing glare, I understood. Emmanuel was the Father's love. And I appealed to that.

I dropped his hand. "First, we can't let it happen this way. We can't do this to them. It is our responsibility. They are our responsibility."

"And their choice." The boy scrubbed his eyes. "The Father gave them the ability to choose, He gave them free will. We cannot remove these gifts He has given them."

"Gifts? They abuse themselves!"

Emmanuel stood now and a brilliant light engulfed him. "Know your place, Watcher! The Father is without error. You know this."

"I know they will die."

"So be it," and Emmanuel stared into the Water. "Maybe that is what is best."

I couldn't contain myself any longer. "Best? The separation of Heaven, the abuse and slaughter of mankind? This is what is best?" I grabbed Emmanuel, felt the snap of electricity surging through my muscles. But I lifted the boy high above me. "I have served you without fail. I have held my tongue and swallowed my anger for eons while I watched my beloveds kill one another in droves. I have watched this world torn apart by the choices we have made. I will not watch—"

"The Father made you to watch, Gabriel! That is your purpose!"

"He did not make me to watch this! You have His voice: speak to them. If you do not, I will act."

"I can't." Emmanuel hung his head, cried tears into my face. "He has not given His word."

"The Father has said nothing?"

"No, He told me," said the boy. "He told me to wash them away. All of them. The Waters are coming, Gabriel. Just as they made Heaven live, they will remake the Earth. They will make it right. If I speak, the Waters will come."

I dropped Emmanuel in the sand, felt my own hot tears on my cheeks. "Too many have died because they did not hear you. They will hear me. I will not let you destroy them all."

He grabbed my hand again. "Gabriel, the Father did not make you for this."

I pushed him away. "Then the Father is wrong."

And I leapt into the Waters. I leapt for Earth.

38
RAPHAEL

"Raphael!"

Michael's voice shook the earth, shook me to my core. It was the Father's voice I heard, the one who called me forth from nothing, from ether, calling me to life. And when he burst through the flames, wings wide, armor burned with the heat of the damned, eyes flaming and furious, I thought he was the Father come to Earth.

Come for me.

"Raphael!" He roared my name, screamed it to the Heavens, even as his swords butchered the four angels shielding me. "Answer me!"

"I'm here," I said and my voice was stronger than expected, stronger than I hoped. The earthiness of my new limb, the mortality of the energy that surged through me now gave my voice a weight, a heaviness I hadn't had before. "Here I am."

"You know why I'm here, Raphael. You turned your back on your duty. You shirked your responsibilities. You misled those in your command. You tried to kill my commander." He ripped the head from a demon, sliced a human in two. "You know what I've come to do."

"I did what I had to do!" I roared at him, leaping with my sabers bared. They flamed, like Lucifer's, and I grinned at the irony. "I did what was required of me!"

Michael sliced for my head, backhanded me in the mouth. "Required? You are the Peace Keeper! What peace is here? What commitment did you keep? To your Sword?"

His blades reached for my abdomen but I rolled aside.

"To your brothers and sisters?"

I evaded another swipe for my neck.

"To me? To the Father?"

I blocked his assault, spun and sliced his face. "To my wife!" A heavy blow from my new hand, my earthly hand, sent Michael careening in the dirt. "To my son!"

"Son?" Michael held his jaw, furrowed his brow and narrowed flaming eyes at me. Past me. To the black hooded demon cradling the wailing baby on a flaming battlefield. To Karan. And to Shiloh.

"Your...son." His growl reached across the field, snaked along the ground until I felt the vibration climbing my legs. "You turned to the demons, you turned against us, for your son?"

I backpedaled. "Michael, no. Sariel was going to—"

His teeth were fanged and spittle flashed out in sparks. "You ordered your Sword to attack their brothers, to attack me, for this monster?" A heavy step forward. Then another. "All of this, for that?!"

I stood between Michael and Karan. "He's my son, Michael."

"And the demon? The Reaper? She is your Chosen?"

"Yes," said Karan. "Raphael loves me."

"I hate you!" I screamed into the air. "I hate all that you've taken from me. I hate what you've become. You are not the angel you were. No longer the one I loved."

"I am the one you need," she said and smiled at me, stroking my son's head.

Michael glared at me. "Why haven't you done what you needed to do? Why haven't you ended this nonsense?"

I dropped my head. There was nothing I could say, nothing I could explain in the moments before Michael would act. I knew this angel, this horrible apparition that stood before me. I knew his brand of justice, his righteous anger. My voice left me.

"I couldn't," I squeaked. "She was going to—I couldn't."

"Lucky for you," Michael said and raised his swords, "I can."

"Careful, Peace Maker," Karan said. She leveled her scythe against Shiloh's throat. "I have no qualms about ending his life."

But Michael only cocked his head, grinned a wicked grin. "Kill him. He's not mine, demon. He means nothing to me."

And in the moment Karan looked at me, the final moment we shared, Michael moved. Faster than I expected. Faster than I could see. A shoulder to my face, toppling me, his sword dragging in a swift, wide arc. Karan's body crumpled into ash, her burning face lolling next to my wailing baby.

"See how easy that was?" Michael said to me. "Now, tell him goodbye, Raphael."

I couldn't see through my tears. "Michael, please! This boy is my son. Flesh of my flesh, blood of my blood. The boy is mine."

"I don't care! He is an abomination, Raphael. He is the product of something that never should have happened and you know he cannot stand." And now Michael growled at me, "I warned you, didn't I? I told you: I was made to do horrible things. That is my purpose. You started this, Raphael. I will see it finished. It will not be pleasant."

I blinked and the world went quiet. Everything was silent. As though the Father robbed me of my hearing so I wouldn't know when my son stopped screaming, stopped crying. Stopped breathing. I blinked. And Michael was wiping the blood of my child from his sword, dragging it on the earth. I blinked and felt the liquid warmth of his life pouring against my feet in slow pulses. I blinked. And everything that ever mattered to me was gone.

Taken from me.

In the blink of an eye.

"That is what obedience looks like, Raphael," Michael said. "It's bloody."

"Funny," I said, and I realized I was smiling amidst my tears, "it looks a lot like revenge."

My hands moved on their own, pulling spears of stone and metal, light and fire from my fists. I charged Michael, I remember, stabbing and twisting and cutting and tearing, screaming as I moved. His armor bent and broke beneath me, blackened at my touch, tore against my blades. I powered him backward through flame and lava and Michael flopped against the earth. But my rage wasn't focused: it was wide and ranging, endless, and I lashed out at anything that moved. Demons. Humans. Angels. My own Sword.

"Kill me," I begged them before tearing limbs from bodies. Before impaling souls with my spears. Before my teeth bit into throats. None could meet with my request. None could match my ferocity.

Except Michael.

He was always there, always coming. Always slashing and ripping, brutal and terrifying. And grinning. Laughing amid the carnage. Coated in blood and sweat and white fire, the Archangel roared and growled, laughed and chuckled, even as he tore living beings apart with his bare hands. Even as his swords bit into angel and demon alike. Even as men and women fell to his fury, bodies cloven beneath his blows. And as I watched him, as I tried to match him, I saw the horror I was becoming. I was becoming him. I was becoming Michael. This was the monster, the beast we all feared, the horror that lurked in our hearts. We'd seen the depravity of Lucifer, we knew what falling truly meant. But, for those of us left behind, Michael was the animal we feared the most. He said he was the Father's justice but he truly was the Father's fury. That rush of anger that led to the destruction of the first Heaven, the one that saw Lucifer bound, the rage that cast us out. That was Michael. That was...me?

That was me. And that was not the angel the Father made me to be. Not the angel I would become. I could not honor my son's memory by being the monster Michael said he was. I was—I would be—better than that. I had to be.

"You failed, Peace Keeper. There is no peace here," Michael said.

"There is no peace here," I whispered.

"I am the one who comes after you. You know me. I am the Peace Maker. And I will make peace."

"Through blood," and I dropped my hands, closed my eyes, waited for the bite of Michael's blade into my throat.

I heard the rush of his blow, the hush of his sword slicing the air. The soft grunt as Michael pressed his weight behind his sword. And then...

The blare of Gabriel's Horn. The true song of the Father.

"Enough!" said the Watcher.

And everything stopped.

39
GABRIEL

Nothing prepared me for the reality I found on Earth. Not the destruction of Heaven at the hands of the Father. Not the death of Lilith. Not the rise of Samael. Not the fall of Lucifer. Nothing.

And I knew what was going to happen.

I knew I'd find wholesale chaos. I knew the Earth would be flooded with the blood of angels and man, that bodies would litter the soil, that hands and fists and weapons and wings, flesh and bone and ash and stone—these things would form the foundation of the world given to man. The world made for our salvation, now covered in the detritus of our sin and sadism. I knew this place would be lost before it would be found, that we would lose ourselves in its beauty and find a way to mar its perfection.

And I knew I'd find Lucifer in the center of the madness.

Basking in the chaos. Arms outstretched. Eyes closed.

Smiling at me.

"Now that," he said without looking at me, "is quite an entrance. Look at that!"

My Horn had brought angel and demon to their knees, covering their ears and wailing in the din. But the humans weren't so fortunate. Humanity is not made for the music of angels; immortality has no place in the mortal: our divinity is destructive. The women and men worn like bedclothes by the fallen became flaming piles of ash against the song of the Horn. I incinerated them simply by making my presence known.

The Father didn't show me that...I didn't know.

"What did you do them?" I said to Lucifer.

He giggled. "Me? Don't insult me with this savagery. You know me by now, Gabriel, my methods are much more subtle. This was you." He kicked at the remains of a woman, her hair still aflame. "So sad."

"Not them," I said, stepping close to him, pointing at the frozen. "Them."

Lucifer said, "Oh! Well, it's been a long time since you and I had a real, sincere heart to heart, you know? And I hate interruptions so," he drummed his fingers on a kneeling dominion, set the angel's armor aflame, "I stopped them. I stopped everything."

"You stopped them?"

"You haven't been here before, have you, Gabriel? Always at the beck and call of that little boy? You should do your research, buddy. Rules here are a little different than what you're used to. I can do *anything*." He put his hand on my chest and the earth moved beneath my feet. "Here I can do what I want."

And the lightest push of his fingertips against my armor sent me reeling across the field, flipping head over heels. I landed on my face next to Michael and Raphael, brothers in peace, one trying to decapitate the other. Lucifer stopped Michael just short of a killing blow: when time resumed, when this little charade was over, so was Raphael. Across the field were similar examples of brother against brother, sister against sister, lover against lover. Even those bound by something greater, bound by affection and affinity for one another—like Uriel and Sariel—were at odds. Sariel was frozen in the middle of shifting her weapon, pulling a sword from the ribs of a fallen and stretching it into her bow. She was turning, aiming, toward the open back of Uriel as he cleaved a group of demons with his mighty sword. Civil war is too simplistic a term for the horrors I beheld: my brothers and sisters were like savages, barbarians, worse than in Heaven, and there was no turning back.

And then there was Lucifer, in my face in a puff of flame, grinning. He crouched, stroked my face. "Not exactly what you were expecting, huh?"

"What did you do to them?"

"Nothing really," and Lucifer slid a finger down the length of Michael's sword. "They did this to themselves. I just opened the door."

"You drove them to this madness!"

"Did I? Gabriel...We both know you can see better than that. Did I send Michael here? Or Raphael? Did I tell him—did I tell any of them—to fall in love with the humans? Did I tell encourage them to forsake their duties, Gabriel? This right here," Lucifer jerked a thumb at Raphael and Michael, "is because Raphael tried to kill her," he pointed at Sariel, "and Michael killed him." Now he nudged the baby with his foot. "Walk with me," and Lucifer pulled me to my feet.

We walked through the maelstrom, frozen as it was, and Lucifer told me the story of each conflict as it unfolded on this battlefield. I knew it, I could see it, but my vision didn't allow me to feel the emotion of it. I was disconnected. Separated. Alone.

He clapped a hand on Uriel's shoulder. "This big fella deserted his post as soon as they got here. I think Michael's going to make him pay for that. He left his soldiers, left Sariel and found a Chosen here. He got her pregnant with something horrible and when Sariel finally found him, she killed his woman. Killed her in front of him and then she left. Did the same thing to Raphael." He dragged my face to his, met my eyes. "This isn't me, Gabriel. This is *them*. You think I'm on some horrible crusade to destroy it all—and that's true—but, honestly, I know it's not worth saving. I know it's all garbage and I wasn't interested in waiting for all of you, or Him, to figure that out. Forgive my impatience. I think I've been vindicated."

"And now you want what, Lucifer? What reward do you seek?"

"Justice. These are monsters, Gabriel, they are abominations. Do you remember what you told me when you called my daughters 'abominations'? Do you remember what you said?"

"That was a long time ago."

"I remember. You said they couldn't stand. You said if I couldn't destroy them, you would. Do you remember that?"

"I remember," but my voice was quiet. I did remember. It was the first time I disagreed with the Father, the first time I tried to challenge him.

Now Lucifer turned from me, dropped his voice and I heard the quivering of tears. "And what happened after that? The Father came and He destroyed everything. He took everything."

"I know," was all I could say.

"Call Him." He spun, looked at me with fire in his eyes. "Call Him. I want the justice I deserve. I want Him to serve His justice on these monstrosities, on these abominations. These are His children, Gabriel. I want Him to tell them they cannot stand. I want Him to take everything."

"Lucifer..."

"CALL HIM! Or I will let them tear themselves apart." He stepped close to me, let the fire die, spoke in soft, intimate tones. "We both know how this ends. It comes one way or the other, Gabriel. Let it come."

Lucifer was right. I knew how it would end. I'd already seen it. He simply followed the madness to its logical conclusion. And he was right. There was nothing I could do to make it stop. Angels had unleashed horror on this world, the fallen had pushed humanity farther from the Father, and the race of men had embraced evil far too willingly. And as I gazed across the field, twirling my Horn between my fingers, I didn't see my brothers and sisters, angels and demons. I saw only monsters.

Lucifer was right.

I brought the Horn to my lips, and with a mighty breath, played the saddest song of my existence. A dirge for the

Earth. A death march for the race of men. And the skies began to darken. A wall of black clouds plumed, blotting out the sun, leaving us in shadow. Wind, first trembling the tips of leaves, the heads of grass, now hushed across the field, blowing shattered angels to nothing and scattering the ashes of the damned. Thunder shook us all and I felt the first drops of many fall between my eyes.

"There we go," said Lucifer.

And the Father came.

40
LUCIFER

Finally.

I don't know how long it had been since the Father last spoke to me, since I last saw His face. I was still in Heaven then, still one of His beloveds, and He was telling me to make the man. He held me in His hand then, blocked out all the nonsense, silenced the cacophony that Heaven had become. That was the last time I saw Him. The last time He held me close and called me His own. And then forsook me in the same breath.

He told me to create a beast that would save us all.

Then He turned His back on me.

"Look how well that turned out," I muttered.

I felt the familiar thump of His footsteps moving through Earth. The Father was coming. He was coming to see the results of His handiwork. To see the good works of His faithful servants. I couldn't help but smile.

His face pressed into the clouds and the fury of wind picked up, pushed against my face. "What are you doing?" But His tones were controlled, forced. Like when He walked away from me.

"Nothing," I said. "This wasn't me. This was—"

But the wind swirled about me, pulling me from my feet and dragging me in air. Pushing me away. "I wasn't speaking to you, Keeper," the Father said.

He dropped me roughly. Beyond the field.

"Michael!" and the skies exploded with lightning. Thunder boomed loud enough to split trees, to burst our ears. To make me cower.

I am often reminded of the truly limited scope of my power. Oh to you, I am a god, capable of working wonders your diminished capacities can barely fathom. I can manipulate your world to whatever my heart desires. You are easily beguiled and concocting illusions, pushing your simple little buttons, appealing to the baser temptations of your heart, are skills I could perform in my sleep. If I ever slept. This world is but putty in my hand.

But next to a true god—the God—I am but a shadow of Him. A wisp of His magnificence. I am nothing, just a disillusioned soul with an ambitious mind and more ability than he knows what to do with. I am paltry next to the Father. I am a plaything, a toy, a puppet for Him to manipulate and discard.

And He knows it.

The Father released my suspended animation, brought Michael to life. Brought him to His face.

"Answer Me!"

"I did what you made me to do," Michael said, hanging in the dark sky, wings outstretched. "I did what had to be done."

"You dare to judge your brother? You believe this is what I made you to do?"

"It *is* what You made me to do!" Michael was furious. "You told me to destroy the wickedness among us! That's what You said!"

"I told you to protect the others, Michael! I told you to end the darkness! Lead the army! That is what I commanded. Look around you, Peace Maker! Is this bloodshed your success?"

"No!" Michael roared. "It's Yours."

"YOU ARE NOT JUDGE! I AM JUDGE" And the Earth shook beneath the Father's voice. The winds bent the trees, tore massive trunks from the ground, spewed black dirt into the air. I watched angels and demons, frozen in my grip, shatter in His gale. "You are My son, Michael. You are My child. Just as Raphael is mine. Just as they are mine. All of them. You were made to love them, not judge them."

"Could have fooled me," Michael said and then he was silent, dropped his head. But I could see the rage building on his face, see the tightness in his jaws. For the briefest of moments, I sympathized with him. I knew how he felt. Doing what he thought was expected of him. Following his true nature. Embracing the darker parts of the soul he was given. I sympathized with Michael then but I couldn't contain myself.

"Look at Your success! These are Your children! Look what they have become!" I screamed in the darkness. And then, "Isn't this what You wanted?"

"You speak out of turn, Lucifer."

My name. He called my name. Not my function, not Keeper. Not the horrible moniker the angels had branded me with. He didn't call me Satan. He called me Lucifer. He called me now as He called me then, in the beginning, when I was but a flicker of light and hope in the palm of His hand. Before everything went wrong. In that instant, at the sound of my name on His tongue, I almost lost my fury. I almost forgot the Hell I'd been sentenced to. I almost forgot the millions of souls He put before me, the souls He took from me, the steps I'd been forced to take. I almost forgave Him.

Almost.

"This deserves justice," I said and my voice was small, weak.

"I told you—" the Father began.

"It deserves justice!" and I screamed in the dark. "Look at this! This is the madness You have ordained. This is the horror You unleashed on this world. These are the works of Your servants. And this world bleeds for justice."

Gabriel appeared next to me, dropped a heavy hand on my shoulder, "What are you doing, Lucifer? You know the penalty for disobedience. You know how this will end."

I smiled at him. "I'm counting on it."

"Father—" Gabriel said.

"He's right." It was Raphael, his voice weary and broken. "Lucifer's right. Look at this. We deserve whatever comes."

Gabriel said, "Raphael, you can't be serious."

Raphael was crying, "My wife—my Chosen—and my son bleed into this place. My brothers and sisters have turned on one another. All of us betrayed the promises we made to man. We earned judgment."

"Then let me finish," Michael growled.

"I made you to be better than this," the Father said, but He was talking more to Himself than to us. "You were meant for so much more." Then, "The sins of this world must be washed away."

"No!" And Gabriel was airborne, flying toward the face of the Father, hanging before His frightening countenance.

It was a dangerous game Gabriel was playing. And wholly unexpected. I crossed my arms and watched. Smiling.

"You cannot destroy them all! No sin is this great!" Gabriel said.

The Father boomed, "Your work here is finished, Watcher. You have done your duty."

And I saw the wind press against Gabriel's body, tumble him through the air. He was being brutalized, swung to and fro, his wings wide and open, struggling to hang there before the Father.

"No!" Gabriel said and the wind stopped. "I stood by before, I let you destroy it all before because I believed You. You said it was right. You said it was just. I believed You and You took everything from Lucifer. You took his heart. And it has only bred distrust and destruction amongst us. You would sow those seeds here?"

The Father seemed to lean forward, press His massive face further into the clouds, closer to Gabriel. Hands of mist and fog cupped the Watcher, pulling him upwards. Up to the Father.

"Disobedience will not be tolerated," the Father said. "Not even from you."

"Father, please," Gabriel whispered.

But the Father smiled a sad smile, spoke in kind tones. "My son, the seeds have already been sown. It is time for reaping. The crimes committed here merit justice, Gabriel. Surely you can see that. This world, these souls, will get the justice deserved. Your work here is finished. My Son needs you now."

And Gabriel was gone, vanished in a wisp of blue fire.

Then, "Raphael, Keeper of the Peace, come forth!"

Raphael stood, hung his head.

"LOOK AT ME!"

The Peace Keeper's head jerked up and he was snatched into the clouds, until he dangled beneath the Father's face.

"Raphael, my son..." and the Father seemed at a loss for words. "You weep for lost love, your heart breaks for a lost child, does it not?"

Raphael wept openly now, heaving great sobs. "He was my son and she—"

"Was forbidden!" The Father's tone changed and thunder shook the Earth. "You swore to serve them, Raphael! You swore to protect them! My heart aches! My children are dead! At your hand! This world cries, Raphael, it weeps the blood of its sons and daughters. And you seek compassion? You beg for mercy? What mercy do you deserve? You were made to be better!"

"I know," Raphael whispered amidst his tears. "I failed you."

I remembered that too, the weight of that responsibility and my failure. In the end, even though I hated the Father for it, the destruction of the first Heaven, Lilith's death and the forcible removal of my daughters fell squarely on my shoulders. I knew it was my actions that led to their horrible ends but I disagreed with the Father's steadfast refusal to find compassion. I found it contemptible that He could not find one iota of empathy in that cold heart of His, that there was no attempt at understanding my pain, my guilt. He just made me pay for it and used my mistake as justification for ruining the rest of my existence. I prayed His brand of justice was universal.

It was.

"You did not fail Me, Raphael. You disobeyed Me. You turned your back on your duties and those who swore their allegiance to you. And you have suffered a greater punishment than any I could mete out. Your brothers and sisters have taken the things you held higher than your duty. Those you have betrayed will decide your fate."

Raphael's body ignited in blue flame and he began to disappear before our eyes.

"Go," the Father said. "Return from whence you came. Never come here again. You are forbidden from this place."

And he was gone in a flash. Michael and I stood amidst chaos frozen, awaiting our own punishment.

"Michael," the Father began, pulling him into the air, "you are the Peace Maker. You are made to deliver peace from the hand of chaos. You are to be light in the midst of darkness. But you have abused the power I have given you. You have lost your way."

"I did what You told me to do," Michael said through clenched teeth. "You made me to do one thing and then you chastise me for doing it. You keep changing the rules!"

"I made you to be My hand! I made you to show your brothers and sisters the consequence of disobedience. You were to lead them away from this madness, not push them toward it! Now," and the Father's voice changed, grew irritated and harsh, "take your place as head of this army. Fulfill my commands. Lead them home."

"No," Michael said. "No. I can't do this anymore. I won't do this anymore. I don't care what You want me to do. I'm done. Sariel is a far better Captain than I am; she can lead them home."

The Father considered this, clearly taken aback. He let Michael fall to earth. Discarded. "Seraph!"

Sariel was pushed to her knees, bathed in a stream of white light. Her chest burned with white fire and swords snaked from her fists. Swords like Michael's, curved and dangerous.

"You are Captain now," the Father's voice boomed. "Lead this army. Take your brethren home. The next time you return, it will be the end."

"Captain?" Sariel said. "What about Michael?"

She met his eyes and I could see the concern, the longing, the love in them. She more than followed the Peace Maker; she idolized him. He was more than her equal, more than her Captain. He moved her, touched her, led her, molded her. She was...smitten. And it was obvious.

"Michael's path is not your concern," the Father said. "Do as I command. Lead this army."

"What about the others?" she said. "What about those that stood against us? What happens to them?"

"The damned are still the damned, Sariel. Nothing changes," He told her. "Now leave this place."

"Father..."

But Sariel was gone before her sentence finished. In flashes of blue, in swirls of wind and fire, angels, followers of Sariel, loyal soldiers of Uriel, slipped away. Their footsteps remained etched in the soil, stones burned in their wake. Standing rigid like statues, the blackened bodies of the fallen littered the battlefield. Locked in combat with adversaries long gone, these souls were little more than headstones, sculpted mausoleums. This place was dead, the world and its promise was dead. And Michael and I stood in it. Alone. Silent.

Until the Father screamed.

I have existed since the beginning. I breathed before light was born, spoke before your world was forged, wept long before the sun burned in the heavens. I have seen countless souls created and destroyed, I have watched brothers and sisters tear one another apart, sons and daughters reduced to blood and bone. I've seen nations rise and empires fall. I have heard the wails of angels and demons, the cries of man and women. But I have heard nothing like the agony of the Father. Nothing like His rage and frustration and disappointment and the very essence of His futility. He is the Father. He is the beginning and the end. The author of it all. Omnipotent. Omnipresent. God. And yet He could not stop His children from tearing themselves apart.

Even the Father could not stop the inevitable.

He began to cry and His tears came down in torrents, in sheets. Incessant. Flooding the world with His grief. Washing it all away. The bodies of the fallen broke beneath the raindrops, beneath the Father's tears, leaching into the earth. Trees, thirsty for the water, soon began to drown in the tumult. We watched rivers rise beside us, overflow their banks and rush, unbidden, across dry land. Water poured down mountainsides, dragging rocks and trees in horrible landslides, devastating whatever lay below. We heard the screams of men and women, children and animals, unable to escape the rush of water. We heard them drowning, begging for mercy.

We heard it all.

Michael sat down in the decay, in the rain, let it wash the detritus of battle from his body. He scrubbed his face, cleaned his hands and stabbed his swords in the dirt. I joined him, grinning.

"You win," Michael said to me. "Happy now?"

I was.

EPILOGUE

Michael

"Why the long face?" Lucifer asked me.

The Earth was dead. Again. Bloated with the weight of the blood of my brothers and sisters, drowning in the sorrow of the Father's tears. The Father cried for forty days and forty nights, more than He ever cried for us, any of us. He drowned this place.

He killed everything.

And I hated Him for it.

For forty days, with the rising of the sun to the setting of the moon, I listened to His wails, His screams in the dark, as the rain fell on torrents, in sheets. I watched millions of humans, begging for mercy at His hand, sinking beneath the depths of His sorrow. I heard their cries, the bargaining with their God, the pleading for deliverance. The Earth itself cried peals of agony, animals and birds, beasts and fowl, screamed to heavens, screamed to nothing. Nothing. Their solicitations drowning in the crushing deep. And I heard the Father's silence. I heard Him turn His back on the humans, the souls made to save us all, condemned to die at His hand.

I hated Him for it.

"What was the point?' I said.

"In this?" and Lucifer was grinning broadly and preening, standing on the water. "Justice."

"I heard that part. There is no justice in this."

"Not true!" Lucifer was terribly excited. "This was what was deserved, Michael. This is what they deserved. I told you this would happen. I told you all."

I was sitting on the water, staring into nothing. "I don't care what you think, Keeper. I know where you sit on this."

"Oh no no no," he crouched down to me, smiled in my face, "I wanted the best for this place. I really wanted the best for them."

And then he began to laugh.

"I'm sorry, I'm sorry," he tried to stifle his joy, drumming fingers on his lips. "You're right: I'm a horrible liar. These monsters got what they deserved. All of them got what they deserved. And so did you."

I moved in a flash, tightening my hand around Lucifer's neck, pulling him from the water. I growled and the earth rippled beneath the waves.

"Do it, Peace Maker," Lucifer gurgled. "See how well that works out for you. I wonder if it'll make a difference."

He grinned at me and I knew he was right. There was nothing I could do. I dropped him in the water.

"Figured you'd see it my way," he said to me, stretching his neck. Then, "So, defiance. That's a new one for you, isn't it? What's that about?"

"It's pointless. Why make them to kill them? Why go through it at all? There has to be more than...," I waved about me, at the endless water, "...this. And, until I figure it out, I'm done with this stupid game."

"Where's the fun in that? Can't you see, Michael? The only thing left is the game. We have to go through these motions, you and I. The Father wants something from us. I don't know what and I don't know why. We have to play this out until it ends."

I stomped away from him, water steaming at my footsteps. I shouted at the sky, "What are You doing to us! What do You want from us?!"

But the Father was silent and my screams simply echoed across this dead world.

Lucifer just smiled at me, chuckled at my tantrum. "You know, I've been here before. I did exactly what you did, screamed for Him. I begged Him to come back. I cried for Him to answer. But He didn't. He left me alone! Just like He left you."

"He came back for you, Lucifer. He came back."

"True, He did come back. Eventually. But the damage was already done. You think this is what I wanted? You think this is the angel I was supposed to be?" Then Lucifer was on me, caressing my face. "Are you the angel you're supposed to be?"

"I'm the angel I have to be," I said.

"And how's that working out for you? Well?" Lucifer smiled, "Because it seems like you're stuck here with me."

Lucifer was right. And I had nothing to say.

"Besides, all the fun stuff happens while He's gone," Lucifer said to me, then grinned broadly and pointed into the distance. "Well, would you look at that?"

Then I saw it. A dot on the horizon. Coming closer. It floated on the water, moved with a current unseen. And it was unnatural. Made by the hands of man. It was a wooden structure, a vessel—massive, long and lean, ambling along the surface of this drowning world. It was a hopeful, ambitious thing, a finite speck of life in the midst of all this death.

The Ark.

The vessel trundled alongside us and Lucifer clapped me on my shoulder. "Time to go," he said. "That's my ride."

And Lucifer the Satan, Keeper of the Light, Lord of the Host of Hell, snaked along the surface of the water and slipped aboard the Ark. A man appeared on the bow of the ship, a man with a thick, white beard and tired eyes. He tossed a bird, a dove, into the sky, watched it disappear in the horizon then looked down at me.

And his eyes flashed red.

My breath caught and the man smiled a little smile, nodded and said, "See you around."

www.ingramcontent.com/pod-product-compliance
Lightning Source LLC
Chambersburg PA
CBHW020458310726
48979CB00016B/2711/J

* 9 7 8 1 7 3 5 0 1 1 4 3 1 *